Pope Mary
and
The Church of
Almighty Good Food

Pope Mary

The Church of Almighty Good Food

A novel by

Gene Logsdon

WICKER
PARK
PRESS Ltd.

**Pope Mary and the Church
of Almighty Good Food**

Copyright ©2011 Gene Logsdon
All Rights Reserved

ISBN 9780978967642

Wicker Park Press, Ltd.
PO Box 5318
River Forest, Illinois 60305-5318
(773) 391-1199
www.wickerparkpressbooks.com

The paper used in this publication meets the minimum requirements
of the American National Standard for Information Sciences—
Permanence of Paper for Printed Library Materials, ANSI Z39.48-1992.

Library of Congress Cataloging-in-Publication Data on file
with publisher.

Printed in Canada

Dedicated To My Grandchildren:
Evan, Rebecca and Alex.
When they are older they will
understand why.
Taking care of the cemetery
and making fine furniture
in his woodworking shop.

Chapter 1

The dark figure lurking among the tombstones across the one-lane country road from St. Philodendra's church watched the lightning flicker in the night sky. The approaching storm was part of the plan that he and God, with the cooperation of the Weather Service, had worked out. In this quiet countryside of Vinal County, Ohio, the least little sound would carry across the corn and soybean fields to farmhouses as much as a mile away. But the thunder, soon to erupt as the storm rolled in, would muffle the noise of his maul as he battered and broke the lock on the church door. He was talking now, evidently to the headstone in front of him. The inscription on it was so weather-worn that only a person who knew what it said would be able to decipher it: *Benedict Berogston: Born 1816 Died 1870.*

"I have sworn an oath on your grave, old Benedict, that I will not let them close the church which you worked so hard to establish. The world has been going bad since you were laid to rest, Benedict, and by God, it has got to stop. We did our best to save our church legal-like, as you well know, but the bishop and his diocesan officials, and the pope of Rome and all his whole nest of goddamned cardinals, has got to be put in their places and the Church returned to the goddamned people." He never used such language ordinarily. A studied innocence was part of his public disguise. No one really knew him. He wasn't sure he knew himself very well. He waited for Benedict to say something but when no voice from the grave spoke, he continued, gradually becoming more agitated. "As you well know, there's no good reason for closing this church. We got the money, or did before that bishop took it, we got the people, we even got the priests. But they still closed us down. Not only closed us down, but locked us out of our own church. Locked us out, mind you, Benedict. *And took our money. All two hundred thousand dollars of it."* He paused then for dramatic effect, having worked himself once more into such righteous anger that he would not have been surprised if old Benedict had risen right up out of the ground, like the Lord Jesus Christ had done in that earlier age.

Benedict did not speak but the Lord did. A streak of lightning pierced the darkness, so close it seemed to strike the steeple of the church, accompanied by an ear splitting crack of thunder. The dark figure took it as a command for action. Time to attack. It was August, 2006, in the year of Our Lord, and he was about to make some history that the people of Vinal County, Ohio, would never forget.

He grabbed up his maul and made his way out of the cemetery, across the road, and to the church door. Rain had started to fall, the wind whipped up, the lightning ripped and the thunder roared as he swung the first time against the knob of the huge red door. Apocalypse. Timing his swings with the thunder, he brought the sledge down solidly on the brass knob and latch until he had smashed the door hardware out of its metal seating in the wood. The fury of the storm drove the fury in the man and he did not stop pounding until the whole wooden area around the knob, latch and lock had been mangled and split asunder and the great door blew open in the storm winds. He stood there, panting to get his breath back, and made the Sign of the Cross. He looked up at the steeple, illumined sporadically by lightning, then entered the church, knelt in the aisle and prayed out loud: "I know, Lord, that I have desecrated holy ground but that lock was the greater desecration as you well know. I have just done your will." And then he slipped out into the darkness, into the standing corn beyond the cemetery, the perfect cover for a getaway, crashed on with his head down to avoid being cut in the face by the sharp edges of corn leaves, until he came to his pickup hidden some thirty acres away at the field's edge, all just as he had planned, and drove off into the night. There was a grim, triumphant smile on his face. He had done it and he was glad. History was full of examples of people breaking out of churches to escape the prayerful life, but he had a notion this was the first time that anyone had broken into a church to pray.

Chapter 2

Mary Barnette thought ruefully that perhaps she had the hots for Father Ray. That gave her just one more reason for being disgusted with herself. She didn't even like him, she kept telling herself. And she definitely didn't belong to his stupid church. She had given up religion fifteen years ago when the nuns tried to tell her that babies couldn't go to heaven if they weren't baptized. Even at age twelve, or especially at age twelve, Mary Barnette loved babies which is why her mother could not understand why she hadn't married yet. Mary had not taken kindly to the notion that a baby couldn't get to heaven without baptism. The poor thing had to go to Limbo instead, so the nuns said. Limbo was not so bad, they stated unctuously, even if it was still part of Hell.

"I don't think so," Mary had said, right out loud in the classroom. She was never the bashful kind. It was not the baby's fault if it died without baptism. When Mary wouldn't back down, the nuns sent her home with one of those notes that nuns were so adept at writing, notes liberally sprinkled with the word, "recalcitrant."

"But Mom, that's just not fair. A baby hasn't done anything wrong yet. You can't keep them out of heaven just because they die before someone can sprinkle water on them."

"Hush up," her mother, Martha, scolded. "It's sinful to question church doctrine." It was obvious from her tone that Martha didn't think too much of that doctrine either.

"Mom, for heaven's sake, that just can't be so."

"Well, Limbo isn't a place of suffering except for not being able to be face to face with God for all eternity."

Mary had stared at her mother in disbelief. Sometimes parents could be really stupid. Evidently the whole Catholic Church. What in the world could make a baby unfit for looking at God for all eternity just because somebody didn't sprinkle water on it? And why would a baby want to look at God for all eternity anyway? Why would anyone want to do that, come to think of it? She had decided, right then and there, that Baptism was as stupid as Limbo.

Once she opened the floodgates of doubt, she realized, as her mother had dolorously warned her, that the whole business of religious doctrine would begin to appear questionable, including Heaven, Hell, Purgatory and papal infallibility. By the time she had gone through two years of college, after which she quit, she had made up her own private religion which she named after the 4-H farm youth club. She announced that she belonged to the 4 H's of hellion, heathen, heretic, and humanist. Probably atheist too, but that didn't start with an H. Besides, by that time, she had learned not to use the A word in public. People were willing to put up with Catholics, Evangelicals, Muslims, Hindus, Democrats, philanderers, drunks, lawyers, even liberals, but, whoa, not atheists. So, she kept her mouth shut, got a good job working in a commodities brokerage firm in Chicago, and saved her money. What difference did it make anyway. All of it was bullshit, including atheism.

So now she was afraid she had the hots for a dumb Catholic priest. Jeeezusss. But, she told herself, she might be forgiven because Fr. Ray was certainly the most extraordinary priest she could ever have imagined. He broke horses. Only people who actually saw him do it believed her, but it was the God's truth, pardon the expression. Not only that, but as pastor of two very rural churches situated about five miles apart out in the middle of the cornfields, he had, at least up until a year ago, been transporting himself on Sunday mornings from one church to the other by horseback. Bishop Feering was askance at this lack of what he called priestly propriety, but when he looked into the matter, he learned that Fr. Ray was in good standing with the farmers he administered to. They liked him for horse-backing from one church to the other, especially the old men who every morning watched old Westerns on TV until lunch time. With the difficult times the bishop knew were coming because of all the miserable pedophilia crap that had infested the Church, he decided that he needed Fr. Ray a whole lot more than to let a stupid horse or two come between them. At least Fr. Ray was not diddling little children. He wasn't even diddling pretty women.

Mary recalled what had brought her to this strange ambivalence about a priest she hardly knew. She had been working on the fence along the road in front of her parents' farm the first time she saw him. She had, at that time, no idea what was behind the apparition flying past her on horseback.

"What in creation was that?" she asked her father after the headed horseman had disappeared in the distance.

"If you went to church once and awhile, you'd know," he replied with a snort, always willing to point out her recalcitrance although he was actually a bit envious of her. He would have liked to quit going to church too but was afraid. It might be bad for business. "That's the Reverend Raymond Tulley and he must have preached too long at St. Philodendra's and now is going to be late starting Mass at St. Clare's unless he really gallops that nag." He waited for her to say something irreverent. She was too amazed for that.

"He really rides a horse between churches? You're kiddin.'"

"Nope. Says its saves quite a bit on the gas bill."

"Well now I've heard everything."

"No you haven't."

"What do you mean."

"He breaks horses. Charges a hundred bucks. Says it's good money."

"C'mon, Dad, you've been watching too many old Westerns on TV."

"Check it out if you don't believe me. A little churchin' might do you good."

The next Sunday, Mary made sure she was out along the road about the time Fr. Ray would be galloping by. To get him to stop without actually seeming to do so, she was wearing a pair of shorts a tad on the short side for someone 26 years old, as her father would have said had he seen her, and wore the bonnet she knew made her look sexy. But just in case that didn't work, she had parked the tractor and wagon, on which she was pretending to load the old posts she had been replacing in the fence, so that the Lone Ranger might at least have to slow down and swerve around the obstruction sticking out into the road.

Probably the wagon ruse was unnecessary, but Mary would never know for sure. Fr. Ray only cantered his horse as he approached—he had of course taken note of Mary the previous Sunday, and recollected that he had not seen her in either of his churches. He pulled up as he drew alongside the wagon.

"Howdy, ma'am." It came out a bit awkward and before he could stop himself. He even tipped his hat to make matters worse.

Mary almost laughed. He sounded like John Wayne spoofing one of his own characters. She could not help herself.

"Haowdee, cal-boy." She even batted her eyes.

Fr. Ray hesitated. He was used to being addressed as "Father." Oh well. He could play the game too.

"Reckon I haven't ever seen you in church, Miss ah—" Talking like a TV cowboy made the reprimand less tense perhaps.

"Miss ah Mary. Reckon you ain't," she accented the bad grammar. "Bein' half way between two of them churches, I ain't never made up my mind which-un to go to." She sported a grin she hoped looked evil.

He kept from laughing only by determined effort. A real smart ass. He looked off toward the skyline. He did not intend to let her get the better of him.

"Reckon you oughten to be working on Sunday either," he observed, mimicking her grammar, but without looking at her, as if he were talking to the horizon.

"Waall, I reckon you know what the Bible says about having to get your ass out of the pit, even on Sunday." Her glare dared him to answer.

Fr. Ray had grown up with six sisters, all of them smart alecks like this one. Women did not confound him very often. He had intended to ask her, as he asked everyone he met, about the church break-in, but now decided not to. He gave a sidelong, overt, exaggerated glance in the general direction of her bare thighs and drawled: "Waal, I'd say there's a greater worry this Sunday of getting one's ass too close to those multi-flora thorn bushes in that fence row." And off he galloped in a cloud of possible future intrigue.

Now recalling that meeting, Mary realized that her mind had been almost entirely preoccupied with the smart ass priest ever since then. That's why she thought she might have the hots for him. He had reacted to her in such an unpriestly way that she just had to know more about him. She had only been back home now about a year, having found the world beyond Vinal County every bit as boring as Vinal County. In

Chicago she had fallen for one of the smart young traders on the Chicago Board of Trade. When he stiffed her, she came back home and in a fit of irritated depression, or perhaps just to prove how contrary she could be, she had decided to farm with her father. She knew that would delight him so much that he would consent even though he had grave doubts about the arrangement and so did she. Much to her surprise, she had found that the work was more interesting than it had seemed when she was in high school. Farming was a tremendously challenging occupation, demanding every ounce of physical and mental ability she possessed and more. Why didn't more people want to be farmers? The opportunities within it were varied with new ideas coming along constantly. And what could be more satisfying than a career producing what everyone had to have, food. Even most of the physically hard work had been reduced to pressing buttons or to knowledge about whom she could call for assistance when pressing buttons didn't work. The truth was, she realized, that not even most farmers encouraged their children to become farmers. Her parents certainly had not. Even most farmers were infected with the cultural attitude she had found so prevalent in Chicago, the lingering notion that farmers were peasants and peasants were at the bottom of the social order. She shook her head at such ignorance. But on second thought, maybe that was good. Less competition for those who did know how exciting and challenging farming could be.

As she drove her tractor back and forth across a field now in September, the huge disk behind the tractor worked the soil into a loamy seedbed in preparation for sowing wheat. The radio in the cab blared rap songs that she didn't like especially, but which she hoped conveyed her rebellion against the world to anyone who might hear them across the otherwise quiet countryside. Her mind was busy, actually, trying to come up with a plan that might accidentally throw her into the company of the priest again. She couldn't just stand out along the road half naked, waiting for him to gallop by, like some slut. As she pondered the situation, she noticed that her father had walked out to the edge of the field and was waiting for her. With him was his brother. Oh God, was Uncle Tom going to get on her again about making something of herself. She stopped when she reached them but let the tractor run at a little louder than idle so that it would be difficult to talk.

"Your uncle would like a word with you," her father said when it became obvious that Mary was not going to speak first.

"What's up, Unc?" she asked, sticking her head a little farther out of the cab.

She was wearing only shorts and halter, which would probably vex her uncle. She hoped.

"Think maybe that disk could stand a little grease," he said. "Could hear it squeaking from the barnyard." He needed, as he did with nearly everyone, to put her on the defensive and thereby appear to be superior.

"Talk to the boss," she replied, nodding at her father. "All I do is work here." All three of them knew that wasn't quite the whole truth and it left Tom having to tread water.

"There's a problem at church," he said, getting to the point. "And we'd like you to maybe help us out."

She glared at him. Of course there was a problem at church. That's all anybody had been talking about for a month, and she was getting tired of it. Damn fools let the bishop lock their church. And then someone broke the door down. She didn't think anyone in the congregation had the guts.

"There's to be a big meeting about the situation. Maybe a showdown. We thought you might have something to say about it."

"Me? I don't go to church, remember? What do you mean, 'showdown'?"

"Now, Mary, you're one to speak out and everyone knows it and we thought you might have something to say about opening the church up again, seeing as how there's about as many dead Barnettes in the church cemetery as there are live ones living here. It's your church whether you want it or not."

"I've told you before, you'd all be better off quitting all that religious stuff."

"That's why we're asking you, Mary. We need someone to speak out who isn't afraid of getting excommunicated."

She stared in disbelief, then had to laugh. Wily old Tom probably was just as much a heathen as she was but too scared to say so out loud. "Oh, you want me to be the fall guy. What a bunch of yellabellies."

"We've got Fr. Ray about half committed to standing up with us with the argument that locking the church again will just mean more trouble. But we need someone like you to be spokesman."

"Spokeswoman." Mary was thinking fast. She cared nothing about the church, or not much anyway, but here was a made-to-order chance to get acquainted with the very reverend Lone Ranger.

"Your grandfather there in his grave would expect it of you," her father added, knowing that Mary had been especially fond of him.

"I'll think about it," she said.

"We're havin' a meeting tomorrow night," Tom said. "Seven o'clock at the church. Fr. Ray will have it open for the meeting."

Mary, somewhat to her own surprise, did think about it. In fact she found herself aroused with enough curiosity that sleep would not come that night. Just who the hell had given the bishop the right to close the church anyway. Just who the hell's church was it. The more she thought, the angrier she got. If the bishop didn't have enough priests, why didn't he ordain women? She had heard there were quite a few fool enough to want the job. Or for that matter, why didn't the bishop just let someone, anyone so inclined, lead the congregation in prayer services. There were plenty willing to do that, the kind who always offered to pray for her when she talked contrarily about religion, so why not give them a shot at the pulpit as long as she didn't have to listen. The church hierarchy of old males just didn't want to give up any power. They would close a church first. What a lot of crap.

She decided she would go to the meeting and maybe raise a little hell. On the farm, far from the drinking and mating sessions of so-called happy hours in the Chicago after-work world, life had grown a little dull.

Chapter 3

Fr. Ray eased himself out of the saddle, patted his horse, and led it into the stable. His flock of sheep watched from their lot next to the barn, waiting patiently until he opened the door that allowed them inside too. He had just chalked up another hundred bucks. "Breaking" horses was the easiest money he ever made but he never said that out loud. By the time he got up on a horse, he had humored and cajoled it into friendly submission not so different from turning a raccoon into a pet. The horse rarely objected to him climbing aboard after it had learned to endure the saddle alone, but customers, culturally brainwashed by watching too many westerns or rodeos, didn't know that. They thought that a hundred dollars was a bargain for taming a bronco and so everyone was happy.

If humans would behave as rationally as animals, Fr. Ray thought, his life would have been almost perfect. But they didn't and now everything was in an uproar. It was good to have a horse to break to take his mind off the breaking and entering at St. Philodendra's. Nothing had been stolen so calling it a B & E was true only in a very literal sense, but that's what the sheriff called it. Closing the church in the first place, even if it were only four miles from St. Clare's in one direction, six miles from Our Lady of Good Patience in the village of Marystone in the opposite direction, and eight miles from the Church of the Resurrection to the east, was a huge mistake in Fr. Ray's opinion.

But the tragedy for him had happened before the break-in. Closing the church had meant the beginning of the end of his dream. He had become a priest because he liked taking care of people almost as much as he liked taking care of farm animals. And being celibate suited him. Sex was not a big issue with him and never had been, neither the heterosexual nor the homosexual variety. He referred to himself secretly not as homosexual or heterosexual, but halfasexual. Men wearied him; women scared him. Bachelorhood suited him fine. Even masturbation required more effort than it was generally worth, he often thought. The only activity that really interested him was farming, and he often wondered why he had left the farm where he grew up. He never really left it in his mind. He maintained a large garden, even in seminary training and then in major seminary, he worked as a farm hand on the attached farm in his spare time. After ordination, when he had learned about the opening of the joint pastorage of St. Philodendra and St. Clare, with nothing much surrounding the churches except corn fields, he had shamelessly plotted to get the job. It did not take much plotting because none of the other priests in the diocese wanted to get stuck "out in the sticks," as they put it. Moreover Bishop Feering wanted to curry Fr. Ray's favor, he being a "real solid" priest by which he meant that Fr. Ray was blessedly untouched by the sexual and alcoholic travails that seemed to be affecting the priesthood everywhere. Not making an ass out of oneself sexually or alcoholically had become the number one priority for the Catholic clergy in the twenty first century. So when Fr. Ray kept up his campaign to become pastor of the two country churches, the bishop gave his blessing. He had other reasons. Both churches were slated for closing, and when the people found that out, they would be so angry that the bishop would need a really unsullied priest as his point guard.

After his assignment, Fr. Ray had rented a house, barn, and forty acres near enough to both churches to pass for a rectory. The owner was a retiring farmer, and Fr. Ray believed if humored, the old man just might donate his land to the church, or better, to Fr. Ray. The priest had settled into what he thought would be a lifelong career as a spiritual shepherd of a human flock and a temporal shepherd of a sheep flock. The duties, he believed, were similar. Put a good fence around your fields, keep your rams happy with plenty of ewes and your ewes happy with plenty of lambs, feed them all well and they would prosper ever after. Likewise, fence in the people, the fence being Holy Mother the Church safeguarding them from the evils of the world, and encourage stable family life along with plenty of good food, winning sports teams and decent incomes. People would then work hard to maintain their good life and peace and plenty would prevail. Being inclined to literal-mindedness, Fr. Ray was as solicitous about feeding his spiritual flock as he was his farm flock. He believed that if he could encourage enough local food production and marketing, he could turn around the decline in rural life and prevent more farms from being swallowed up by giant corn and soybean enterprises. He wanted rural people to know that there was more to a vigorous local economy than raising grain for world markets and buying groceries at the supermart. If his parishioners would again establish food independence, he thought, all else would follow. Therefore, he, as their vicar, would function not only as dispenser of spiritual advice but of farm and garden advice too. That's how he justified spending so much priestly time at farming. He was preaching by example, he told himself. He would raise chickens, eggs, pigs, vegetables, fruits, and lamb chops and sell them locally.

His attempts had already borne fruit. Times were uncertain. Far away war bombs were exploding almost daily and near at hand financial bombs were bursting in air. More and more parishioners were keeping hens again, planting big gardens, even raising a few livestock. He had added a farmers' market to the popular summer festivals at both St. Philo's and St. Clare's, featuring fresh food stands along with the usual games of chance and the traditional beer garden. People from as far away as Lima, Findlay and Bowling Green had started to come for the fresh farm produce. He could see great promise in the event, somewhat like the auctions that flourished in eastern Ohio where Amish farmers were active, but with beer and gambling enhancing the profit picture. He was sure he was inventing, or re-inventing, the salvation of the local rural church.

But then circumstances began to unravel his whole agenda. When the bishop had called him a few months earlier to his countryside mansion outside Bowling Green for a conference, Fr. Ray thought it was because of his new approach to Catholic action.

"How are things going out in the hinterlands, Ray?" the bishop had intoned magnanimously, seeming not to recognize that he in his country mansion was out in the hinterlands too.

"Very well. We're about two hundred thousand in the black at St. Philo's and about half that at St. Clare's. But council doesn't publicize the fact for fear people might decide to contribute less." He had meant that as a sort of joke, but the Bishop did not smile.

"What do you think of the mess we're in?" the Bishop had asked.

"Which mess are you talking about?" Fr. Ray had thought that was funny too, but the bishop's face seemed molded in concrete.

"We're in real trouble over this confounded pedophilia crap, you know," he said, "and I'm the one catching hell. Confound it, I didn't know this was going on. I mean I'm as shocked as anyone. And now we are getting sued and I don't know which way to turn. Christ, we may be the first diocese in history to have to declare bankruptcy."

Fr. Ray knew better than to remind his boss that the warning flags had been flying for years about the pedophilia problem. It was important not to get on the bishop's wrong side. The subject was extremely obnoxious to Fr. Ray anyway, and he didn't want to talk about it. He could not imagine anyone—especially a priest for God's sake— being so depraved as to sexually abuse children. His secret solution was to castrate the whole lot of them but he was careful never to say that out loud except where only his real sheep could hear. Besides, experts had told him, castration wasn't effective either.

"But there's another problem, as you well know," the Bishop had continued.

Fr. Ray had nodded. He could think of a number of other problems but again was not going to be stupid enough to try to guess which one the bishop was stewing about now.

"We aren't getting enough vocations to the priesthood, confound it anyway."

Silence from Fr. Ray.

"We're going to have to start clustering parishes. Parishes are going to have to share a pastor. We can't afford so many little independent parishes anymore."

Fr. Ray felt relief. He was already doing clustering, being pastor of two churches. That must be why the bishop had called him into his office. He wanted advice on how clustering worked.

"I rather like the idea," he said. "Sort of fun having two parishes. You can appeal to their competitiveness. If St. Philo's votes for a new furnace, it will be easier to sell the idea to St. Clare's."

"That's not exactly what I mean." The bishop had cleared his throat. "We might have to cluster the people of both your churches into the Church of the Resurrection in Bredsocken."

Cicadas buzzing outside the window could be clearly heard in the silence that followed. Fr. Ray had once again shown how smart he could be. He said nothing. Mostly it was not mental acumen that kept him silent this time but total shock. That louse of a Fr. Lemming had engineered the clustering in his direction, into Bredsocken. Fr. Ray loathed Fr. Lemming who wanted to be called Pastor Lemming like the Lutheran ministers were addressed.

The bishop waited. Fr. Ray, although full of dread at the announcement, waited longer.

"Well, whatever am I supposed to do?" the bishop demanded defensively.

"Go slow." Fr. Ray figured if the Church proceeded slowly enough, which it usually did, nothing might happen at all, or not at least until he was ready for retirement.

"Well, we can't go slow. We must act. Soon."

"We?"

"I am hoping for your full cooperation. The people will not go along with this easily, as we know from other church closings, but your people respect you and I'm depending on you to make this happen without too much, ah, trouble."

"Go slow."

"Well, we'll only close St. Philodendra's for the time being. When we get everyone used to that, we'll close the other one."

Thinking back over those past events now, Fr. Ray realized that the bishop had not gone slow, at least not in Fr. Ray's sense of the word. He had closed the church and transferred two hundred thousand dollars out of St. Philo's treasury into Resurrection while Fr. Lemming tried to make his gloating demeanor look like pious concern. Lemming cared only about one thing in Fr. Ray's opinion. He wanted to be the next bishop of the Bowling Green diocese. He probably prayed every night that Feering would croak soon.

And so now someone had broken down the locked door of the closed St. Philo's and there would be no peace for the diocese after that. Fr. Ray thought about volunteering for missionary duty overseas, but then he thought maybe the ruckus would delay closing St. Clare's indefinitely and so keep him safely on his farm. He had to go to another dreadful meeting that very night, to discuss the smashed door, and he knew that those who had opposed the closing and locking of the church were going to be there in force this time. The break-in had emboldened them. They were getting more organized. They called themselves People For a Democratic Church. The bishop's advisers said that PFDC had been infiltrated by members of the heretical group, Call To Faith, headquartered in Chicago. Whether that was true or not, People For A Democratic Church had a lawyer now and the lawyer had a precedent. A judge had ruled against a bishop in a church closing in rural Iowa, and though the diocese had immediately appealed, and since the ruling had been only preliminary and did not directly address the real issues involved, like who really did own title to the church, it might be years before the matter was settled.

Why me, Fr. Ray wondered, when he thought about the meeting coming up. Why didn't that conniving Fr. Lemming have to hold court. It was Lemming who had insisted on keeping the church locked. Fr. Ray would much rather have spent a quiet evening doing his farm chores and then watching television or playing cribbage with his doctor, Jacob Tinnius, whom everyone called Dr. Jake. Dr. Jake told irreverent jokes about religion which the priest pretended not to enjoy. He would have liked to be as irreverent as Dr. Jake, but that might get him excommunicated and what could an excommunicated priest do to make a living except maybe break horses?

Chapter 4

B oth the People For A Democratic Church (PFDC) and the people loyal to the bishop, now calling themselves the Defenders of the Door (DOD) hung back from entering the church. Normally they would have been engaged in hearty conversation about important matters—like the price of corn. They all knew each other and each other's families going back to the early 1880s, when their ancestors arrived in Vinal County. But tonight, the subject was religion. No one ever talked about religion any more than they would talk about how much money they had in the bank.

Being of a practical bent of mind, most of them had come to the meeting to see if, and how, the church door had been repaired. What they found was a crude arrangement of 2 by 4s reminiscent of a barn door, hanging rather gingerly on the original church door's hinges. The original door was nowhere to be seen. One rumor had it that Dow Kapier, the respected community woodworker and caretaker of the cemetery and church, had it in his shop where it was undergoing intensive surgery. But Dow wasn't talking much—never did. Another story said the door was locked in the church basement and that Fr. Ray intended to keep it there indefinitely. The twin spinster sisters, Mabel and Ding Duholland, who always parked their hulking 1967 Cadillac on the cemetery side of the road as far from the church as possible so as not to seem to be "puttin' on airs," giggled at that rumor. Locking a door to hide a door that wouldn't lock struck them as somehow funny. But no one else seemed in a humorous mood. The conversations among the little knots of people in front of the church all pursued the same kind of logic with remarkably similar words.

"Whoever it was, he sure had balls."

"Maybe it was a she."

"Not likely. Anyone who could swing a sledge that hard had to be a man and a pretty hefty one to boot."

"Twern't a sledge, the sheriff says."

"Whatcha mean?"

"A splittin' maul."

"How can he tell."

"Some of the blows to the wood were from something sharper, like an ax, only heavier."

"Well that narrows it down some. Who's been splitting wood a lot lately?"

"Wouldn't mean a thing. People got mauls in their barns that ain't seen a block of wood since their grandpaws died."

"I sure would like to shake his hand, whoever done it. Bishop had no right lockin' us out of our church."

"Shush. You want to get excommunicated too?"

"Whatcha mean?"

"They said the bishop is going to excommunicate whoever did it."

"You're kiddin'. You can't excommunicate someone incognito."

"In what?"

"In absentia."

"I didn't know we had so many foreign speaking people in our midst."

"Well that's what my lawyer says."

"All your lawyer knows is how to do is execute wills and he's not very good at that."

Another Cadillac, a newer one, oozed up to the church entrance. Tom Barnette's car, everyone knew. He didn't care if he was "puttin' on airs." He'd park in the vestibule of the church if he could. He was a big-time farmer now, several thousand acres, a man to be reckoned with. Not that anyone present cared. What the crowd was craning its collective neck to see was not the car nor their very own farm czar but to see if Mary Barnette, the heathen bitch, was inside. Rumor had it she was coming.

Sure enough. She stepped out of the car, looked around, nodded at some, ignored others, and stalked through the crude two by four make-shift door into the church. It was what the others had been waiting for. Someone to take the lead. They trooped in behind her and took seats, mostly towards the back, the PFDCs on one side, the DODs on the other. The sanctuary was dark, shrouding the magnificent, hand-carved cherry reredos looming up in the gloom behind the altar. The sanctuary lamp, which had flickered continuously for a hundred years, denoting the presence of God, or the "Blessed Sacrament" as the faithful would say, was no longer lit. The tabernacle door hung open, showing the emptiness inside, underlining the symbolism of the unlighted lamp. God no longer dwelt in the church, or so the bishop said.

Mary Barnette continued her stalking, straight up the aisle, coming to rest in the pew right in front of Fr. Ray, who was standing with his back to the sanctuary, about halfway down the aisle from the communion rail. She was trying to look brazen although in her mind, she was as uncomfortable as he was trying not to appear. He was forcing a smile. He had known that none of the people would venture to the front of the church so he was meeting them halfway. Sort of a gesture, but he doubted that they would realize it. He recognized the young woman in front of him as the one he had met along the roadside. But he pretended not to, pretended to look past her at the rest of the people filing into the church. Although he took pride in knowing as much about his human flock as he did about his sheep flock, he was surprised to see her there after what she had said. He wished now that he had taken the time to learn a little about her.

Her father, Don, and uncle, Tom, flanked her like bodyguards, which is about how they viewed themselves. They were afraid, but also hopeful, that Mary would live up to her reputation of troublemaker. If she did, she might need protection from the DODs. Mary, for her part, studied the priest and decided she didn't have the hots for him after all. In black trousers, white shirt, black vest and Roman collar he seemed more the insipid clergyman than the dashing Lone Ranger she had encountered along the road. She began to regret that she had come to the stupid meeting.

"Let us all kneel in prayer," Fr. Ray intoned, "and ask God to look kindly on all of us"—he accented the 'all'—"as we strive to bring peace and solidarity to our troubled community." He then turned toward the altar, which technically was no longer an altar, knelt on one knee, and recited the first part of the Our Father, to which the audience responded with the second part. Mary Barnette, they all noticed, did not kneel, did not bow her head, did not move her lips in prayer. She remained seated and stared straight ahead, scrutinizing her Lone Ranger out of the corner of her eye. Fr. Ray then recited the first part of the Hail Mary and the congregation dutifully chimed in with the second part, Mary still not participating. The people were finding it difficult to bow in prayer and watch her at the same time. The prayer over, the priest turned back to the congregation and motioned for all to be seated. He got right to the point.

"I doubt very much that any parishioner of St. Philo's committed the heinous crime against the house of God that we have suffered here," he lied, "but we are here this evening to share whatever information anyone might have leading to the arrest of the vandal or vandals."

Mary went right to work, too, the way her uncle had hoped she would. "How can it be a heinous crime against the house of God when the bishop has declared the church no longer is the house of God?" Her heart was quaking, but she managed to look brazen anyway.

There was just the faintest titter from the PFDC side of the pews, while all the DOD eyes from across the aisle raked over her in disgust. Maybe she was the culprit herself, more than one of them thought, especially Alvin Farkow, who, having tried to date her once long ago, and having been turned down, was trying to despise her now. Fr. Ray stared at her too, for the first time, and found, to his chagrin that his stare was not entirely without a bit, just a tiny bit, of sexual buzz. Damn.

"We would all appreciate it if everyone would identity themselves before speaking," he said, archly.

"Everybody knows who I am," Mary replied, gaining strength in audacity, grinning wickedly. "In fact everybody knows everybody here forever. Maybe all the way back to the Mayflower. Unfortunately."

Both the group on the right and the group on the left laughed. Fr. Ray was forced to smile. If this was going to turn into a contest of wit, he knew he had lost the first two innings. He wondered if this bold brat knew who had broken down the door. He doubted it. People open enough to speak out in public were usually not the kind to slink around in the dark breaking down doors. He could see now that the whole idea of having this meeting was going to turn into one grand mistake. It was the bishop, again, who had demanded that Fr. Ray "do something"—hopefully to scare the offender enough so that he or she would not vandalize again.

"Well, Miss Mary Barnette, who do you think broke the door down." Fr. Ray believed in going straight to the heart of danger. He read that in a Graham Greene novel.

"I expect it was somebody who doesn't like the bishop," she replied crisply. "But that doesn't narrow it down much, does it?"

More tittering from PFDC; frowns from DOD.

"Let me remind one and all," Fr. Ray said, although his voice did not reflect very strong conviction, "that we are gathered here as members of the Mystical Body of Christ, faithfully obedient to our beliefs in the one, true church and with all due respect to church authority."

"Amen," said George Dribble, suntanned below where a ball cap always sat except in church. The suntan was a dead giveaway that he farmed only a few acres and worked in a factory for his main income. Farmers who farmed for a living lived out their days in tractors that had cabs. They no longer felt the hot breath of summer anymore than an Eskimo did. His arms and shoulders looked middle thirtyish but a ballooning stomach suggested maybe forty plus. He sat safe in the heart of the DOD side of the aisle and amened loud enough for all to hear.

Tom Barnette stared at him with the look he usually reserved for a tractor that wouldn't start, but said nothing.

"What we know now is not much," Fr. Ray continued. "The door was beaten in by some heavy object, something on the order of a sledge hammer or maul. Nothing seems to have been stolen or harmed in the church, and so robbery has been ruled out. No fingerprints, no tracks, no evidence of any kind has been found. The sheriff has no leads at all. Which is why we have asked you to come here tonight in the hope that someone has heard talk or knows of anything out of the ordinary on the night of August 7 when the break-in occurred."

"Our dog was howling extra loud," Ding Duholland said, "but I expect that was the thunder. She hates thunder."

"Some guys were talkin' in the Yellow Saloon in Bredsocken. Said it was an outside job," Lloyd McTicken volunteered, from deep in the DOD section. Thin and wiry, too swarthy to show the effects of sunlight even if he hadn't spent much of his work time in a tractor with a cab, he quivered nervously at the fact that he was speaking up. "Someone from that parish up north where they have sued the bishop for closing their church."

That was enough to encourage Alvin Farkow, who never needed much encouragement anyway. After all, he was a deacon now, officially ordained as such, and he had to act the part. He was also second in command at the grain elevator which commanded quite a bit more respect. He raised his hand, got a nod from Fr. Ray, and stood up. "As we all know, this happened about the same time those street preachers were carrying on in Marystone during the last pilgrimage. Trying to disrupt the pilgrims at the shrine, you know." A murmur went through the crowd. Everyone knew about the street preachers. They had been coming the last few years to the shrine of Our Lady of Good Patience to talk against the Catholics for what they called worshiping Mary the mother of Jesus as if she were God. The street preachers' most grievous act of desecration, the one that almost always started a fight, was to shout "Mary is a whore, Mary is a whore," at pious pilgrims coming to and from the shrine. Troublemakers, those street preachers. Alvin was probably right.

Fr. Ray tried to nod sagely without committing himself. He had talked to the street preachers himself and while he thought they were idiots in their own right, they were so well-trained and focused on embarrassing the Catholic Church only within the law that they would hardly break into a church. They had nothing to gain from that and everything to lose. He also doubted the theory that the culprits came from the parish in Toledo where several churches had been closed. They would surely break down their own locked church doors. Nothing good ever came out of public meetings, Fr. Ray was thinking. It just gave people a forum to say stupid things. He began to wish that Mary Barnette would speak up again. His instinct told him her kind of rebellion was safer.

She obliged. It was not in her genetic makeup to remain silent when she heard what struck her as poppycock.

"Oh sure. Next thing you know, it'll be Muslim terrorists come all the way to an Ohio corn field, dodging the full force of the U.S. government all the way, just to beat a door down."

This made Mary's bodyguards smile broadly. Also Dan Bandy, reporter for the local *Weekly Carrier*, and Doctor Jake along with a sprinkling of others on both sides of the aisle. Fr. Ray was rapidly trying to take note of everyone who considered her remark funny. Knowledge like that might come in handy down the road.

"Please now, let us remain in peace and good will here," he intervened. "Let us all be vigilant and patient as the bishop and his advisers work through this problem and the larger problem of closing the church."

Tom Barnette stood up. He did not ask for permission to speak. When you farm more acres than anyone else in the county, you do not need permission for anything. "Some of us think," he began, clearing his throat, "that a further discussion of the underlying problem might insure that this kind of vandalism not occur again. We would like to raise the issue about whether the bishop might allow us access to the church again, at least for social functions."

Fr. Ray wished fervently that he was back at his barn, feeding his real sheep. They were a whole lot better suited for his pastoral role, "feed my lambs, feed my sheep." Christ himself had tried to do that for human sheep and they put him to death for his trouble. One thing for sure, if Fr. Ray's real sheep were like the Barnette type of human sheep, he'd have to get rid of them. They would find ways to get through any fence he might put up. But he could hardly ignore Tom Barnette's request. He nodded. Tom turned to Mary. "I believe you had something you wanted to say, Mary?"

She had known this was coming because they had planned it that way, but her contempt for her uncle was plain to see on her face. Sure, make contrary bitch Mary do the talking. She stood up, stared at the ceiling, heart pounding and began. She had nothing to lose. It wasn't her dumb church. "We have heard of a parish north of here that is suing the bishop. Up at Broken Cross, Ohio." All of a sudden she realized what a fitting name for a place that was suing a bishop. But she forced her mind back to the subject at hand. "We are wondering, Mister Father Ray" (she had thought she would try calling him that, just to see his reaction), "what you would think if we sued too. As I am sure you know, a judge ruled against the bishop out in Iowa."

"Upon what grounds might such a suit be made?" Fr. Ray heard himself ask. He was going to have to defend the bishop and he didn't want to.

Mary was still looking at the ceiling. "Well for one thing," she said, "the bishop says we have a priest shortage. But I have an idea that the

Josephians in Marystone, who served St. Philo's for so many years, could keep on doing it, if they were asked properly. Anyway why not ordain women since I understand there are plenty of them fool enough to want the job. Secondly, St. Philo's was not broke but two hundred thousand in the black, and more could come easily from all these rich, tightwad farmers hereabouts." She glanced sideways at her uncle. "And thirdly, St. Philo's is not a dying church. Looks more like a well-heeled suburb around here than a farm community and getting worse that way every day."

Fr. Ray stared at her, as much in admiration as in dismay. Where in heaven's name had this woman come from.

"I'm afraid, Mister Miss Barnette," he leveled his eyes at her, playing her name game back at her, "that it's a little late to be making these points. They have all been made before and taken into consideration, and the bishop, representing Holy Mother the Church, has ruled to close the church."

"Parishioners want you to take the message to the bishop again," she answered, not at all flustered. "They are talking to lawyers and there is evidently good reason to argue that this church property does not belong to the diocese. It is not the bishop's to close. You tell him that, if you please. You know, Mister Father Ray, these people won't say what they really think because they are afraid of excommunication. They asked me to speak because they know I would love to get excommunicated."

A very audible murmur of shock and dismay arose from the pews. Who had ever heard of such arrogance, such sacrilege. Alvin Farkow could not keep silent. He had promised God and man that he would defend the Pope and the Church from any attack, and he intended to live up to his promise. He stood up, not asking for permission this time.

"And just who do you think your are, Mary Barnette, the pope or somethin'?"

Utter silence enveloped the church. On both sides of the aisle, people craned to see how Mister Miss Barnette would respond to that.

A nervous chuckle stirred in her throat, louder than she really would have called upon for the occasion. She nodded. "Pope Mary. That has a nice ring to it. Well, Alvin, I've got a hunch I could do as well as that old man over there in Rome."

A tide of shocked faces turned toward Fr. Ray, demanding rebuke and retribution. But Fr. Ray was saved by Alvin, intent on doing his duty.

"We don't have to listen to this blasphemy," he shouted. "This woman seems possessed by the devil. I will not stand for it. I am going home." Out into the aisle he stomped, glaring at Pope Mary. Most of the DODs followed him. Fr. Ray knew that the coming days were going to be very long ones.

The person most upset by what happened at the church meeting was Fr. Louis Lemming, pastor of the Church of the Resurrection in Bredsocken where the St. Philo parishioners were supposed to be going to church now. He had not been invited to the meeting though it seemed to him that he was the priest now in authority over what went on at St. Philo's. Actually he was relieved that he had not been invited because he did not relish having to face those renegades out there in the country who just might get violent if provoked. He made sure that his faithful lieutenant, Alvin Farkow, and his spies, Alice Dribble and Plover Venale, firm DOD members, would be there. They would give him a complete report on the proceedings.

Fr. Lemming preferred to be called Pastor Lemming, like the Lutherans were calling their ministers. This was his one and only deviation from conservative Catholic tradition and the real reason he did it was to set himself apart from other priests. Pastor Lemming's consuming ambition was to become a bishop, and setting himself apart from the other middle-aged priests who might also desire a bishopric could not hurt him. In his conservative eyes, too many priests his age were either liberal whiners or alcoholics, or womanizers, or sex offenders. Or weird characters like Fr. Ray. More of the young priests coming out of the seminary now were neo-cons and they would support him when the time came for choosing a new bishop.

"Mary Barnette dominated the meeting," Plover told him as they sat in the parlor of Pastor Lemming's rectory. "She doesn't even go to church."

"She's real trouble," added Alice, "but only Alvin stood up to her. Said she was possessed by the devil. Even George wouldn't stand up." Using last names was not necessary. All three of them knew Alvin was Alvin Farkow, and George was Alice's husband, George Dribble. "That heathen said she would like to get excommunicated, if you can imagine that." Alice looked over at Plover somewhat condescendingly. She figured her juicy little detail would grab the priest's attention more than what her rival had said, and it did. The two women forever competed for what other parishioners humorously referred to as the position of Pastor Lemming's Numero Uno. The irony of the situation was that both of them would have been shocked and outraged had anyone accused them of anything even remotely sexual in this competition. They fawned over him as a mother does a son, and the fact that he appeared to be delicate, almost effeminate, only strengthened them in their resolve to help him through the travails of pastoral office. As for Pastor Lemming, he enjoyed their attention but found them otherwise difficult to endure. He cultivated them for their role as devoted spies and council members.

"She said that?" Pastor Lemming blurted. Such irreverence was completely beyond his comprehension. "Is she a church member?"

"She's a Barnette. You just have to know the Barnettes. Think they own the county. But her father and uncle give generously to the church. Or did."

"What do you mean, 'did'?"

"Well, I don't need to tell you contributions are way down."

"Yes, I know. It is deplorable. What has happened to people? Don't they know we must all stand firm in bad times like these."

"They want more voice in affairs," Plover said. "That Mary Barnette— Alvin asked her if she thought she was the pope—was making that same old point. Not enough democracy in the church."

"But the church is not a democracy," Pastor Lemming said in his soft but earnest voice. "Democracy is an imperfect form of government. Only with the absolute authority of an infallible pope can we find our way through this vale of tears."

The two women nodded. The fact that they were women who considered themselves capable of running the parish and were more or less doing so, did not seem to shake their faith in male dominance. The pope said that he was infallible and since he could not make mistakes in such matters, then of course he was infallible.

"When Alvin asked Mary Barnette if she thought she was the pope, she practically took it as a compliment," said Alice. "Said she wouldn't mind at all being called the pope."

"She did?" And again Pastor Lemming gasped in genuine shock. "See, that's what comes from liberalizing the church." And again Alice beamed, knowing her detail had registered higher on the priest's shock-meter than Plover's.

"Was there anything new about the break-in?" Pastor Lemming wanted to know.

"No, but now some people are wondering if Pope Mary did it." Alice said.

Pastor Lemming: "Please, don't desecrate the pope's office that way. Do you think she could have?"

"Well, she was out in Chicago for a few years. That's where all those Unroman Catholics are headquartered, isn't it?" Plover said.

Pastor Lemming: "Who?"

Plover: "Oh, that's what we call them sometimes. You know. The ones who want to break away from Rome."

Alice: "Maybe we should call those Chicago Catholics." She thought that was funny but the priest only looked puzzled at her. Humor almost always escaped him.

"Well, to the matter at hand," he said briskly. "We must continue to stand firm. St. Philo's is closed. It will remain closed. Please help me get that word out. Legally, this is a matter for church law—Canon Law—not civil law. The church, the Mystical Body of Christ, has title to that church property and we must all accept that decision whether we like it or not."

The two nodded in agreement, if a bit mystified. All their lives they had heard the church referred to as the Mystical Body of Christ, but they weren't at all sure what that meant.

Chapter 5

A lvin Farkow was sure he could figure out who had knocked down the church door at St. Philo's. Basing his undercover operation on his years of watching detective shows on TV, he scheduled a series of meetings in the Yellow Room Saloon in Bredsocken with his buddies, Lloyd McTicken and George Dribble. Invariably in this setting, well-irrigated with beer, they recognized a cleverness in each other that they did not ordinarily notice. But at the moment he could not get his two compatriots focused on the subject at hand. They were into one of their favorite arguments with two other farmers.

"No Lloyd. Canada thistle is a bad weed but it is not by far the worst. Get a bunch of morning glories climbing all over your corn, then you know what bad is."

"Oh my, morning glories is as nice as tulips compared to that new horse weed thing that is taking over. Roundup won't even faze it anymore."

"You guys are babes in the woods about weeds. The worst of all is giant ragweed. I've seen it stop a 16 row combine right in its tracks."

"No, no, the granddaddy of all weeds in quack grass. Roots will grow right through potatoes in the ground."

"You fellas are not going to believe me, but if you want a real weed problem, try mulberry trees. You got a mulberry tree in a fence row and two weeks later you'll have a hundred. And by the time they are four inches high, they have a root half way to China and you cannot pull 'em out."

"Pooh, pooh. You gotta talk to my cousin in Tennessee. They let that stuff from Japan get started—kudzu. It'll climb a sheepshed and pull it right over to the ground in two years, he says."

"But sheep'll eat kudzu. Nothing'll eat horse weed."

"Be that as it may," Farkow raised his voice above the others, "we've got work to do here tonight. All right?"

In no time at all, which is to say, about six beers later, they had weeded out about two-thirds of the people in the county as possible suspects in the break-in. Farkow did it with one masterful stroke of a ball point on a napkin:

"People who can't swing maul accurately—out."

Three more nights and 17 beers later, came a second flash of wisdom:

"People who don't know church is closed—out."

After considerable argument, they also agreed that:

"People who aren't Catholic and never were—out. Non-Catholics would not care if the church was locked or not."

That narrowed the playing field considerably, except that, as Farkow pointed out, their list of suspects still had to include people who maybe weren't Catholic now but who once had been. "Once a Catholic, always a Catholic," McTicken observed.

"Even Pope Mary Barnette." Farkow said, and then after a little thought, added: "In fact, people who are not Catholic, but are supposed to be, are the very kind most likely to have done it."

All nodded. A plan of investigation was emerging. They would focus their attention on "fallen away Catholics." But this did not much simplify the matter because it was difficult to know who was "fallen away" and who was merely falling in and out on a month by month basis. That was the case for Hem Judin, the village philosopher, accountant, and official adviser to the finance department at Resurrection of the Lord parish in Bredsocken who happened to be sitting right then at the far end of the bar. Farkow leaned over, looked past his two partners in anti-crime, and shouted: "Hem, are you still going to church?"

Hem eyed him suspiciously and sucked elaborately on his beer bottle. As the accountant for Resurrection of the Lord, a post he held more out of wanting to know what was going on in the parish than in having any special allegiance to the church, he had to be careful. "What's it to you?"

"Oh, we were just wondering," Dribble said hastily. "Not meaning to pry. Now that nobody can get into St. Philo's, it's hard to tell who's going to Bredsocken like they are supposed to and who's not going at all."

Hem, who had been on his cell phone but listening to their talk too, eased himself carefully down off his stool and weaved over to the three budding detectives. He leaned carefully against the bar next to Dribble, studied the rows of liquor bottles on the shelves behind the bartender, took several belabored breaths, searched to find the right words. Finally: "Tell you gentlemen something. I'm no farmer but if you want to know the worst weed you ought to watch that chickweed stuff in the garden." He waited for a reaction but got none. "On the other subject at hand, I just don't know what to believe anymore. I feel like quitting church altogether but I'd hate to miss out on anything."

"Who do you think broke down that church door," Farkow asked.

Again, Hem stared ahead, ran his forefinger through the drips of moisture on the bar where Dribble's beer bottle had sat, as if he were trying to write something on the bar top, and took a few more mind-clearing breaths. Then he remembered he might need more fortification and shuffled all the way back to where he had left his own beer, picked it up, made a pretend-call on his cell phone for extra effect, and made his way slowly back to his questioners.

"I think you guys are missing one batch of suspects altogether. People that still despise the Catholic Church from the old days." He looked around as if maybe he was being spied on. "It could be the Masons, you know. They've been against Catholics from the beginning of this town."

"Oh, hell, Hem, I know most of those guys personally." McTicken replied. "They aren't that way any more. Fact is they asked me to join. Me, a Catholic, of all people. Anyway, there's not enough gumption in that entire bunch of old potbellies to do something like that."

"Did you join?" Dribble wanted to know, finding that question momentarily at least as fascinating as the broken-down door.

"Course not. I'm a Knight of Columbus. You want me to get excommunicated?"

"That contrary bitch of a Mary Barnette said last night that she'd like to get excommunicated," Farkow reminded them.

"You mean Pope Mary?" McTicken smiled in spite of himself.

"Just what does it mean to get excommunicated?" Dribble asked. So much about the Catholic Church mystified him, even in his solid allegiance to it.

"It means you get kicked out of the church," Farkow said.

"But we already been kicked out of our church. And they locked the door behind us."

"That's just a church building, not *the* church. The church is not a building. It's the Mystical Body of Christ. That's what the bishop keeps trying to tell us." Farkow was proud of his grasp of church doctrine. Not many deacons were so well informed.

"Well, just what the hell does that mean? What is a church if there's no building?"

"I'll tell you what it means," Hem said, looking around again and lowering his voice. "It's the cardinals and archbishops and such over there in Rome pulling all the strings. Nothing mystical about it."

"You're starting to sound like Tom Barnette."

"Tell you what I really think," Hem said in an even lower tone of voice. He was sizing himself up in the mirror behind the bar now, trying to look wise. "I bet you even money it was one of those pedophile priests broke that door down. Wanting to get even with the pope, the real one, for crackin' down on those sex loonies."

"We don't have any of them around here," McTicken said.

"And how do you know that?"

"Just what do those pedophile characters do, anyway?" Dribble said, the beer allowing him to speak with more candor than usual.

"First you don't know what the church is and now you don't know what a pedophile is," Farkow, the deacon, scolded. "Don't you ever read anything about religion?"

"If you're so smart," Dribble shot back, bold with the buzz of alcohol. "Unless you are one, just how the hell do you know WHAT they do?"

Everyone laughed uneasily except Farkow who decided they were straying too far from the subject at hand. Besides he wasn't sure what pedophiles did either. And he had a message on his cell phone. He flipped it open in the proper, practiced way, like the detectives on television. It was a text message from his wife: "Get hell home or dogs r eatin ur supper."

"Looks to me like we have to split up the investigation," he said, rolling his eyes at the message. Each of us take a different detail. OK?" When no one said anything, he went on. "Hem, you in on this?" Hem willy-nillyed around, finally nodded assent.

"OK, you are in charge of checkin' out priests around here who seem to be acting strange." Now it was Hem's turn to roll his eyes.

"And you, Lloyd, since you are on good terms with the Masons, you mince around and see if you can pick up anything suspicious about them." McTicken rolled his eyes too, but agreed to give it a try.

"George and I will make up a list of Catholics on shaky grounds with the church and start checkin' them out. I already know a few of them were up in Cleveland that night at a ball game so we can off them from the list already. And I think we ought to check out Pope Mary a little more."

"I still want you to tell me how anyone knows what those pedophiles do if you aren't one," Dribble said, not wishing to let Farkow off the hook.

"Meeting adjourned. I'll get the beer tonight." Farkow was thinking about his text message.

Chapter 6

A new rumor floating through Balem Township as winter approached made people forget about the vandalism at St. Philo's for awhile. An ethanol plant was coming to Vinal County, or so it was whispered. That in itself might not have caused the news to ricochet with such speed from the Yellow Room Saloon in Bredsocken to the Corner Pocket in Derby to the Last Ditch Cafe in Marystone. There were always rumors of new factories sifting through the ragweeds but nothing much usually came of them. This one, however, arrived in a most appealing gift wrapper.

"This could mean four dollar corn, you know," Tom Barnette was saying to Floyd Gowler at the Sheepshit Golf Course near the village of Gowler, in Jergin County. The course came by its weird local name because a few years earlier, Emmet Gowler, Floyd's father, had made history of sorts by grazing sheep on the fairways and roughs. Perhaps because of that notoriety, the golf course had become one of the main intellectual centers of agriculture in north-central Ohio—a place where new ideas were often discussed even before the agricultural professors at Ohio State found out about them. For a Barnette to be in Jergin County at all meant that something unusual was in the wind. Jergin and Vinal counties lay side by side, but might as well have been in different states as far as the local people were concerned. Floyd Gowler visited Las Vegas more often than he visited Vinal County and Tom Barnette went fishing in Canada a whole lot more than he went fishing in the lakes on Killdeer Plains Wildlife Refuge close to some of his farms. Hem Judin philosophized that the real division between the two counties was more like the northern halves of both versus the southern halves because of the "watershed enigma" as he called it. South of Gowler village, the water flowed eventually into the Gulf of Mexico and so Gowlerites looked southward for salvation, he claimed, doing their serious shopping in Columbus. On the other hand, Marystone, farther north where the water flowed into Lake Erie, looked toward the Great Lakes for rescue from boredom, and the people shopped in Findlay or Toledo. Terry Speckle, who sold John Deere tractors on both sides of the divide said that Hem was "full of it" because Bredsocken was on the north side of the divide too, but shopped in Columbus nevertheless. Speckle claimed that Bredsocken villagers were not about to do anything that Marystone villagers would do for a reason no one talked about. Marystone was the location of the Shrine of Our Lady of Good Patience which towered benevolently above the village. People got cured of diseases at the shrine, so tradition said, but that "Catholic stuff" sounded creepy to the Protestant majority in the two counties, Speckle often explained. Some of them would travel all the way to Italy to marvel at the churches there but had never set foot in the Marystone shrine even though it was just as magnificent as most of the ones in Rome— "just not any nekkid statues like in Italy," Speckle pointed out. Another reason for avoiding the shrine was that it attracted "foreigners" of middle Eastern backgrounds from Detroit and Cleveland, and was therefore viewed with suspicion by the majority of the natives, including many of the Catholics. Also Marystone often voted Democratic, which didn't advance local good will. Bredsocken considered itself Lutheran and Republican, the two halves of the one true religion.

"Maybe even five dollar corn," Floyd Gowler replied to Tom Barnette's suggestion. Floyd, in his fifties, had become a little more comfortable with taking over the mantle of patriarchy that the Gowler name cursed him with, now that his father, Emmet, had passed away. His eyes gleamed. The vision of five dollar corn appealed to farmers like the vision of a naked cheerleader cavorting along the sidelines at an Ohio State football game, which was something else that just might happen any day now. Corn had gone to five dollars back in 1995 and the result had been not riches for struggling farmers but the consolidation of farm land into fewer hands. Younger farmers did not remember that; older ones didn't want to remember.

"It's supposed to be built somewhere around Marystone, between the highway and the railroad," Speckle elaborated.

"Maybe in Balem Township," Barnette said, unable to keep desire out of his voice. "They say it will take up a whole farm and that they intend to buy even more land so they can have a big hog factory to feed the spent grains to. That'll make farm land values jump, you better believe it."

Gowler snorted and repeated what he remembered his father saying in earlier spasms of spiraling prices. "There isn't any prevailing price anymore. Every time you sneeze land goes up again. Bringin' five thousand an acre and more in Iowa."

"What's spent grains?" George Dribble asked. Wherever rumors simmered, Dribble could be counted on to be taking the temperature of the gossip.

"It's what's left over after you distill the ethanol. That's what makes this thing go, you see," Barnette explained. "You make fuel out of the corn and then you can still feed it."

"Isn't but half true," Hem Judin replied. He was the most revered of local accountants because he knew a lot about agriculture. He had also become the unofficial Father Confessor of Vinal County and nearly that in Jergin County. He knew the numbers and so seemed smarter than anyone else. "Once you take the spirits out of the corn, you take out most of the feed value too."

"You don't say," Barnette replied, a bit of surprise in his voice. "The boys at the bank didn't point that out." He jotted a note in the pad he always kept in his bib overalls. He did not get to be a well-to-do farmer by overlooking details.

"What is ethanol anyway?" Dribble, always the questioner, wanted to know.

"Same as whiskey," Gowler said. He had a special interest in the subject because his father had always had another dream—to make bourbon out of his corn if he could get some tax breaks like on-farm wineries got.

"You mean ethanol that you can run tractors on is actually whiskey?" Dribble was by turn totally in disbelief and totally in awe.

"Well, they make you put something in it so you can't drink it. They add regular gas to it. Otherwise the entire corn belt would fall to alcoholism." Gowler said.

"But if we use all the corn for ethanol, how we gonna feed the hogs and cattle?" Dribble was thinking ahead.

"If I can get five dollar corn, I don't care if all the hogs in Ohio starve to death," Gowler replied.

The older farmers stared at him. What was going to come of the world with brash men like Floyd Gowler coming into leadership roles? But none of them said it out loud. Tom Barnette was still staring at his notes and the numbers he had jotted down earlier.

"Tell you what, gentleman. I don't think I'd get too rambunctious about this ethanol thing. It's gotta have subsidies with two dollar corn. With five dollar corn I can't imagine even politicians wanting to fund it. And it appears to me that Saudi Arabia could still make money selling oil at ten dollars a barrel."

Don Barnette would have been with his brother at the golf course were he not having a meeting of his own, with his daughter. And it wasn't pretty. Pope Mary was handing out ultimatums like a real pope.

"If I'm to do all the work here, or most of it," she was pounding the table, "I am going to have some say-so about how this farm is run."

"Now, child, don't get so—

"Don't you dare refer to me as 'child.'"

"All right, all right." Don was not as confrontational as his brother could be, which is why Tom usually made farming decisions for both of them even though they did not farm together. Now it was obvious, at least to Martha, his wife, that he was about to let Mary have her way.

"I've been studying the markets real close," Mary said. "It is all plain as day and I can't understand why farmers can't see the handwriting on the wall. Grain prices are going to go higher than a kite. So I say we should *not* sell our 2006 grain yet, I don't care what that imbecile up at the elevator says. He *wants* us to sell, don't you see, Dad. He wants us to sell ahead of the upturn. Or else he's just as dumb as the farmers."

"Mary, this kind of talk about high prices is nothing new. Farmers wishfully-think the market that way all the time and then they overproduce and the price goes nowhere," Don tried to explain to her. "You really haven't had enough experience in farming to be so sure of yourself."

"The heck I haven't," she replied hotly. "What do you think I was doing in Chicago at that commodity brokerage firm? That's by far the best experience for farming that you can get. I'm telling you we are not going to sell any grain right now. Nor tomorrow, nor any time soon and you can either agree or I'm outta here."

"How can you be so sure?" Martha said. No wonder they were calling her Pope Mary. "Do you think you're infallible?" She had always been half afraid of her daughter. She was convinced that Mary wanted to farm only because she wanted to embarrass men by doing it better than they could. She asked another question. "Why are you so bitter anyway?"

Mary stared at her. The face of the handsome grain trader who had jilted her in Chicago came into her mind but she was not about to bring that episode up. "Look, this isn't about me," she replied, trying to sound patient. "All you have to do is be able to add and subtract. Carryover is down. World demand seems to be up. Land's going out of farming by thousands of acres a month. Whenever you have war, and we are in a war, don't forget, farm prices go up. And now we have ethanol and biodiesel pushing up prices. All you have to do is study the numbers on that computer there that you refuse to touch. We've got information from all over the world right there at our fingertips. I know just as much as those stupid traders do. Maybe more. We... are ... not... going ... to ... sell ... yet. OK?"

"Oh, I've heard that all before," Don said. "You'll learn eventually. Hope springs eternal within the farmer's heart." Then he stormed out of the house.

"I take that as you are agreeing?" Mary shouted out the door at her retreating father. He just kept going, not looking back. Mary smiled. She knew she had won. Their 2006 corn and soybeans would go into storage and stay there until she said sell.

"And one more thing," she shouted at the retreating figure. "We're gonna build more grain storage. If the elevator can make money storing grain, then we can too. That's something else I learned in Chicago."

Don, in his machine shop, slammed a few tools around. Without a son to take over, he had been thrilled, if a little nervous, when Mary came home and announced her intentions to farm with him. He did not agree with what she was saying at the moment, but what the hell. He had enough money socked away to weather just about any storm, and if worst came to worst, he could sell the farm and be a millionaire several more times over. Let her have her way. Let her fall flat on her face once. Do her some good. And building more storage was a good idea, something he would have done on his own, if he were younger.

He stalked back to the house and sat down at the kitchen table in a great show of ceremony.

"All right, Miss Prissy. You do the marketing. You build more storage. If you lose your ass, don't come whining to me."

"Put it in writing," she said, unmoved. She already had an agreement typed up.

He hardly glanced at it, just picked up the pen she offered, signed, and stared out the window with the look of a man expecting to see a tornado on the horizon. She looked at his signature and then smiled wickedly.

"And as my first order of business," she said. "We are planting all soybeans next year. No corn."

He whirled around. He thought she must be kidding. Next year was going to be the best corn market ever. Ethanol was going to make them rich. Not to grow corn, not to grow *any* corn was folly beyond any cornbelt farmer's imagination.

"Just think it out now," she said, trying once again to show patience. "Everyone is going to plant corn. If they do, soybean prices must go up. Historically beans are always about two and a half times the price of corn. So if corn goes up, like you say, beans will go up too. And beans are not nearly as expensive as corn to grow. You know as night follows day the damned suppliers will up their prices for fertilizer and herbicides just as fast as the price of corn goes up. And you're the one always telling me, it costs twice as much to grow corn as beans even in normal times."

"This is the corn belt. You grow corn in the corn belt. It produces twice as many bushels as beans and then some. You can't *not* grow corn in the corn belt."

"Watch me."

Chapter 7

Fr. Ray was leaning on the sheep pen gate, his right foot on the second board from the bottom, watching his sheep munching on their hay. He heard a throat clear behind him. Startled, he turned to see Dow Kapier standing in the mellow glow of the barn light above them. The priest relaxed. Kapier was one of the few people he always felt comfortable around. He liked to sit in Dow's woodworking shop and watch the carpenter at work. Being with Kapier did not require conversation.

"Father, I've got the door repair done. You want I should put it back up."

Fr. Ray heaved a sigh. Kapier was always bugging him about the door, as if it were important to get it fixed and back up again as soon as possible. The priest did not like to think about the door. "Nice bunch of lambs, don't you think? Gotta get them wormed again. Hate feeding hay already in November, but pastures dried up." He waited for Kapier to say something. Silence. "Don't you think if we put the door up now it just might antagonize whoever broke it down to do it again?"

"Doubtful," Kapier replied. "He made his point, I'd say."

"Think so?"

"Yep." Kapier seemed uneasy. Eight words amounted to a speech to him.

"I think we'll just leave the temporary door in place for now," the priest said. "At least till we get this thing settled."

Kapier started to leave, his face showing disappointment, then turned back. He had more to say, but the words came only laboriously. "You think the bishop will let us use the church again? After this?"

"Perhaps."

"You think it's right for him to lock up the church?" Kapier's eyes bore into the priest's face. Something about his manner precluded any quibbling.

"Actually, Dow, I don't, but you know, we have to obey church authority."

"Puke on church authority," Kapier said and then retreated into the night, leaving the priest gasping. The quiet woodworker had never talked to him that way before.

He barely recovered from the shock of Kapier's remark when another visitor arrived. Dan Bandy from the newspaper. Since the break-in they had gotten to know each other a little.

"Just driving by, saw you in the barn door," he said. "Who was that guy just left. He dang near ran into me. Looked mad."

"Dow Kapier. He's fixed the door. A good woodworker. He takes care of the cemetery and the church at St. Philo's. And what can I do for you?" A bit of annoyance had crept into his tone. His barn time was his happy hour. He didn't like being disturbed there.

"Just wondering if there's anything new to report. About the break-in." Although like most everyone else, Bandy had relatives in the cemetery, he was not Catholic and viewed the whole affair like an anthropologist studying the behavior of primitive societies, a category not too far removed from Balem Township in his estimation.

"Nice lambs, don't you think?" the priest countered. "But need worming."

Bandy looked slightly uneasy. Brought up mostly in urban society, he was not accustomed to casual conversation about internal parasites, least of all with a priest. Fr. Ray noted his discomfort with some secret satisfaction. Modern society was rearing humans who felt uncomfortable when forced to face the real world of nature. Then he answered Bandy's question. "No. Haven't a clue. How about you?"

Bandy shrugged. "I think it was an outside job. Meaning no offense, Catholics around here generally do what their church tells them to do in my experience. Way too gutless to break down a church door. No, I think it was just pranksters. Kids. Out for a lark. Probably drinking. Beats knocking over mailboxes."

Fr. Ray liked his answer. Bandy was a good reporter. He would no doubt get a better job at a bigger newspaper one of these days and move on. That was the fate of village newspapers. Always a brain drain in progress.

"How long have you been working for the *Weekly Carrier* anyway, Dan?"

"Long enough. Eight years I guess now." He paused. He felt that he needed an excuse for not having moved on to higher pay somewhere. "There's something to be said for staying put and really getting to know a place. My family goes way back here, you know. Staying here might make a real writer out of me."

"Maybe you'll make editor someday."

"Oh Lord no. Being editor of a small town newspaper is almost as thankless as being mayor. Somebody's bitching at you all the time, you know."

"Almost as thankless as being a parish priest." They both smiled. The priest decided that Bandy might be all right. Bandy thought the same of the priest.

"Well, if some of our local swains did the break-in, we'll know eventually," he said. "They won't be able to keep their mouths shut. I've been hanging out at the Yellow Room Saloon. Surely hear something there."

Fr. Ray was seized by an impulse. "Why don't we go there right now. I could use a little change of scenery."

Bandy looked surprised. "You sure you want to be seen in there? Especially with me? I'm not exactly a church goer, you know."

"I could say I was trying to convert you." Again they both smiled.

"I'll drive," Bandy said.

"So you were a Catholic at one time," the priest inquired, as if he were going to pursue his threat of trying to convert Bandy. They had taken a table in the darkest corner of the bar, the better to observe while not being observed.

"Hardly. Oh, I was raised Catholic but soon grew out of it. Sort of like Santa Claus. Meaning no insult, but no one can really believe all that God stuff, can they?" To his surprise, the priest did not seem offended.

"You sound like my father," Fr. Ray replied. "He used to say things like that. Just to get my goat, I think."

"I bet there's more disbelievers than believers," Bandy said. "But most of them are afraid to admit it. Not like that Mary Barnette."

Fr. Ray perked up. "You know her?"

"Well, yes. I was pretty interested in her in high school. Then she went away to college. I tried to keep track of her. She went to work in Chicago and fell in love with some hotshot commodity trader. Turned out he traded in everything, including girls, and he broke her heart, the way I understand it. Made her bitter, everyone says. She came back here to heal I suppose."

"Have you tried to date her?"

Bandy smiled resignedly. "She won't have anything to do with me. Nor any other man, far as I can see. I think she uses all that bravado to hide her unhappiness."

"Maybe she's a lesbian."

Bandy looked at him sharply. What kind of priest would say that right out in public? Strange. "No, I think I can vouch for that. She was what we used to call boy crazy in high school. Hot. I can tell you one thing, she was the smartest girl who ever went through our school. That's probably the reason she doesn't have a man. Men are afraid of women like her."

"You think she could have knocked the door down?"

Bandy looked surprised again. Just what kind of character was this priest anyway. He paused a moment before he answered. "Nah. Not her style. But then anything is possible. I've quit trying to figure out human behavior."

The door to the Yellow Room Saloon opened and in came Alvin Farkow. He looked around, blinking in the dim light, spotted Fr. Ray and Bandy, and after a moment's surprise, walked on over to their table.

"Didn't expect to find you in here, Father, but you're just the man I wanted to see," he said. "Got some news for you." He looked at Bandy, his eyes narrowing. "This is off the record, newsboy." He tried to look like a character on television saying that. Bandy rolled his eyes. He would have been amused, but he more or less loathed Alvin Farkow.

"Gotten a piece of that Barnette girl yet?" he asked, knowing that would irritate Farkow.

Farkow reddened. Only Dan Bandy would say something like that in front of a priest. Or to a deacon. Alvin Farkow was faithful to his wife and you better believe it. He looked at Fr. Ray for some evidence of shock or disapproval, saw only dismay, and went to the bar. What he had to tell the priest could wait.

But Fr. Ray was curious. He was also feeling the beer. "Well Alvin, I think you can speak what's on your mind. Dan will honor your privacy. Won't you?"

"I'm sure I already know his gossip, and now if I repeat it, he'll accuse me of breaking a confidence."

"You're so smart, newsboy, what did you think I was going to say?"

"That Binky Small over in Marystone had another nervous breakdown in church and took a communion wafer back to his mobile home instead of consuming it like he was supposed to, and then said this is what comes when bishops lock up churches."

Farkow glared at Bandy. Did the smart ass know everything first? Fr. Ray's eyes widened. He had not heard that one.

"What I was going to say was that maybe Binky knocked the door down," Farkow said. "Anyone crazy enough to steal a Sacred Host is crazy enough to do anything."

"Except that Binky doesn't drive anymore and was seen in town at a time that would disallow him from walking all the way out to St. Philo's and back," Bandy said.

"Maybe he had an accomplice to do the driving." Farkow loved words like accomplice. He flashed out his cell phone, flipped it open expertly and expertly text- messaged Lloyd McTicken. "Check out Binky. Have access to car?"

"Wait a minute," Fr. Ray interjected, wide-eyed. "Did I just hear you say someone stole a consecrated communion wafer?" His voice was full of disbelief.

"Oh, it's very, very hush up stuff at the Shrine," Farkow said, delighted that he, a mere deacon, was for once better informed than the priest.

"But how—"

"He just took the Sacred Host in his hands and walked out of church with it. Fortunately the priest noticed and got the sheriff after him. But no one knows what happened to the Host."

"I find it somehow odd to think of a sheriff tracking down the body of Christ in the form of bread," Fr. Ray said, feeling the beer, feeling suddenly like he was out of his own body, trying to be cute. Trying to be cute was his weakness and beer didn't help. The other two looked at him uncomprehendingly, not catching what the priest thought was a very sophisticated bit of theological humor.

"Well, Binky supposedly said he was going to use it for secret communion services if the bishop didn't unlock St. Philo's," Bandy said. He had told the sheriff he'd not write about the incident because it was so shocking to Catholics, but since the news must be all over if Farkow knew it, he could at least talk about it.

Fr. Ray was indignant. He should have been notified, if not by the sheriff, then by church authorities. None of the Josephians who ran Our Lady of Good Patience had said a word, and he was often their confidante. Nor had the Bishop bothered to tell him. Was he an anachronism now that one of his churches was closed? Maybe he was spending too much time at his farming.

"Who is this Binky Small for heaven's sake?" he asked.

"Oh, you know about him, Father. He's always doing something weird. Last year he started drinking holy water right out of the baptismal font. Thought it might cure his cold. He's kind of a nut case, but not quite crazy enough to pen up. Or so we thought anyway."

Farkow's cell phone was buzzing. He glanced at it. "Lloyd's getting right on it," he announced, hoping he looked very detective-like. Then he added: "He says no one will give Binky a ride anywhere because God's going to punish him for sacrilege and might decide to do it when Binky's riding in their car."

Bandy broke out laughing. He knew why he stayed in Vinal County.

The front door to the bar opened and in walked Lloyd McTicken and George Dribble. They came straight to the table where the trio was sitting, and without any invitation, pulled up chairs from another table and sat down. They both stared curiously at the priest, nodded to him, did not say what was obvious from the look on their faces, that they were wondering what he was doing in a bar. Priests weren't supposed to go into bars, were they?

"Got something you might like to hear," Dribble said, beaming, his gaze taking in the priest too. "Got a lead."

"A motorcycle gang was actually seen out in the vicinity of St. Philo's," Bandy said, watching Dribble visibly deflate.

"I think I hate you," Dribble said. "But that's not the best part of it."

Now it was Bandy's turn to look curious.

"Lester Swart was ridin' with 'em." Dribble smiled triumphantly.

"Lester? That could figure. He's always into devilment." Bandy conceded a point to Dribble.

" But I can't imagine him knocking a door down." Farkow said. "Too much work."

"He'd just pick the lock instead." Bandy elaborated.

"Remember when Johnny Reamer dared him to slip a pint of cow piss in a whiskey bottle onto the bar at the Knights of Columbus, right next to the bourbon?" McTicken said, "Begging your pardon, padre." They all laughed.

"Whaaaat?" The priest's eyes seemed to cover his whole face. Where had he been all his life. He decided part of his priestly work should mean frequenting bars. .

McTicken was delighted to tell the story. "Well, he wouldn't try to do that when the place was open. That would have been too easy. You just have to know Lester. He decided to break in after closing time and put the vile liquid on the bar among the other bottles. He's a real good lock picker. With the pint of cow piss in his hip pocket, he was about half way through jiggling at the lock when our defenders of law and order, the Buste brothers, spotted him." McTicken had slipped into a kind of laid-back drawl, a trademark part of his story-telling. "When he spotted the cops he walked right straight up to them, as if not a bit dismayed. 'It's not what it looks like,' he said to them. 'You know I'm good at pickin' locks and I was just tryin' to help out a fellow citizen. Grady Graham borrowed this pint of whiskey out of the bar, and then felt guilty about it and so I said, well, Grady, I'll just put it back for you.'"

"What do you mean, he borrowed the whiskey?" the priest asked, by now thoroughly puzzled. He really was spending too much time on his farm.

"He's our resident klepto," Bandy broke in. "Nine times out of ten if someone is missing something, the police will find it in Grady's apartment and nobody presses charges."

"You're kidding."

"Nope." McTicken was back on the story. "You see, Lester knew that the Buste brothers would have suspected that his story about Grady was made up but more believable than if he had told the truth, if you get my meaning. So anyways, our local enforcers who often move back and forth a tad over the fine line of the law themselves, they nod, pretending belief, because they see a chance to enjoy a little free liquor. They confiscate the bottle, and tell Lester to get the hell home—pardon, Father—and they'd fix it up with Grady and the Knights of Columbus. Just for Lester to keep his mouth shut. You can figure out what happened. Lester lit out for home and the Buste brothers got a big laugh out of it." He paused for just exactly the right length of time. "Until they tasted the bourbon."

Everyone around the table except the priest broke into raucous laughter even though they had heard the story a hundred times. Fr. Ray just stared, astonished to silence.

"Of course, you understand, Padre, they could never make an issue out of it because that would be admitting they opened the bottle which meant that they would be accomplices to a crime," McTicken explained. "It was sooooo poetic. Lester had 'em sort of blackmailed."

Finally Fr. Ray did laugh, and once laughing, found it difficult to stop. A realization was sweeping over him, heightened by the beer. These guys were all characters, just like the guys in seminary. But of course. Everyone was a character. He had never allowed himself the pleasure of embracing the individuality of his parishioners. Always kept to the aloof, professional oversight befitting a clergyman. But here he was in this bar with these men and for the first time in his priesthood, maybe in his whole life, he was seeing, quite clearly, what had never been clear to him before. People were real, live, individual persons. He had been in the habit of thinking of them as bodies, numbers, digits, parishioners, *subjects*. Undifferentiated "members of the Mystical Body of Christ," as the theology books put it. Now he was realizing that they were each unique, each different from the others. He knew that was true of sheep. Every one of his ewes had her own personality. Of course people did too, only more so. He was at once ashamed that he had been so blind, and elated to have made the discovery. His training, if not his own natural reserve, had brainwashed him into thinking of people always in the plural, as a flock, to be handled as if one size fits all. How stupid he had been.

"Isn't that such a fit now," he said, using an expression his mother always said in reaction to a story like McTicken's. He knew he sounded a little woozy because he was a little woozy. Then he tried to sound sober: "I think it's time for me to head back to the rectory." He paused. "Yep, I know it's hard to maintain that a farmhouse two miles from the church is a rectory. But life is full of mystery." And before the puzzled eyes of his companions, he laughed, threw a twenty dollar bill on the table, and walked out. "Keep the change for the fund to find the door knocker-downer." His laughter trailed behind him.

Dan Bandy was smiling. "He's forgotten that he came here with me. He's going to have to come back in."

The real reason Fr. Ray wanted to get back to the rectory was that he needed to talk to the bishop about this stolen consecrated communion wafer business before it got too late in the evening. The bishop did not like to be called after eleven o'clock. It was fortunate that he did not have a cell phone because if he had called right at the moment, he might have been reckless enough with beer to violate his rule of not ever saying anything to provoke anybody, especially a bishop.

Chapter 8

The first thing he did next morning was to call the bishop. This communion wafer business was bothering him more than it should. After all, anything that can happen will happen, and the more unlikely the happening, the more probable will be its happening.

"Do you know anything about a mentally-disadvantaged man in Marystone desecrating a sacred host?" he asked, after the usual greetings.

Silence. Then the Bishop answered. "Nobody tells me anything anymore, you ought to know that." His voice sounded complaining. Oh, Lord, the bishop had not been informed either. "What do you mean? Someone desecrating the Blessed Sacrament?"

Fr. Ray immediately realized he had made a mistake. Never tell the bishop anything disturbing that he will eventually find out from someone else. The messenger always gets the blame. Now he had to extricate himself with minimal fallout.

"It must be just more silly gossip, nothing to concern yourself about, Your Excellency. You know how it is in the autumn. Rumor season. People beginning to fear the coming winter I believe. You ever wonder why there's more paranoia in the fall?"

"Ray, what the hell are you talking about? Every day is paranoid season around here and confound it, it's getting worse. You found out anything yet about that confounded break-in?"

"Well, actually no, but the rumor is that there was a motorcycle gang cruising around Marystone that night. Might lead to something." Fr. Ray did not think it was going to lead to anything, but it would give the Bishop's mind something to chew on.

"Well, I'm glad you called. Something I need to talk over with you. What with the break-in at, at, at, —"

"St. Philo's."

"Yes, St. Philo's. There's been a growing fear that there might be more vandalism—at closed churches everywhere. What if the stained glass windows were broken? They're worth a lot of money, you know."

"I suppose so."

"Anyway, we've been approached by an antiquary business that is interested in purchasing stained glass windows."

"What's an antiquary business?" Fr. Ray's mind was going numb with what he thought he was going to hear.

"Well, you know, high class salvage. An art recycling company."

"Are you suggesting that we remove the windows at St. Philo's and sell them?" Fr. Ray could barely squeeze out the words without revealing anger and contempt.

"Well they're worth really big money, not just the windows, but some of the altar carvings. There's a real demand for this stuff. People are using it to decorate with. Real upsmanship to have a span of communion rail in your house."

"Are you saying," Fr. Ray tried to maintain a calm, even voice. "Are you saying the plan is to tear down the church and sell it piece by piece?"

"Well, you make it sound really awful. It's really just being practical. I told you this before. Didn't I? Confound it, I'm sure I told you that."

"I see." Fr. Ray dared say nothing more because he knew that whatever he said would be full of anger. For the first time in his life, a spark of rebellion caught embers in his soul and began to smolder.

"You do know I tell you this in strictest confidence," the bishop continued hurriedly. "I know I can trust you in this regard. Yes, I understand how repulsive this must sound, if not to you, to your congregation, but all things considered, I don't need to tell you how badly we need money."

"I see," Fr. Ray said again. Nothing more.

"Oh, and there's another thing," the bishop said. "You've been nominated to become an auxiliary bishop. It's a great honor and I don't know anyone who deserves it more."

"I see." Fr. Ray's voice now sounded as cold as a wind blowing off a polar ice cap. But the bishop sailed on, not hearing the edge in the priest's words.

"Can't tell you any more than that right now. Nothing's been completely decided, but I wanted you to know I'm backing you. My old ticker isn't working like it used to, and I want someone I can rely on in a pinch."

"I see."

For a long time after he put the phone down, Fr. Ray sat in his office, staring out at his barn looming in the darkness beyond the window. At first he merely rejected what he had heard as impossible. In the arms of the institutional church, he had known only comfort and safe harbor, never the frigid hand of monarchical power that other people and other churches complained about down through the centuries. He had thought that any criticism of Catholicism was merely prejudice from those too ignorant to understand how much good the church accomplished. Even when sexual scandals engulfed the clergy, he had remained steadfast in defense of his fellow priests. Less that 15% of the clergy were involved, he repeated in the face of the rising storm. And half of those were, he figured, victims of liars seeking money for abuse that they merely fancied or that lawyers had conjured up out of dim and shadowy memories.

But his new-found realization from the conversations at the Yellow Room Saloon, that when dealing with church members one size does not fit all, came rising again to the surface of his brain. His abhorrence of what he had just heard from the bishop ballooned in his mind out of control. It was bad enough to close churches that did not need to be closed except in the hope of making those still open more profitable, but to auction off the art treasures of these churches as if they were mere antiques, that he found unconscionable. And did Bishop Feering think his priests were venal enough to accept an honorary title as payment for loyalty? Right out loud in the empty room, he spoke his thoughts: "One size does not fit all, Mister Bishop Feering, and you are about to learn that." His customary timidness told him to hold his peace and be glad that he still had St. Clare's. But when a man slow to anger finally gets aroused, he is more dangerous than the quick-tempered. Could he slink, yellow-bellied, away from the fight that was sure to come if anyone tried to take the windows out of St. Philo's and sell them? That was like Judas selling out Christ.

A strange thought came to him. Did, maybe, an auxiliary bishop have any real power? Maybe he could raise real hell if he were one. What was an auxiliary bishop anyway? He pulled a book about Canon Law off the shelves nearby and leafed through it. It appeared that when a need arose for an auxiliary bishop, recommendations were requested from the priests in the diocese. The bishop then submitted a number of names to the Apostolic Nuncio who after some deliberation recommended to the Pope several candidates. The bishop was then informed which candidate had been picked and if the candidate would accept the offer. Then came the part Fr. Ray was looking for. An auxiliary had all the powers of a bishop including ordination but had no fiscal authority in the diocese unless the local bishop were absent. Of course. Another Catch-22. Hold tight to the money. That was the only real power. But an auxiliary did have all the other powers of a bishop. Hmmm.

For a reason he could not articulate, he decided that he wanted to talk to Mary Barnette at the first opportunity.

It was not easy to find an excuse to talk to her, to appear to have only accidentally happened upon her while pursuing other business. He drove past her farm several times, hoping to see her at work in the barnyard or in fields close to the road. His plan was to use as an excuse for stopping to ask if she knew anyone who sheared sheep in the neighborhood although he already knew of several shearers. When he was unable to "happen by" casually, he inquired discreetly of parishioners about why he had not seen any of the Barnettes in church lately. Perhaps with the fall work more or less finished, they had gone to Florida like so many of the "poor farmers" in his human flock did these days. But discreet inquiry drew no information either. The Barnettes were not Defenders of the Door and the church-goers were apparently pretending they did not exist.

Finally he saw her pickup parked in Dow Kapier's driveway and since he was a frequent visitor to Dow's woodworking shop, he had a good excuse to drop in. As he pushed through the shop door, the two people inside stopped their conversation abruptly and eyed the priest as if he were interrupting important talk. Fr. Ray pretended surprise at Mary's presence, pretended not to have recognized her pickup.

"Well, if it isn't the Lone Ranger," she said and then looked out the shop window. "Where's Silver?"

Fr. Ray smiled. Although unaccustomed to being treated in what he considered a disrespectful, even snotty fashion, he was surprised that he didn't mind. Kind of liked it in fact. Certainly better than the fake respect with which he was confronted most of the time.

"Just passing by. Thought Dow had traded pickups. Was going to tease you,"—he nodded towards the woodworker—"about finally getting rid of that old jalopy."

"The jalopy may be 25 years old but she's got only 31,000 miles on her," Dow said. "Not good math to trade yet." He looked sharply at the priest. "I'm surprised you pay attention to what people drive. You always do that?" He seemed to be making more than just conversation.

"That's a really beautiful cabinet you're working on," Fr. Ray said by way of answer. He did not care a bit about what kind of car or truck Dow or anyone else drove and had only said what he had said as an excuse to visit.

"It's for Mary."

"Actually for my mother," Mary said.

Silence all around. Fr. Ray had a distinct feeling the other two wanted him to leave so they could continue their conversation. But he was not about to pass up what seemed to him a perfect opportunity. Having Dow there helped. Dow rarely talked to anyone and could be counted on not to gossip if asked not to. And the woodworker could act as sort of foil between the priest and the woman. In case of, well, good grief, Ray, he thought to himself, in case of *what*?

Out loud, he addressed the two, as if they were co-conspirators. "I've learned something I want to share with you." He wondered if he were making the biggest mistake of his life, maybe his first big mistake. Or maybe for the first time in his life, he was standing up for what he truly believed. "But you must promise to keep it between us for now. You really must."

"Why would you start trusting me?" Mary asked sarcastically.

"When I tell you, if I do, you'll know why. I really need to tell someone, and I really need secrecy at least for a little while." The priest felt himself oozing into quicksand from which he would never be able to extricate himself.

Both Mary and Dow stared at him. Whatever was going on was not in character with the priest they thought they knew. Mary made her usual quick decision.

"OK. You've got my word." Then, not wanting to be drawn too far into anything churchy, she added: "For a month."

Fr. Ray could not repress a smile. This woman was very, *very* clever. Dow, meanwhile, merely nodded assent to the asked-for promise. The priest took a deep breath.

"The bishop plans to take the stained glass windows out of the church and sell them." Fr. Ray knew, with those words, that he had crossed over into a life he had not planned for himself.

The wonder on the faces of his two listeners was obvious. Neither could even imagine such an action, let alone believe it. But Fr. Ray was riveted not by Mary's stony silence, but by the anger he could see building up on Dow's face. He had thought that it would be Mary who would express outrage. Even when she spoke, the priest could not take his eyes off the woodworker. The man seemed about to explode.

"Why do you think I would care," Mary said, saucy now, realizing that she did care, but not yet ready to let her true feelings show.

"You care because you know that such action is grossly unjust," the priest said. He was still watching Dow who had picked up a hammer and was tapping the worktable in front of him with it. Suddenly, the hammer rose over Dow's head and smashed hard into the table's surface.

"Like the living hell he will," the woodworker muttered. "Those windows go out only over my dead body and it won't be the only dead one."

Even Mary drew back, her eyes bugging out. For once no words came to her lips.

Nor had Fr. Ray anticipated such an outburst. Dow had always seemed a gentle soul. Where was all this anger coming from?

"We have to figure out a plan," the priest said, staring hard at Dow as if he were afraid the latter would become violent. "We have to figure a civilized way out of this."

"Does the lawyer my uncle retained know about this yet?" Mary asked.

"I will break the windows out before I let anyone take them," Dow muttered.

"Now, let's not overreact," the priest said hastily, regretting that he had shared the news with Dow at all.

"There's no way they can dismantle that church if we, I mean the congregation, is against it," Mary said.

Fr. Ray shook his head. "The bishop says the diocese has legal title to the church so he can do as he pleases with it."

"Our lawyer seems to have some guts," Mary said. She was not supposed to be telling Fr. Ray just how far along their legal proceedings had gone because he was deemed to be the opposition. That had been what she was really visiting Dow about. And there were other strategies in the works that even the lawyer didn't know about. "You want us to keep a secret, Lone Ranger. We need to know if you are with us or against us?"

The priest's mind all but seized up. The last thing he wanted to do was commit himself, even though he knew he could never condone the sale of the church windows. Something in Mary's eyes, boring into his very soul, made it impossible for him to evade her question.

"I am with you." He finally said, evenly, deliberately, knowing that his answer meant the end of life as he had known it.

Chapter 9

Something she saw in the parking spaces in front of the church made Mabel Duholland slam on the brakes and pull up.

"Think that's them, Ding?" she queried her sister beside her.

Ding shrugged. "Better check it out."

After the not-so secret meeting at the Barnettes, the two had volunteered to keep an eye out for the "salvationists," as they called the salvage company that was rumored to be coming after the church windows. Keeping an eye out meant that every two hours or so they would drive "Black Beauty," as they called their old Cadillac, from their farmhouse a mile away, past the church, turn around at the next crossroad, and drive back past again. Through the cold winter they had kept up their vigil and now with a February break in the weather, the air felt almost warm. It was good to be out and about. Becoming watchdogs of their church was proving to be most exciting. All their lives they had lived in the house where they were born, seldom straying far from it, never dreaming that some day great adventure would come their way. It was even more exciting than working at the bank and knowing how much money all the farmers roundabout had on deposit. The ones who poor-mouthed the most almost always had the most, they liked to say. The two spinster sisters sat in their car now and stared through the windshield. Three men standing beside a truck were watching a fourth bracing a ladder up alongside one of the stained glass windows.

"It's them surely," Ding finally said.

Mabel pulled a cell phone from her purse and started dialing. That was their job. To notify Dow Kapier if anything looked suspicious.

"Yep, it's me." Dow always answered the phone that way.

"Mabel here. I think the salvationists have arrived."

"I'll be right over."

With backup on the way, the two elderly women slid out of the car and marched resolutely up to the group.

"I am the president of the Altar and Rosary Society," Ding announced officiously, as if that information could put fear into the heart of a mafia assassin, which it just might in some places. "What are you doing on that ladder?"

The men all stared at her, hints of smiles on their faces.

"We are looking into how much of a job it is going to be to dismantle the windows," one of them, evidently the leader, replied, as if everyone who needed to know that had already been informed.

"You touch that window," Mabel said archly, "and the thing that is going to get dismantled is you."

The men stared at each other in astonishment but before any of them could say anything, Ding grabbed the ladder and started shaking it. "You come down from there, young man. Those windows don't belong to you."

The man looked off into the distance, shrugged, and climbed down the ladder. They all seemed baffled at the idea of two little old ladies threatening to get physical with them.

"Ma'am, we're just doing what we're being paid to do," the leader said. "I don't want no trouble."

"Don't you ma'am me, young man. I am not a ma'am. I'm an old bitch. I'll have the law on you."

"Look, ladies, there must be some misunderstanding," the leader continued. One of the others muttered, "Unreal." They all started laughing nervously.

About that time, two pickup trucks skidded to a stop beside the truck. Dow Kapier stepped briskly out of one, Mary Barnette the other. Dow walked up to the men, did not speak at all, but grabbed the ladder and practically threw it back on the salvagers' truck.

Mary made a big show of flourishing a cell phone. "If I were you guys, I'd rethink this thing," she said, enjoying herself but very nervously. "There's a gang of very upset parishioners on their way here and they won't take kindly to losing their church windows." Dow's glowering visage spoke even louder than Mary's words. The four men retreated a bit to discuss the matter, occasionally glancing fearfully at the man who had handled their ladder as if it weighed no more than a chicken feather. More cars were pulling into the parking spaces. The salvagers reached a quick decision.

"There's evidently been a lack of communication," the leader said. They crowded unceremoniously back into their truck and drove away.

News of the encounter rolled like a dust storm across Vinal County, taking on more mythic proportions as it advanced. Two little old ladies ran four grown men off the church property. Dan Bandy referred to it in his weekly column as "The Great Routing of the Salvationists," obviously enjoying himself immensely. Hitherto not many people, other than those immediately involved in church affairs, had been aware of the effort to sell off the stained glass windows, and now even the Defenders of the Door were dismayed. Just didn't seem right. Hem Judin said it was like selling off the church for thirty pieces of silver. Alvin Farkow wondered why Mary Barnette was meddling into church matters if she didn't care about churches. Fr. Ray was furious because he had not been informed that the salvationists were coming. Perhaps they were just sizing up the job before they announced themselves properly. Perhaps not. Perhaps they had a key to the church.

Dow Kapier also thought of that. He asked Fr. Ray if he might replace the lock. Fr. Ray thought a second or two and shrugged. He was allowing himself to be dragged into something he did not want to be dragged into. The sheriff had provided the present lock and it would probably be against the law to change it. Then again the idea was most alluring. "Maybe just put two locks on the door," he said. "See if that bothers the sheriff any. But I never said that, OK?"

Dow nodded.

Fr. Ray soon got a call from the bishop's assistant, Madeleine McMurry. Her voice was icy. "We understand that various principals ran off the workers hired to take out the windows," she said. "Is there any truth to that?"

Fr. Ray did not like Madeleine McMurry. Whenever he thought of her the word barracuda came to mind. And he resented male officials who hired women to do their controversial public relations work for them. Male officials thought that women's voices were less confrontational than men's. McMurry's voice was about as soft and yielding as a hammer head.

"Various principals?" the priest answered. "What's that?" He loved it that he had thought of such an innocuous reply on the spur of the moment. He was becoming bolder, now that he had realized that people were more than just nameless digitalized members of the Mystical Body of Christ. Probably even Madeleine was a real, individual human being when she wasn't acting as spokesperson for the bishop.

"You know what I mean," she answered, sounding, to the priest, very much like a digitalized, nameless member of the Mystical Body should sound.

"Well, I would think that the bishop would have told me the salvationists, er, the salvagers were coming. After all, it could have been anybody, feigning proper authority, out to steal the windows."

Pause. "Hmmm. I was under the impression that you had been brought into the loop."

The loop? Fr. Ray was wondering if Madeleine was watching too much of the news from Washington D.C. But he pushed his advantage.

"No I was not brought into the loop."

"You did know the decision. I know the bishop shared that with you."

Fr. Ray was sure that she knew. Madeleine McMurry knew everything the bishop knew. Some priests believed there were times when she knew before the bishop did.

"In any case, shouldn't I be forewarned about precise times? To avoid possible confrontations?"

"Do you know who was involved?" Madeleine was not to be deterred.

"Not until it happened. I'm sure by now you know the various principals as well as I do. It was all over the papers."

"Who are these Duholland sisters, anyway?"

Jeez. The woman was worse than the reporters from Channel 11 in Toledo. He wanted to tell her that the Duhollands were more than a match for a mere diocesan spokesperson but knew talking like that would only get him into deeper trouble. "Oh, just parishioners. Er, former parishioners."

"Is there some kind of organized effort going on here?" Her voice suggested hostility.

Good grief. "Let us say I was not surprised." He tried to sound as if he knew of nothing to be surprised about. He could play Channel 11 news too. Saying he was not surprised was not a lie, nor was it an actual admittance of what he did know.

"The bishop wants to know what your advice would be now about proceeding with dismantling the windows."

"As I said before, I think we should move very slowly in anything that affects the church and the congregation, er, the former congregation. Like maybe wait a year before doing anything drastic."

"I see. Well, I shall let the bishop know. I think you will be hearing from him soon."

Fr. Ray put down the phone. He was sure he'd be hearing from the bishop soon. He was surprised when "soon" was two days later.

" 'Lo, there, Ray," Bishop Feering announced himself, trying to sound jovial and avuncular. "Got some good news for you. You are one of two who have been nominated for the position of Auxiliary Bishop. The procedure now requires that you formally make a statement that you are willing to accept the post." Pause. "You do wish to be appointed, I'm sure."

Being an auxiliary bishop was the very last thing that Fr. Ray wanted but he had thought about it now for awhile and had made up his mind. He liked to play chess and if he made his moves right, he just might save his remaining parish and therefore his little farm.

"It is a great honor, Your Excellency. I am totally flabbergasted that I should be nominated and shall do my best to carry out the duties of that office should I be appointed." The priest was amazed to hear himself talk that way, to realize that he could be so deceptive, that there was some dangerous outlaw character lurking down inside himself somewhere. And even more thrilling, he realized that his ability to be duplicitous did not make him feel at all guilty. In his view, St. Philo's did not belong to the bishop or to the diocese so they couldn't tear it down, no matter what Canon Law had to say on the subject. Maybe as an episcopal clone, which is what an auxiliary really was, he could stop it. Or at least make the whole business so difficult that he would save St. Clare's and his farm.

"You are definitely the man for the job," Bishop Feering replied. "It is of course up to the Holy See and all that, but I shall be testifying most favorably for you."

"I am most humbly grateful."

"Which reminds me, can you tell me anything about those people who are suing us?"

"Suing us?" Fr. Ray did his best to sound shocked and surprised even though the only surprise to him was that the suit had not moved forward sooner.

"Yes. We've heard from lawyers now and they seem to mean business, now that the church windows have ahhh, received so much attention lately."

"On what basis do they sue?" Fr. Ray tried to sound nettled. "It is very clear in Canon Law that the diocese owns the church. Isn't it?" Again he could hardly believe that he could be so hypocritical.

"Well, of course, but that is not obvious to everyone. A judge ruled in favor of a similar suit against a bishop out west. But the kind of people who make trouble like this fortunately don't usually have the financial resources to stay in the game as long as we can."

"But it will still cost the diocese quite a lot of money, will it not? Right when we need the money most?"

The bishop chuckled. "Well yes, but we have decided to use the money left over in St. Philo's banking account. That $200,000."

"You mean you will use the parish's money to fight the parish in court?" Fr. Ray could not believe his ears.

"Well, money is money. Who knows whose money goes where once it gets thrown into the general pot. And some of the parishioners are not against using the money this way. The truly faithful want to protect the broader welfare of the church."

"I see." The outlaw spirit lurking inside Fr. Ray was seeping to the surface. He could feel it. But with some effort he kept his voice even and noncommittal.

"Yes, in hard times like this we must remember that we are all members of the Mystical Body."

"No better way to put it," the bishop responded. "And now I must get moving here. Please keep me informed about anything you hear. For instance do you know anything about this group that calls itself People For A Democratic Church?"

"Sounds like an offshoot of that group headquartered in Chicago. Call To Action, I think it's called." Fr. Ray realized that he had neatly avoided admitting what he knew or did not know about PFDC.

Bishop Feering grunted only, not demanding to know more, not realizing that Fr. Ray had not really answered the question. "Well I must be moving on. But let me know if you hear anything, confound it. I'd like to know who's all behind the opposition."

Fr. Ray did not reply. There was an edge in the bishop's voice. Did he suspect that Fr. Ray might be sliding toward the opposition? Evidently not, or he would not be appointing him an auxiliary.

Chapter 10

Tom Barnette thought he would try once more to talk some sense into his niece's head. Her father could not make her give up this notion of planting all beans, but maybe he could.

"It's the ethanol, don't you see, Mary? Gonna put upward pressure on the corn market."

"You said yourself that ethanol is a trap. It will make the corn price go up so high the ethanol people won't be able to afford it." Mary found sheer economic poetry in that observation.

"So? They can dump all the ethanol in the ocean for all I care so long as it keeps the price of corn high."

"But all it means is that land rents, fertilizer, fuel, pesticides and seed will go sky high. It happens every time. The only money to be made will be from last year's crop which is why I'm not selling it yet."

"It never makes sense to put all your eggs in one basket, Mary. You've got no idea what's going to happen. What if some disease problem takes the beans? A farmer needs to be able to jump more than one way when the bullets start flying."

"Yep. Maybe some disease will get the corn. Anyway, what I've really been thinking about is making whiskey. Micro-distilleries, they're calling them. Why make ethanol if you can sell it for bourbon at 50 times the price."

It took Tom almost a minute to digest that one. "You've been talking to Floyd Gowler, haven't you?

"You mean there's someone else getting smart?"

"That Gowler is sort of brash, you know. Got it from his father. Emmet was always talking about making bourbon. Not the only fool idea he ever had."

"Not a fool idea. They're doing it all over now."

"Costs too much to get a license and build brand recognition. Emmet thought he could persuade the politicians to ease up on that here in Ohio, but never got the job done."

"They're already lowering the fees in some states. Just makes sense for everyone involved. Same sense that microbreweries made."

"You've been studying up on this, haven't you?"

Mary nodded. "Gotta have more than one way to jump when the bullets start flying."

Tom winced. "But don't you see. If the ethanol thing doesn't pan out, those ethanol plants could turn themselves into distilleries and then there wouldn't be much money in whiskey either."

Mary glared at him, wondering if that were true. She hadn't thought of that possibility. "It's not that easy to switch over. Think I will talk to this Floyd Gowler."

"Actually, the man you want to see is Amish Bump, if he's still alive. Lives over there in Jergin County near Gowler. He's the one gave the idea to Emmet Gowler, so they always said. Bump's father was a moonshiner, so they said. He also gave Emmet Gowler the idea to graze sheep on his golf course, so they say." Tom grinned at that recollection. So did Mary. Everyone knew about Sheepshit Golf Course, all the way to Scotland where the earliest golf courses could not have existed without grazing sheep. "Amish Bump was quite the fellow."

"Why did they call him Amish?"

"He farmed with horses. The contrariest man in these parts."

Mary thought that might be a compliment. "I'm not changing my mind about planting all beans."

"Huh. After you farm a little while, you'll not be that dumb, young lady."

She had no problem finding Amish Bump, real name Ben Bump. When she asked for him in Gowler, everyone pointed down the road to the east and rattled off directions as if they had done it often. Bump was evidently something of a local celebrity. Going past the golf course, she noted that there were still a token half-dozen sheep grazing where once Emmet Gowler made history with a larger flock. Farther down the road, she began seeing signs directing the traveler on to "Amish Bump's Giant

Open-Pollinated Corn." Other signs read "Natty Bump's Leatherstocking Woolens" and "Killdeer Sheep Cheeses." By the time she had come to the place to which the signs had directed her, Mary was brimming with curiosity. She had been accustomed to such novel food and craft ideas in Chicago where there were people rich and fool enough to buy them, but not out here in the corn and soybean boonies. She suddenly realized that she knew more about Chicago than she knew about her own neighborhood.

The store, if it could be called that, was an old farmhouse with a porch facing the road. She wondered if the old man dozing there in a rocking chair was a prop, part of the old-timey ambience the store exuded. As she got out of the car and slammed the door shut, the prop awoke with a little jerk and smiled at her.

"I'm looking for a Mr. Ben Bump," Mary said.

"Well, you've found him, young lady, and he doesn't mind that you have."

She laughed at such a strange reply. Surely part of the décor. "Do you really sell what those signs say?"

"Unless we're sold out. Go on inside. My son Natty's in there. He actually runs the place. I just sit around and gather shade unto myself."

Again Mary laughed. A great prop, sure enough. Not surprising either. Anyone who knew how to make whiskey would have to be a real character. "Actually, it's you I wanted to talk to, on a different subject. But I surely will check out your store."

The man said nothing so Mary continued. "I hear tell that you know how to make whiskey." Saying "hear tell" was excellent down-home, colloquial talk, she figured.

Ben squinted at her. "You a revenooer or something? Or have you been talkin' to Floyd Gowler?"

"Neither. My uncle says you're the one who knows."

"Your uncle?"

"Tom Barnette. I'm Mary Barnette. Farming my dad's place now. Don Barnette's farm. Over in Vinal County."

"The Barnettes. Well, yes, I've heard of your family. Don't know any personally, I don't think. You're the ones trying to out-farm the Gowlers, so I hear."

She laughed. "I guess you could say that about my uncle and his boys. My father is not quite so ambitious."

"The local weathervanes say that the Gowlers are to farm all of Jergin County and the Barnettes all of Vinal County." The old man smiled in a way that meant he thought that was foolishness.

"Well, anyway I'm interested in starting a micro-distillery. There's quite a few of them cropping up here and there. It got me to wondering, what with all this ethanol talk. Ethanol from corn is bourbon and so I got to thinking about doing bourbon instead. Everyone sort of laughs and says to talk to you."

"My father truly was a moonshiner," Ben said with a smile. He could not keep the pride out of his voice. "Paid for his farm that way."

"You're kidding."

"So help me. But what I learned from him is that there is throat-burner whiskey and then there is good whiskey and making it is not like making ethanol once past the main chemistry of it all. Good whiskey is art. You just don't whup off a batch. Even the corn that farmers mostly grow today isn't the best for bourbon. You want an old-fashioned variety, like our open-pollinated corn." That was one thing he had learned late in life. Never miss an opportunity to push your product.

"Could you show me how to do it?" Mary asked

"Oh my. I know some of it. But you'd need a real master distiller to get serious about it. Making the whiskey is only part of the secret. You need to have a good yeast. Bourbon makers in Kentucky guard their yeast like it was gold. And anyway, I'd want to make sure you were legal before I helped out. A person can go to jail just for helping out at an illegal still."

"Don't want to do it illegal."

"Then you got to pay some fancy fees. Don't know what it is right now, but enough to keep the little guy out."

" I think it only costs $500 for a federal permit."

"But the state wants its share of your blood like Uncle Sam only more so. You need to talk to Floyd. He's up on that."

"You really do make cheese from your own sheep milk?"

"Sure. You think the Europeans are smarter than we are? Go inside. Natty'll give you a taste."

Inside the store, Mary looked around. What she saw was hard to believe. Right here in her stomping grounds were people just as aware of the growing interest in unusual local foods as anyone in Chicago. Who would have thought she could find gourmet European-type cheeses made in Ohio near a forlorn, dying village like Gowler. And, good heavens, where did those long ears of corn come from. Must be two glued together. She inspected a ear from the cluster hanging above the counter.

"No, they aren't two glued together," said the young man behind the counter, smiling. His looks undeniably reflected the man on the porch.

"I'll be durned," she said, shaking her head in disbelief. " I live just one county over, and I had no idea anyone was doing this sort of thing around here. Are you Natty?"

"No, I'm Jack, Natty's son. There's been so much talk about us I thought everyone knew about the cheese and the corn."

"Have you been at this long?"

"My grandpa started it back in the late eighties. Then Dad and Mom came home to help with the marketing, so they said. They weren't sure they wanted to stay on but I found out I loved farming with Grandpa so I said if they went back to the city, they'd have to go without me. I was just in high school and it kind of took them aback. They decided to stay. We've been here since just before the new century started. What makes it work is the Internet. There's no such thing as being isolated from markets now."

"That would be true of selling specialty whiskeys too, wouldn't it."

Jack smiled. "I suppose so. Works with wines."

"So you came home too. I came back from Chicago about a year ago. Never thought I would."

"I guess farming is in my bones. My main job is not in the store here. I do the farming, sort of taking over for Grandpa as he tries to retire. I like taking care of the sheep."

"I'm Mary Barnette from over in Vinal County. I am farming with my Dad. All corn and soybeans."

She kept staring at him. He was good-looking in a rough sort of way, spare, tall, Lincolnesque like the man on the porch, but with a shock of black hair where old Ben's was about gone and grey. Unlike the old man, he seemed shy, almost reluctant to talk. He looked as if he belonged on a farm, as he said, not clerking in a store.

"Who does your shearing?" Mary asked.

"I do," said Jack. "We were having a hard time finding a shearer who would measure up to our standards, so I learned how to do it myself."

"Do you ever shear for hire?"

"Well, no, but I might if the job's not too big."

"This guy has only about 40 head."

"I expect I might do that. Your husband?"

"Oh no. I'm not married. But I'll tell him you're available if that's all right with you." She didn't want to go into details. At the moment the Lone Ranger and his church problem were something she was trying not to think about.

Jack nodded assent, just a wee bit of an impish grin on his face now that he knew she was not married. "Yes I expect I could shear a few sheep up your way." Mary could tell that he was implying that he would like an excuse to see her again, but she did not react. She still bore the wound of one man's rejection and was not ready, yet, to risk another's.

"Where can I find Floyd Gowler?"

"Surely at the golf course. He hangs out there mostly when there's no field work to do. Unless he's in Florida."

"I want to see what he knows about making whiskey. Maybe I'll see you when you come over to shear." It was more of a question. Tentative.

Again he smiled. "That would be nice."

Chapter 11

Her visit to the Bump farm had left Mary brimming over with ideas about new farming prospects. She had been brought up to the tune of corn, soybeans, and maybe wheat, which seemed kind of boring. That whole industrial grain procedure had been committed to computer-driven machinery. All the farmer had to do was keep his tractors running, push the right buttons at the right time and hope the weather cooperated. With the latest GPS technology, the tractor would even guide itself. Her uncle Tom's boys kept magazines in the cab so they stayed awake to turn the tractors around when they reached the end of a field. Like anything else that could be done with robots, grain farming, at least from her previous vantage point at the Chicago Board of Trade, was not very profitable. Even with the $17.2 billion in direct subsidies that the government was pouring into farming, it was often not very profitable. Farmers had a good year once a decade and lived on hope and rising land prices the rest of the time. Her own long-term plan had been that, as sole heir of her parents' farm, she would sell it after her parents died, and live in modest luxury ever after. But the idea of producing new products and marketing them right from the farm was challenging and enticing. Sheep cheese, for heaven's sake. Who would have thought. Or making a business of selling open-pollinated corn for seed or corn meal. Fantastic. Declaring independence from the commercial hybrid seed corn companies would be in itself a revolution akin to suing the bishop for closing a church.

With the church problem and the farm problem both on her mind, she wondered, playfully at first, then sort of seriously, if they might not be one and the same problem. Small churches shutting down in favor of large ones was a reflection of the same kind of economy that shut down small farms in favor of large ones. It was all about cost per unit of production—

fewer but bigger churches, fewer but bigger farms. Agribusiness dictated how a farmer had to farm and how much he had to pay for agribusiness's help. Church officials dictated how the faithful had to live if they wanted to make it to heaven and how much money they ought to contribute to make sure. What the world needed, she mused, smiling at the thought, was a new vision of agriculture, a sheep cheese agriculture, as well as a new vision of religion, a sheep cheese religion. Why not combine the two. She giggled at the thought. Combining religion and farming just might make both of them profitable again. Fr. Ray didn't know it, but he might be the prophet of just such a farming religion. Blessed are they who grow their own organic food, for they shall see God.

Yes! She hooted and closed with a clap the book that she had been trying to read about making homemade diesel fuel out of hamburger grease. Her mother, reading beside her on the sofa, jumped with a start.

"What on earth is the matter?" she asked, a bit alarmed.

"You don't want to know, Mother." And out the door she hustled, straightaway to her pickup, and down the road. Destination: the Lone Ranger. She wanted to tease him about her insight. About a new future for him. Or so she told herself.

"I found you a sheep shearer," she said after parking at the priest's barn and sauntering inside. He was currying a horse that was in the process of being broken to riding but didn't know it yet. Seeing her, he turned his head away and rolled his eyes. He had, early on, felt some interest in her, but that interest had turned the way it always did in his relationship with women. Women made him nervous. This one especially. She spelled trouble, especially since he knew he liked her. He tried not to look dissembling when he did turn to face her. He had pretended ignorance about sheep shearers earlier just as an excuse to talk to her. He didn't know it, but she was up to the same trick now in reverse, using the shearing issue merely as an excuse to talk to him. Two dissemblers earnestly dissembling.

"You did?" He really was surprised that she remembered.

"Guy over in Jergin County. Name of Bump. Doesn't normally shear other people's sheep, but says he might make an exception." She paused, grinned mischievously and added. "He really thinks it will give him an excuse to see me again." She didn't know that for sure, but wanted to see how the priest would react. She found herself slightly disappointed when no hint of possible jealous rivalry registered on his face.

"Why would he want to see you again," he answered, neatly parrying her taunt. "Do you have sheep to shear, too?" He knew full well she did not have any sheep.

"You would find these Bumps interesting," she said, acknowledging with a nod that he had bested her and wanting to get to her real reason for her visit. "They make cheese from their sheep milk. They have a sheep dairy. Really neat. Making money too."

"I've read about that idea," Fr. Ray responded, with genuine interest now. "It has always seemed like a good one to me. A good example of the kind of sustainable, local farming that I try to encourage in my sermons. Like combining a farmer's market with our summer church festival. Sheep cheese would be a great product to sell there. I will try to get these Bumps to come to our farm market."

"You talk about this kind of stuff in the pulpit?" Mary sounded incredulous.

"If you'd come to church you'd know that," he said, pointedly, but without accusation. He was glad she didn't come to church. She'd be a problem for sure. "I am trying to show the congregation how Christianity, especially in a rural parish like this one, should be concerned about not letting big business take our food independence away from us. Seems to me food has a spiritual value, sort of, that it is at the heart of a healthy, virtuous life."

A day earlier Mary would have been hard put not to laugh at the impracticality of his remark. Now she squelched a smile. The poor man was playing right into her hands. She pretended studied seriousness.

"You know something, Lone Ranger. You have a great idea there. Why don't you start a new religion based on sustainable farming instead of praying to some God that doesn't exist. Change St. Philo's name to Our Lady of Good Food. Or maybe The Church of the Divine Wine. Or how about Good Spirits Chapel." She still tried not to smile. "You know how people are. Once they got converted to the religion of good food, they'd load up the collection plate. Not for reward in the hereafter, but for right now. Something delicious to eat. And drink. What a great idea you have there, Lone Ranger."

Fr. Ray stared at her, aware that she was making fun of him. But just maybe she was on to something that he had not dared put into words even to himself. To her surprise, he nodded.

"And then we could make sense out of changing the bread and wine into the body and blood of Christ at Mass. If a person could understand that the food chain is the creative force we call God, then bread and wine would indeed become body and blood, literally."

It was one of his pet ideas, but one which, being utterly heretical, he had never talked about out loud before. Why had he now?

Mary was taken aback at this leap into church doctrine, but she quickly recovered. "Hey, there, Lone Ranger, that's heresy, isn't it? Wait'll I tell the bishop." She tried to look naughty.

Fr. Ray hardly heard her. He was wondering why this vixen could so easily pry his deeper thoughts out of him.

Mary, on her part, was trying to build on her teasing, wondering if she could draw him out even farther. Maybe he wasn't a stuffy clergy type at all. Why she wanted to find out she was not sure. But something else had suddenly inserted itself into her mind. That food chain analogy he had suggested was the first time the Eucharist theology she had been raised on had ever made any sense to her. In a sudden flash, she realized that the whole idea of a church of good food might be more than just a joke.

"Tell you what, Lone Ranger. I know, and you know, that you don't really go along with the bishop on this church closing. I have a hunch you don't really go along with all that religious stuff you pretend to believe either. It's time to give serious thought to what you've really been up to. Turn that parish of yours into the Church of Good Spirits. Tell the Pope to go fly a kite."

And she sailed off to her truck, her laughter trailing behind her. As she slid into the driver's seat, she had one more thought. Sticking her head out the window, she shouted: "And I'll be your first convert!"

Chapter 12

Would-be detectives, Farkow, Dribble, and McTicken, who now referred to themselves as PEG, the Private Eyes of God, were meeting as usual around the back table of the Yellow Room Saloon in Bredsocken, each giving the results of his latest efforts to find the vandal or vandals who had broken down St. Philo's church door. Hem Judin had joined them in earnest now, and from the way he twisted his fingers nervously around his beer bottle, he had something he wanted to say.

"Nothing new on the motorcycle boys." Dribble reported. He was fidgety, knowing he should be out disking corn ground in this good April weather.

"The Masons are definitely not involved. Gawd, the ones I talked to about died laughing." McTicken added.

"It can't be that bitchy Barnette woman. She was in Columbus that night far as I can find out." Farkow growled, disappointment in his voice.

They waited then for Judin to speak.

"I've got a new theory I've been workin' on," he announced dramatically. "I think we need to investigate this Fr. Ray himself a little more." He waited for appropriate expressions of wonder and surprise.

"Oh, come on. Why would he break down the door when all he had to do was get the key and open it?" Farkow asked.

"Oh, ye of simple faith," Judin said, after a perfectly-timed swig on his beer bottle. "He wouldn't be wanting to get in, stupid. He would merely be wanting to make a statement. Everybody wants to make a statement these days."

"A statement about what," McTicken wanted to know.

"Ah, you look for a motive, my dear sir. As well you should. I ask you one question. Who is hurt the most by closing that church? Is it not Fr. Ray himself?

Total silence followed that question, as Hem was sure it would.

"The people out there don't really care that much about the church. Or only a few do. Most of them are trooping right along behind the bishop and going over to Our Lady of Good Patience or into Resurrection. So who stands to lose anything personally?"

"Wait a sec. Not all of them are trooping right along," McTicken said. "Speckle pulled his whole family out and they are going to that Full Gospel Christian Church. They've got a basketball court right in that church and you know how Speckle likes his basketball."

"I hear the Barnettes have quit altogether and that's going to cost us a bundle at Resurrection," Farkow scowled.

"I just happened to be in the right spot and at the right time after Mass at Resurrection the other night," Hem continued, mysteriously. "A bunch of people were standing around outside church talking to Fr. Lemming. He let it slip. He said there was some reason to believe that St. Clare is going to be closed too. Now if that's true, would that not be another blow to Fr. Ray? Losing both his parishes?"

"Why would he care? He can always get another church, with the priest shortage."

"Well, maybe, but not one that has a farm attached." Hem went on. "I decided to visit him at his barn the other evening to check out my theory. It has always mystified me that a priest would be so devoted to that little one horse farm of his. Just doesn't make sense. But I was, like, real respectful and showed an interest in what he was doing. Would you believe that before long, he was pouring his soul out about how much he had always wanted to be a farmer, almost as much as he wanted to be a priest, and how fortunate he had been to be able to get an appointment over two rural churches because it allowed him to show people how important it was to have a society of small-scale farms to keep the rural church viable. He really carried on about it. It occurred to me that he might be upset, I mean seriously upset if both churches closed. When I told him the St. Clare rumor, he got real agitated."

"Doesn't he know it's the big farmers who contribute the real money to the parish, not the little guys," Dribble observed. "They want to buy favor with the Lord for all the cheating they do on their taxes."

"I wonder if maybe he is screwing those sheep," Farkow leered at his comrades, hoping to make a joke. No one seemed to see anything funny in the remark.

"Is that what a pedophile does?" Dribble asked. The others stared at him contemptuously but said nothing. They weren't sure what pedophiles did either.

"There's more," Hem continued, ignoring that exchange as beneath his dignity. "As I was going out the barn door what is it I spy leaning against the wall? A maul, that's what."

"Well, c'mon, Hem, everybody's got a maul. How you gonna connect that one to the scene of the crime?" Dribble sounded disgusted. He was beginning to wonder about his cohorts.

"I'm workin' on that. I dropped by Dow Kapier's place, told him about the maul and asked him if he saved any of the splintered wood from the door when he fixed it. Might be some minute splinters or paint specks on the maul that would match, I said. I've never seen him appear so amused. He's usually as solemn as an owl. I don't know what he found so funny but he just kept laughing and shaking his head. Then he got real serious-like and searched around and did find some splinters he said had flaked off the busted door frame and gave them to me. Got 'em right here in my pocket. Now all I have to do is get hold of that maul."

If any of the Private Eyes of God found Hem's reasoning far-fetched, they did not say so. The only thought any of them had at the moment was inspired by Farkow's joke about screwing sheep. Just why *did* the priest keep sheep? They all knew the hoary jokes about lonely shepherds and their flocks. Now that the notion was on the table so to speak, none of the members of PEG could dislodge it from their minds. Who knew what the hell was going on in this day and age, what with pedophiles and such. Besides, the idea of sneaking into the priest's barn for the maul resonated with an air of high adventure. Apart from the maul, maybe they could catch him in an act too revolting to give name to.

"Look," McTicken said. "Why don't the four of us just go talk to him when he's working in the barn, and while three of us keep him occupied,

Hem can inspect the maul for splinters or paint specks." They all nodded. Sounded exciting even if they did not catch the priest in the act.

Fr. Ray glanced up at the four men standing in his light as he worked feverishly to get a new lamb he had pulled earlier from the ewe's bloody birth canal on its feet and up to the tight udder. He was not happy to see them. Nothing could disconcert a ewe with a new lamb more than idiot human beings standing around scaring her. But as it was, he needed help. Before they could even say anything, he spoke. "Just in time. Will a couple of you get in here and hold that ewe's head. She won't stand still, and I need to get that lamb to nurse." He knew that at least McTicken and Dribble were farm boys and would know how to help. "But keep an eye out on Sam the Ram over there. He'd like nothing better than to sneak up and knock you flat on your butt."

Dribble and McTicken, husbandry in their culture if not in their brains, eyed the ram and stepped over the gate into the protection of the pen holding the ewe and lamb. While they held the ewe's head, Fr. Ray pushed the lamb toward the teat. It merely stood there shivering.

"That'll never work," McTicken finally said. "Never did for my Dad. That lamb is scared out of its wits and so is the ewe and they are communicating total terror to each other."

Fr. Ray nodded, knowing McTicken was right. He let the lamb drop into the straw and grabbed a beer bottle out of his hip pocket. Pulling on the ewe's teat with thumb and forefinger of one hand and holding the bottle close to catch the squirts with the other, he soon had a couple of inches of milk in the bottle.

"Ain't that somethin'," Farkow said. "Never saw a sheep milked before."

"Actually, there are people doing it commercially now," Fr. Ray replied, pulling a rubber nipple from another pocket and stretching it over the mouth of the bottle.

"Milk sheep?"

"Yep. Where you think roquefort cheese comes from?"

"From sheep milk? I'll be damned, er pardon me, Father, darned."

"You can say damn," the priest replied almost graciously. "Makes no damn difference to me."

The three men (Hem had suddenly disappeared) stared at each other in surprise. But then why be surprised. A priest who broke horses and played nursemaid to sheep would surely have to know how to cuss.

Straddling the lamb, Fr. Ray gently pressed the sides of its face to force its mouth open, and inserted the nipple between its teeth. The human entourage in assistance lapsed to rigid silence and watched in total absorption. Hem had returned but they paid no attention to him. Wrapped in the drama of saving a life, they had almost forgotten the purpose of their mission. A good five minutes passed. Then the ewe, reassured by the silence, started making little gurgling noises. As if in response, as indeed it was, the lamb made a first hesitant sucking action on the nipple in its mouth. At the taste of the warm colostrum, its tail jerked, and it sucked harder and then harder still. Before long it was tugging at the nipple with eagerness, its tail flailing right and left, its legs coming back into action as it pushed against the nipple.

"Well, I'll be," said Farkow.

For a few minutes all five men watched in silence, welded together in the kind of commonality that comes when all petty strivings and agendas are suspended in a grand effort to save a life. For a little time they were all on the same side. When it was obvious that the lamb was secure with its mother, at least for the moment, Fr. Ray straightened up and wearily addressed the others.

"I surely thank you for your help. And what can I do for you?"

The other four were still watching the lamb, which the ewe was licking comfortingly. None of them could quite recall directly just what it was that they wanted from the priest. When they did remember, the excuse that they had agreed upon seemed more than a little lame, but they had to say something.

"We were just wondering if there was any more news about the break in," Hem said and then more to the point. "Or anything more about taking the windows out."

Fr. Ray knew all of the men before him, except Hem, were DOD members, that is faithful followers of the bishop. It was hard to tell about Hem who, as an accountant, had honed to perfection the art of not taking sides while showing empathy for all. None of them knew for sure exactly where the priest stood either. He had to watch his words.

"Nothing new, I guess. You know that the people who oppose the church closing have a lawyer and they've gotten a temporary injunction to stop any more attempts to dismantle the church. Don't know how long that will stand. Do you?"

Silence.

The priest pressed them. "I'm interested in what you think. Do you really want the church furnishings sold off and the church bulldozed down?"

A sudden shifting of feet. Clearing of throats.

"We have to obey the church, don't we?" Dribble replied.

"Of course we must," Farkow quickly responded, relieving Fr. Ray of having to say something he didn't want to say. The priest only nodded, hoping that he looked both humble and wise in doing so. No one volunteered an answer to his question.

"Look at that lamb," Fr. Ray said suddenly, pointing. The lamb was dancing around, totally recovered from its birthing difficulties. "Isn't that something miraculous?" The delight in his voice was so honest that Dribble decided right then and there that the priest could not have knocked down the church door.

As the quartet drove away from the barn, he said it out loud. "Fr. Ray is A-OK."

He waited for a reaction. None came.

A mile of silence followed. Finally someone remembered why they had gone to the farm.

"Did you get the maul, Hem?"

"It is old and rusty and the handle about rotted off. Hasn't been used in years."

"So he didn't knock that door down," George Dribble said and then he repeated his earlier observation, liking the rhyme. "Fr. Ray is A-OK."

An idle thought, however ridiculous, achieves a kind of reality when once brought into the realm of the spoken word if it has about it some sense of forbidden allurement. And the more improbable the thought, especially if it is a lurid one, the better the chance that the human mind will become fascinated by it. Alvin Farkow kept telling himself that he had meant only to make a crude joke about the priest and his sheep but now the remark was out there where anybody might hear it, and however unbelievable it might seem to nearly everyone, the more tantalizing was the temptation to repeat it. And so the story spread, at least in the company of males made crude or brazen by beer. It was never articulated explicitly, but only by slyly-delivered innuendo.

"You know why he keeps those sheep, don't you?" The question would be accompanied by a Farkow-patented leer, the listener would grin, and nothing more would be said. When Doc Jake was thus informed, as he sat at his favorite spot in The Yellow Room Saloon, he laughed much louder than the situation warranted and shook his head in disgust. He seemed to know something the others did not. This was just so Vinal County, he thought, surely now in firm possession of first place in the universal sport of churchly sex gossip. But this particular crudity resolved Doc Jake's mind over something that had been worrying him for days. Although he had always considered himself to be a stalwart Catholic, he had been taken aback by the closing of St. Philodendra's. When he heard about the attempt to dismantle the church windows and sell them, his faith was challenged even more. How could he force himself to continue defending a church authority that would do such a thing? Now, the innuendo of bestiality being laid on poor Fr. Ray brought him to a decision. Enough of the bishop. Enough of the bishop's ditto-head followers. He would henceforth throw his considerable influence on the side of the opposition. He knew one thing: he had information that could be devastating to the perpetrators of this new cruel gossip. He just must compare notes with Dan Bandy who knew everything in Vinal County. Well, almost everything.

Chapter 13

———————

What Fr. Ray needed was more time. Now that he had made up his mind to try to save St. Philodendra's, he was surprised at how coyly, even diffidently, he could go about plotting against the bishop even though it might mean losing his safe refuge, the institutional church. What could he ever do as a defrocked priest to make a living? Did priests still get defrocked? What the hell did defrocked mean, come to think of it. Who cared? The attempted removal of the church windows had been like shock therapy. It had clarified in his mind what he really believed, and what he really believed was that much of the church doctrine that he had promised God and man to uphold was a matter of opinion. No authority that would allow a bishop to sell church windows against the will of the people who paid for them could be theologically correct.

But he needed time. If the court order staying the removal of the windows came through, that would help. But if it did not, how much longer could he masquerade as the bishop's stalwart defender. Sooner or later he would have to come out of the closet of righteousness and into the glare of apostasy. But if he did not have to show his hand just yet, then something that seemed to be coming straight from God might occur. It appeared that his confirmation as an auxiliary bishop was moving forward. The prospect of that happening was mind-numbing. He would suddenly have a little power, and power was what organized religion was really all about, wasn't it? Sitting in his kitchen, sipping coffee, he smiled. Quite sardonically, he realized.

A knock on the door startled him. Visitors almost always came to the barn. He was startled a second time when Dan Bandy and Doc Jake walked through the door. But he was not displeased as he usually was with unexpected visitors. He had enjoyed his conversation with Bandy in the bar, even if the newspaperman was a disbeliever. Doc Jake's irreverent jokes about religion he found amusing too. Fr. Ray had an uncanny feeling that there was between himself and these two men, a special kind of understanding, of trust in shared intelligence, that did not have to be articulated.

"We were just passing by," Bandy lied. "Saw the light in the kitchen. Thought we'd check out the latest on the church closing."

Fr. Ray knew that nobody who stopped in to talk to him was ever just passing by, but he played along. "Nothing new, far as I know. Want coffee? Got a fresh pot. And what's on your minds today."

"Well, as you know, I had no personal interest in this whole controversy at first," Dan Bandy began. "But when I heard that they were going to loot the church I just, well, let's just say I'm no longer a disinterested third party. I just can't stand aside on this. Talking to Doc, he's reached the same conclusion. We need to know where you stand." He stopped and glanced at the doctor, waiting for him to resume the train of thought.

"You see, Father," Doc took up the conversation. "I hear you speak in support of the Bishop and all, but my brain doesn't tell me that you really mean it. We need to know if you stand with us or against us."

Fr. Ray was thinking fast. He had declared his disobedience in front of Pope Mary and intimated it to Dow Kapier, but they had evidently not passed on that news. Until now, he had thought Doc Jake would go along with the church authorities no matter what because of his deep personal loyalty to the church—even if he did like to make jokes about religion. The doctor's change of heart was promising but would he keep on opposing the bishop if things got really tight? The priest was not worried about Bandy who prided himself in keeping confidences and who didn't really care about the details of church matters anyway.

"I am in something of a dilemma," Fr. Ray finally said. "You are correct that my heart is not into this church closing business, but if I am to oppose it effectively, not just make noise, I might have to follow a course of action that would offend your religious sensibilities, Doc."

"Try me."

"Not until I have absolute assurance that you will not repeat what I need to tell you. Like me hearing your confession." He looked at Bandy. "And this is totally off the record for you too, all right?" He had never trusted anyone like he was trusting the two men staring intently at him. He was probably making the biggest mistake of his life if he hadn't done that already. But for a priest to take on the power of the Catholic hierarchy demanded taking big chances, so it might as well start now. He repeated his demand. "If you really care about re-opening the church, I must have your solemn promise not to reveal what I am about to tell you. At least not for awhile."

"We're professionals," Doc said. "And we may have secrets to share with you too, you know, under the same terms."

Fr. Ray was silent for a moment, gathering strength. He could almost hear the bridges collapsing behind him as he headed down this new road of revolution. "My thought is that we should keep on pursuing a legal course of action, which the People For A More Democratic Church are doing. But I don't have much faith in laws and lawyering or movements of any kind. The church authorities can out-wait and outspend us, I'm sure. I have another idea. Don't know whether it will work, but it might." He paused. "It looks as though I am going to be appointed an auxiliary bishop." He let that sink in. "If that happens I may have enough leverage to save St. Philo's."

"Terrific," Doc Jake said.

"Well, maybe. But do you appreciate how far I might have to go on this?" Again he paused while the other two stared at him. It was obvious that they had never thought of him as having talents for Byzantine plotting. "Lately I have been thinking that, well, just maybe the only way I can get the church reopened is outside the pale of Vatican officialdom."

"Oh." Doc Jake blurted. He obviously had not thought yet about becoming a heretic and getting excommunicated.

But Bandy laughed. "Now you are starting to make some sense. I've said for years that Rome needs some healthy competition."

"Do you understand that an auxiliary bishop can ordain priests?" Fr. Ray went on. "What would happen if I started ordaining women into the priesthood? How would you feel about that, Doc?" Actually until that moment, he had not thought of ordaining women, but now that he had, he found the idea enticing. Mary Barnette would make one heck of a priest. "I don't really think I would do it, but the threat of that possibility might give me powerful leverage."

Doc Jake's face took on the color and texture of lightly fried veal liver. "I must admit that I totally underestimated you," he gasped.

"That's been my secret weapon," Fr. Ray replied with a little smile. "I've always been considered a pushover, somebody who won't make trouble. I guess that's because I never have gotten as provoked as I am now. I expect that's why they are making me an auxiliary. They think I'm a pushover." He laughed at that. Byzantine plotting was fun.

"You actually mean you are prepared to start a schism in the Catholic Church, right here in Vinal County?" Doc did not know whether to tell a pope joke or to continue gasping.

"Oh, it's not all that melodramatic," Fr. Ray said. "Those Call To Action folks out in Chicago are much farther down that track than I want to go. They are all hung up on theological debates. Not me. I've always thought that the Church ought to be about real things, food, clothing, shelter, medicine, not all this wrangling about the definition of God and all that. Who cares how many divine persons there are in one God, for God's sake." He paused, considering the possible humor of his words. "Or whether there is such a thing as original sin? Or how many angels can dance on the head of a pin? I'm not going to get involved that way. I just think maybe a big bluff will get the authorities to go along with opening the church back up."

Bandy was nodding vigorously, pleased to hear someone start acting the way action had to go if anything was going to be accomplished. Doc was just staring, a sort of embarrassed, metallic grin spreading over his ashen face. Never had he ever thought he would expose himself to excommunication. Then suddenly he erupted into a nervous cackle, sort of like an insane person giggling. In truth he had always thought, privately, along the lines of what Fr. Ray was saying. But he had always considered himself rock solid loyal to the Catholic Church, even when he was telling jokes about it. He never heard a priest talk that way, had never thought that he dared speak, or agree with, such audaciously un-Catholic views.

While Fr. Ray poured more coffee, he remembered his visit from the Private Eyes of God. "I had a feeling there was something on their minds, but I put them to work helping with lambing and they never did get around to saying much of anything. I don't think they could get over a priest playing midwife to a sheep."

That remark brought a dry laugh from Doc Jake who glanced at Bandy momentarily and then back at Fr. Ray. "That reminds me of another reason we wanted to talk to you. There's some nasty business I think you ought to know about."

"Yes?"

"I think Dan ought to know too, but it involves your permission for me to violate my professional secrecy about your physical condition."

Fr. Ray wrinkled his face in puzzlement. "You mean my…"

"Yes."

"What are you getting at for heaven's sake."

"I'll just say it straight out. Some of the less savory elements around here who think you aren't being forceful enough in supporting the church closing, are passing around some vicious slander about you. About why you keep those sheep. You know, the old sheepherder jokes."

Fr. Ray stared at the other two men, first one and then the other. Then, much to their surprise, he laughed a very genuine laugh. Doc Jake joined him, but nervously. Bandy was totally baffled.

"You think that's funny?" Bandy asked, eyes wide.

"Well, no, it's despicable, of course," said Fr. Ray, "but the thing is—" he paused and looked at Doc Jake for some kind of reassurance, and then explained— "thing is, I would have a hard time having sex with a beautiful woman let alone anything else." He watched the surprise spread over Bandy's face. "I suffered quite an injury to my sexual organs when I was young, and it left me with less libido than normal and great difficulty getting an erection. Doc here knows all about it. Maybe that's why I became a priest. My failing sure has come in handy a time or two, that's for sure." He smiled, relieved that his deep secret was now out in the open.

Bandy went slowly from astonishment to a grim smile at the irony of the situation. Always with an eye out for a good story, a headline appeared in his mind's eye: "Priest Accused of Sexual Deviance Found Incapable."

"I must ask you to please keep this in strictest confidence," the priest continued, perhaps reading Bandy's thoughts. "Best to ignore idiocy like this. Reminds me of all that political hate stuff on the Internet these days. If I deny it, the gossipers will only be more convinced. We'll just save the truth for a last resort should it become necessary. I don't think anyone with any brains will take talk like that seriously."

Doc Jake looked at Bandy. "I've told Fr. Ray that it is quite possible with the way medicine is going these days, that the situation could be corrected. Or perhaps overcome with a healthy infusion of Viagra." Now the three of them laughed together even though Fr. Ray was not sure that it was really funny.

"Anyway," he said, "We need to stall off any church demolition activity. I am thinking that many of the Bishop's local supporters might side with us on this. I doubt even the Private Eyes of God will stand for tearing the church down."

Chapter 14

M ary Barnette gazed wearily from the tractor cab, watching the little furrow in the fresh soil made by the planter marker, guiding her as her tractor roared along pulling a drill nearly wide enough to stretch across a four lane highway. She was planting soybeans on another seemingly endless stretch of dark Vinal County soil. Rap music blared from the console radio to her right. Banks of little lights and buttons blinked at her from underneath the vast windshield, making the padded and cushioned compartment look more like an airliner cockpit than a tractor cab. Or as Mary would say, like a luxury hotel room shrunk down to a five by five foot cubicle. Should even the slightest aberration quiver through the monstrous hulk of motorized metal under her or in the drill trailing behind the drawbar, and lights would start blinking or warning sensors tweet from the controls, telling her not only that something was amiss but exactly what was amiss. Glancing at one dial, she knew her ground speed; another gave the depth and rate at which the drill was inserting seed into the soil, yet another told her exact position in the solar system. She switched on the air conditioner. It was hardly warm enough in May for it, but why have air conditioning if you weren't going to use it? She sighed. Only 200 acres left to go and all of her father's farm would be planted to soybeans. Not one kernel of corn on the whole 1,000 acres.

Her cell phone kept ringing. Now that everyone wore phones as part of their apparel, farmers could pass the long, lonesome hours in their cabs talking to each other. Invariably the message was the same in Mary's case.

"Are you really planting all beans?"

"Yep."

If the caller were an older farmer, there would be a pause and then a hesitant question: "How do you figure coming out on that?" in a tone that indicated the farmer thought she was daft and no surprise there because she was a woman who had no business doing men's work.

"A little bird told me," she would say, in a tone that indicated she thought the caller was stupid.

If the question came from a younger man, and single, or perhaps not single, the message was not only about her all-beans philosophy—that just provided an excuse to maybe, well, get to know her better. In that case, the caller would say something like: "What are you seeing on DTN that makes you think you will come out better with all beans?"

To which she would reply: "The same things you would see on DTN if you watched or studied it a little more."

"Ain't got time."

"You got time to call me."

"Well, that's different."

"How so."

"Well, you know. You're the talk of the town."

"I was the talk of the town before this."

"Yeah. I remember you in high school."

"I don't remember you." The way she figured it, if some local swain was trying to start up a relationship, he'd have to work harder than that.

"Well, I was just wondering about you planting all beans. Couldn't believe it. Gotta run. Corn planter needs refilling."

Contrarily, while Mary was ignoring corn for this planting year, the grain was very much on her mind. Not just any corn but Amish Bump's open-pollinated corn. She was wondering if it might be the key element in her wild scheme to produce organic bourbon. She wondered if maybe it was because of sitting in a tractor cab for hours on end that drove her mind to such fantasies. But it made the time pass more pleasantly than listening to what she called blowfart radio talk shows like most farmers did. Wild thinking about organic bourbon led her on to another wild idea but one possibly more practical: organic corn meal. She could surely grow corn and grind it into meal a whole lot easier than distilling liquor with it. A century ago, even half a century ago, there were local flour mills everywhere. Then women decided they didn't want to bake at home anymore. Now the culture was coming around to older ways again. A loaf of homemade bread was such a sign of upper class success that even men were taking up bread-making. There were new kitchen gadgets to make it easier too, and gadgets had a way of mass producing male hormones. But how could she convince her father to grow organic corn. Corn without chemical fertilizer was like a pond without water to him.

On a whim, she dialed Jack Bump. Actually it wasn't a whim. She even suspected that all her dreaming about bourbon and cornmeal might be just an excuse to call him. She couldn't get him out of her mind.

"Bumpy here." The voice sounded bored.

"This is Mary Barnette."

"Oh?" The voice sounded suddenly not so bored.

"Was just wondering. The Lone Ranger, er, that priest I told you about with the sheep, he asked again if you might come to shear. He'd hoped to get it done by now. He is already into lambing."

"Oh yes. I'd forgotten. How about day after tomorrow."

"I'll tell him to contact you." Pause. "That's not really the reason I called. I've been thinking about your corn."

"I thought you were against corn."

"You heard that too, huh?" She chuckled. "What I'm really thinking about is making cornmeal. On a commercial scale. Organic cornmeal. And then maybe organic wheat flour too. Just wondered what you think of that idea, with your focus on producing locally-grown foods."

"We've thought about some kind of gristmill for a long time, to tell the truth," Jack said. "Mostly we haven't pursued it because we've got too many irons in the fire already. Grandpa is really keen on the idea."

"So is the Lone Ranger—that priest. And he wants to talk to you about bringing your sheep cheese to the farmer's market festival this year."

"The what?"

"Well the church is closed, as you might know, and they can't have religious services there anymore, but seems like they can continue to have the church festival, and a farmer's market has become a part of that."

"Sounds interesting." Jack was not sure it was interesting but he liked talking to her. Any excuse would do. "When I come over that way to shear the padre's sheep, maybe we can all get together."

"Sounds good."

"By the way do you belong to that church?"

"Are you kidding? I'm a heathen."

Jack laughed. He sounded relieved.

"Why do you ask?"

"No special reason."

"What about you?"

"Oh, I don't know. Some days I believe in nothing. Other days I believe in everything."

Mary laughed. She liked that answer.

The meeting turned out to be more enjoyable than any of the three had anticipated. For one thing, Mary realized that while she might not have the hots for Fr. Ray, that she still liked him. There was something about the way he related to her. Just as a person. Not in that kind of barely-concealed, sexual-leering, gingerly-smiling way that seemed to take hold of most men when talking to her. He talked to her as if, well, as if she were a person, not a woman. She liked that. Maybe she did have the hots for him after all. Through a mouthful of fresh asparagus and lamb chops that Fr. Ray had prepared himself, she asked: "Did you really fix this meal yourself, Lone Ranger?"

"Yes. Having a cook around would make me nervous."

"It is very good. I didn't think I liked mutton."

"Not mutton and you know it," Fr. Ray replied with a smile. "Grass-fed lamb. Nothing like it."

Jack Bump laughed. "Grandpa says when he was growing up, all that his parents would put on the table in the way of sheep meat was old ewe or as he called it, 'old yo'. The good stuff went to market to pay the bills. He said they served mint jelly with it to kill the taste. First time he had a good lamb chop he didn't believe it could actually have come from a sheep."

Mary found herself unable to keep from comparing the two men as if they were suitors or might become such. She felt comfortable with both of them. There was a certain settled demeanor about them, as if they knew their worth and were satisfied. Jack however was full of that grace that she could not put a name to: unconsciously sexy, yes, but not bold or crass or even attempting to impress her with his maleness. He kept glancing at her however, shyly but with latent interest. The Lone Ranger, on the other hand, rarely looked directly at her and when he did, his expression was one of amused fondness, the way a grandfather eyes a favorite grandchild. But he could cook.

Jack on his part, was finding Mary fascinatingly unlike other girls he knew. Never before had he met a woman so attractive, but without the delicate kind of femininity that he customarily associated with attractiveness. It was like visualizing one of those Victoria Secret models out in the barn, pitching manure in her almost invisible, three-way-flex, form-fitting, uplifting, cleavage-accentuating bra. As for the priest, Jack was relieved to find him very matter-of-fact, unpretentious, even worldly—certainly devoid of that studied piety that he normally associated with the clergy.

"Do you two know each other?" Jack asked, sensing a certain easy familiarity between them.

Mary laughed. "How well can a priest and a heathen know each other?"

Fr. Ray tried to look bored. "Oh my dear Mary, priests know more about heresy than you ever dreamed." He paused, relishing his answer before addressing Jack. "Mr. Bump, this young lady and I have had several go-arounds over the church vandalism. She has suggested that worrying about church buildings might be a waste of time and energy."

"That was before they were going to steal the windows and sell them," Mary interjected. "The Barnettes paid for at least one of those windows, so even as a heathen, I have a vested interest in them."

"Steal the windows?" Jack sounded incredulous.

"They'd like to make the church disappear with a bulldozer, but then they found out it has antique value." She laughed again, finding that amusing. She looked at Fr. Ray for some sign of agreement. He did not see anything amusing about it at all.

"So anyway about the farmer's market festival you were talking about while we were shearing," Jack asked. "That's a great idea and we'd be most obliged to set up a booth and display our cheeses."

"Would you now," Fr. Ray beamed. "That would be splendid. We've got a local winemaker coming, and several market gardeners. It'll be in August when there's lots of fresh produce. Last year we sold almost as much sweet corn as beer." He found that amusing and the other two laughed appropriately.

"That's one thing about Catholics, they like their beer," Mary said.

"Not to mention those Methodists who come out from Bredsocken and drink their share where their neighbors may not see them," Fr. Ray added sarcastically. Jack laughed. He just might end up liking this guy.

"I've been thinking," Mary said. "Talked to Jack here about it too. I've been thinking about selling cornmeal and wheat flour at the social just kind of to see if there's a possible interest in such a product around here."

Fr. Ray beamed again. "Why that's a wonderful idea. I thought you were against the whole thing."

"Never said that. Just think you should be pushing your local foods thing and dispense with all that doctrinal crap." She turned to look at Jack. "I've been telling him to change the name to The Church of Fine Food and make a religion out of producing it."

Jack laughed forthrightly. This woman was something else for sure. "Jeez, I might even join," he said.

"I've thought of a slightly different name," Fr. Ray said. "How about The Church of Almighty Good Food. Sounds a bit more heavenly."

"Hey, yes, that's perfect," Mary added. "Think I might join too." Her eyes met Jack's and there was a delight reflecting between them not entirely over the idea of The Church of Almighty Good Food.

As they left the rectory, on the way to their pickups, Jack slipped ahead and opened the truck door for Mary.

She had a sudden thought. "You know what? I think we should do a little research on this business of making bourbon."

"Like what do you have in mind?"

"Well, I think we ought to stop at the Yellow Room Saloon and see which one tastes the best."

If Jack had smiled any wider, his face might have cracked. "Not a bad idea."

Over a corner table, Jack's first remark after sipping his bourbon could be heard by just about everyone at the bar. "It surely would be a waste to burn this stuff in a tractor."

Mary giggled. She was more elated than the whiskey could account for. She had not felt this way, well, since her early days at the Chicago Board of Trade, when she thought the world was her garden, to plow and plant as she saw fit. The man across the table from her was perhaps shy, but certainly not at all tongue-tied. Once he started talking, and perhaps influenced a bit by what he was sipping, she could hardly get a word in.

"It's kind of funny, I guess," he said. "I've never thought too highly of big tractor farmers hogging up every acre of ground they can get their hands on."

"Like my uncle?"

"Well, that's what I mean. I never really got to know any big tractor farmers. I surely never thought any of them would be as pretty as you."

Mary actually blushed. She had thought she was beyond that. "But we're not big. A thousand acres is small potatoes these days."

"Big to me. I can barely take care of 200 acres the right way."

"There's a lot of big farmers can't properly take care of 200 either. But what if you had a chance to farm more acres. Could you be happy doing that?" There was a look in her eyes. He was fairly sure he knew what she was getting at.

"I expect so." He paused and smiled ever so faintly. "What if you had to get up in the night and go pull a lamb? Think you could handle that?"

"I expect so. If it didn't happen too often."

They both laughed. And changed the subject back to micro-distilleries.

In the darkness of the cemetery across from St. Philodendra's church, a distraught voice was talking to God again, or perhaps to the remains of Benedict Berogston in front of whose tombstone the shadowy figure loomed.

"I did as you directed me to do. I broke down the door. But it seems to have done no good. No good a'tall." The figure paused then, as if waiting for an answer either from on high or from under the stone. None came.

"I now have another plan which I know came from you, Lord, as it would not have occurred to my poor mind. But I need your further help. Can you hear me, Lord, or dear old Benedict, can you intercede for me?"

Silence.

"I think I have figured out a way to get back the $200,000 that the bishop stole from us," the figure in the dark continued. "That money, as you well know, is now deposited in the account of the Resurrection of the Lord church in Bredsocken. I have been reading about the scams on the Internet. I don't know how people can be so stupid as to fall for them but they do. It has given me an idea. What I ask of you now, oh Lord, is that you befuddle the mind of that conniving Pastor Lemming at Resurrection and blind him with greed and ambition. If you will do that, oh Lord, I will do the rest."

The figure in front of the tombstone waited for some sign of acknowledgment and when none came he decided that silence meant approval. He then wended his way out of the cemetery and into the cornfields which as in every summer surrounded the church and cemetery. The corn was barely knee high, as it should be by the fourth of July, so if anyone had approached on the road, he would have had to fall flat on the ground between the corn rows to escape discovery. But no one passed and soon he was back in his pickup, parked along the edge of the field, and drove away.

Chapter 15

———————

Dow Kapier was working unusually late and was surprised when there was a knock on the open door of his woodworking shop. He looked up to see someone he did not recognize, which was also a surprise. Never had anyone come to his shop that he did not know. He beckoned the stranger on in, a frail, drawn man who leaned heavily on a cane.

"I'm sure you don't recognize me," the stranger said by way of introduction. "I left Balem Township when you were hardly more than a boy. I've lived in Toledo all these years, but this is home to me." He shifted his cane to his left hand, stretched out his right. "Name's Lambert Closk. My mother was a Durner."

Dow nodded. "There's Durners in the cemetery."

"Yes, she's buried there. We lived here and went to St. Philo's all those many years ago. After Mother died unexpectedly, Father moved to Toledo and I had to go too. I never wanted to. And that is my reason for coming to you. I want to come home when I die. I have a favor to ask, you being the cemetery caretaker and all. I'd like for you to make sure I get buried next to Mother."

"I think I can handle that," Dow said, somewhat mystified.

"Mr. Kapier, I am dying. Doctors give me a month or two. I want to be buried in our family plot. I will be cremated so there is no need for a big grave. I am a bachelor. I don't have any immediate relatives left, far as I know. I would pay you whatever you require to stick my ashes in there next to Mom's stone."

Dow scratched his ear. "Well, Mr. Closk, I am somewhat taken aback."

"My undertaker knows my intentions. I have my little tombstone already. Just stick it in there beside my mother's."

"I see." Dow could think of nothing to say, but silence was his usual habit. Finally he continued. "Do you know that St. Philo's is closed. It is no longer a church. You couldn't have your funeral here, way things are right now."

Closk stared in disbelief.

"I was just here to Mass a year ago."

"Not anymore."

"They can't do that."

"Well, they did."

Closk looked befuddled, then stung, then something akin to anger. "But they can't do that. We built that church. My ancestors did. I've got money in it myself."

"Lots of us feel that way, and we're very upset about it too." Dow was watching Closk closely, scrutinizing his reactions.

"I don't see how they can get away with that," was all the frail old man said, but he was visibly disturbed.

"You can still be buried here," Dow continued. "I'll look to getting the hole dug if you wish. With only ashes to bury, I can dig it with a shovel myself if that's all right with you." The man looked so helpless and forlorn that Dow really wanted to help. But something more was looming up in his mind. This Lambert Closk just might be the sort of miracle he was looking for.

"You say you've got a month or so?"

Closk laughed dryly. "I expect." Dow liked the laugh. A man who could laugh about his approaching death might go along with what the woodworker had in mind.

"Tell you what, Mr. Closk, I have a proposition for you. I'll take care of your burial free of charge. But I need a favor too. Come on into the house and let me explain."

An hour later, they emerged from their meeting, both of them laughing more than their short acquaintance seemed to justify. Dow helped his new friend, limping on his cane, to his car. They shook hands again, obviously sharing some conspiracy, and the stranger drove away. Dow went back into his house and did a little jig around the kitchen. No one in Vinal County would have believed it. The Dow they knew never did little jigs. Then he looked down at some numbers he had scribbled on a piece of paper, and did another little jig.

Hem Judin tossed the letter in the wastebasket, then thought a bit, fished it back out, re-read it, and pondered the possibilities.

> Dear Mr. Hemmerly Judin:
>
> A wonderful investment opportunity is about to be offered to select people in the Vinal County area. We think that your close knowledge of the economy might make you one of the few with the foresight and means to help us take advantage of it. An ethanol plant is being planned for the area as you probably know. Although the Federal Government is involved financially, thereby insuring the safety of the investment, the new plant will need support from the private sector. It is a golden opportunity, one that we at Intimate Insider Investments would like to make available first to charitable organizations and religious institutions as is our policy when possible. Our mission statement is to help such organizations in their good work while encouraging environmentally-conscious business investments. Since we understand that you are the accountant for at least one church in the area, we thought you might want to get involved.
>
> As plans for the ethanol plant develop, we will send you pertinent information. Needless to say, secrecy is of the utmost importance at least for the moment because if this offering is made to the public at large, demand will surely drive the price of the stock too high to keep a really good profit for initial investors. We are sure that you understand this.
>
> We are a green environmental investment business headquartered in Minnesota, where we have been active in helping the state become a leader in the ethanol industry.
>
> Intimate Inside Investments Ltd.
> "Serving the alternative fuels industry since day one"

Hem's inclination was to share the letter with business cronies in his accounting circles, to get a good laugh out of how far scammers were willing to go these days. But on second thought, he decided to file the letter and keep his mouth shut, just in case it might be legit. After all, unlike most scams, the letter asked nothing from him directly, not even a reply, nor did it infer personal aggrandizement for him. And there were certainly strong rumors in the air that an ethanol plant was coming to the area.

In due time, a second letter arrived.

Dear Mr. Hemmerly Judin:

Plans are moving forward regarding the ethanol plant we apprised you of in our earlier letter of 7/22/07. Cost of the project is estimated at $15,000,000. The Federal Government will provide about half of that directly or indirectly leaving $7,500,000 to be raised privately. As the company chosen to handle the stock offering because of our experience in funding similar plants in Minnesota, we would like to give charitable organizations first chance at this opportunity as we wrote to you earlier. Investments are limited to no more than $200,000 per organization, as we believe in spreading the rewards out as much as is practical. Such an involvement would mean a position on the board of directors too and so for the first time that we know of, a successful commercial business might funnel some of its excess profits directly into charitable causes to avoid taxes. We estimate that the plant at full capacity will produce 50,000,000 gallons of ethanol per year which will sell competitively with regular gasoline, with the government supplying a subsidy making up for the higher cost of ethanol. In other words, this is an opportunity that can hardly lose unless the U.S. government collapses. You can therefore see the need for secrecy so as to give one or more of your clients a chance for substantial returns. It is quite possible that an investment of $200,000 could double in value within a year or so. We will keep you apprised in case you are interested. You can call our regional office at the number given below if you wish to receive detailed information.

Intimate Insider Investments, Inc.
"Serving the alternative fuel industry since day one."

Hem decided it couldn't hurt to check the offer out. The letter was postmarked Toledo, no doubt where the regional office was located. A phone call to the number listed brought him a recorded message. "We are pleased to learn of your interest. Please leave your name and postal address and we will forward information about ethanol production to guide you in your decision." Hem left his post office box address.

In a few days a large packet arrived. Hem blinked at page after page of detailed information and statistics about ethanol production, from the U.S. Dept. of Agriculture, from companies producing ethanol, from corn utilization studies done by land grant universities, from farmer groups, and at least a hundred pages of statistics and studies downloaded from the Internet, all bristling with the latest facts and findings about distilling alcohol from corn. Hem had not realized how much the ethanol industry had grown, with production figures being cited in the billions of gallons of fuel. He knew from other articles that the total represented hardly more than one percent of the motor fuel market but rather than inspiring caution, that fact only suggested to him that expansion was unlimited. He waded through perhaps a third of the material before being totally overwhelmed and wearied by it. But he did take special note of those pages of data that originated from a Minnesota investment company on which was rubber-stamped: "Confidential to Intimate Insider Investments Inc." He checked out the investment firm on Google. Sure enough, it existed. He could find nothing on Intimate Insider Investments itself, but the accompanying letter did indicate an account in Toledo Flyway Bank. If it were a scam, it was a good one, he thought.

Hem started paying closer attention to the small talk at the Yellow Room Saloon. He asked discrete questions. There was talk aplenty circulating about an ethanol plant, but nothing solid. Wily old Tom Barnette seemed to know something, but replied evasively when asked. Was he another of those chosen few selected to get in on the ground floor of the deal? Or was the evasiveness simply because of all the criticism in the news about the practicality of making ethanol from corn. Dan Bandy was having fun in his column pointing out that if all the arable land in the world were planted to corn for ethanol, the amount it would produce was less that 20% of the automotive fuel needed by modern society. And since that took all the land, everyone would have to starve to death in order to keep on driving.

But what did that smartass reporter know?

Hem was surprised at how the first breakthrough in the mystery came his way. He was having his regular monthly meeting with the pastor and the council of Resurrection of the Lord church, whose books he kept. As is almost always true, accountants tend to become the unofficial directors of whatever firms they handle because, as the classic saying has it, "he who has his thumb on the purse, has the power." Inevitably, the owners, directors, decision-makers in any enterprise rely on the advice of accountants simply because accountants are in charge of adding and subtracting the figures. Being able to spout off numbers with precision takes on the appearance of knowhow and wisdom. So it should not have surprised Hem when, as the meeting broke up, Pastor Lemming asked him if he had time to stick around a little longer. He needed some advice about what he called a "financial matter of some urgency."

"Recently I have received certain intelligence of an investment nature," Pastor Lemming began, trying to sound important. "It is about the ethanol plant that is slated for our county. I would like your opinion in the matter. I must insist that you keep this in strictest confidence, do you understand?"

Hem's response gave proof, had any been necessary, of why he was successful in his accounting business and why he had become Father Confessor to most of the local businesspeople. He did not respond at all. Outwardly, he appeared as blandly expressionless as a cow chewing her cud while inwardly he rejoiced at his good fortune. Now he could proceed with his own investigation of the ethanol mystery without any personal risk or involvement. He never invested in stocks of any kind himself. He considered that risky business, especially since he had all the money he really cared to worry about. If there were money to be made in this ethanol thing, he would make his the sure way. He would increase the fees for his services. Besides he did not like Pastor Lemming. Pastor Lemming was a pompous ass and not too bright to Hem's way of thinking. The priest did not even catch the most obvious jokes that the accountant tried to tell him. Hem figured that the poor man had gone to seminary early in his life and had never had the chance to encounter the real world.

"You should know by now, Pastor Lemming, that you can trust me on such matters." He tried to sound a bit offended. "Like you in the confessional, I would not dare betray confidences. I'd soon be out of work."

Pastor Lemming opened a desk drawer, pulled out a sheaf of papers, and handed them to Hem. "What do you think of this? I have never heard of investment opportunities being offered directly to a church like this, but then again it makes sense to me. And so opportune. I don't need to tell you how stretched the diocese is for money because of the pedophilia mess. This offer could be a godsend for the diocese. It is also very appropriate, no doubt a sign of God's infinite wisdom, since you will notice that the investment sought is exactly the amount of St. Philo's money that the bishop has entrusted with us."

Hem swept his eyes over the letters. He did not have to read them because they were about the same as the ones he had received. He nevertheless pretended great curiosity.

"Most interesting," he murmured several times, just loud enough for Pastor Lemming to hear. Pause. "Have you checked out this company?"

"They have an account, Federal ID number, in Toledo Flyway," Pastor Lemming replied proudly. "And look here at some of the material they sent. It apparently comes from a legitimate business in Minnesota that deals exclusively with funding environmentally-dedicated companies. Apparently, I.I.I. works closely with this company. Lots of these papers specifically flag the attention of I.I.I. I called the number listed there in the letter and so far got only a recording and then this stack of scientific data about ethanol plants. What appealed to me was the way they urge me to study the matter closely and not to do anything hastily. Sounds pretty honest."

"I will certainly review all of this and get back to you," Hem said. He could see the desire welling up in the pastor's eyes. If this offer were for real, obviously Pastor Lemming could score big with the bishop.

Pastor Lemming was thinking the same thing of course. The bishop had given no specific instructions about the money from St. Philo's but only said there were no plans for its immediate use. It certainly needed to be invested somewhere better than a plain old certificate of deposit. Pastor Lemming would invest the money in the ethanol plant and before anyone knew, it would double in value. Pastor Lemming would be hailed as one of the saviors of the diocese and ride his success right into a bishopric someday. Out loud, he only voiced his hope that Mr. Judin would continue to counsel him on the project.

Back in his office, Hem paced in front of his desk. What he faced was not exactly a moral dilemma but not exactly not a moral dilemma either. This I.I.I. business was just too good to be true, but his addiction to wanting to know everything that was going on in the community tempted him sorely to let the matter resolve itself on its own. After all, in all financial matters it was his policy to remain aloof from the schemes of his clients, trying always to look wise, hedge his advice so that whatever happened could not be construed as either his fault or his wisdom. All he really cared about in all such matters was getting paid. That's what financial advisers did: they got paid. They did not make investments themselves but invested in the greed of investors. Who was behind this I.I.I.? Local people had to be involved, he decided. How else would they have known to contact him? But who in Vinal County was smart enough to divine that Hem Judin would be precisely the one to get involved? Who would know that he, Hem, might go along with the deal even if he thought it were a scam. Who knew that he was uncontrollably curious about everything that passed through his little world and also that he would not mind seeing Pastor Lemming done in. He, Hem Judin, would think of the $200,000 of St. Philo money in Resurrection's account as quickly as Pastor Lemming thought of it and would understand that using that particular figure could not be mere coincidence. The scammer, if it were a scam, would also have to know that he, Hem Judin, privately thought that the confiscation of St. Philo money was a miscarriage of justice and so he just might go along with the scheme even if he thought it was a scam. Somebody out there was smart enough to figure that he, Hem Judin, would consider the scheme's success to be a sign of God's justice working its way in the pathetic world of human greed. It would, in this case, be just punishment for the Catholic Church for taking the money from St. Philo's in the first place. The former parishioners of St.

Philo's would hardly lament the loss of the money either because they had already lost it once. Many of them would secretly rejoice. If this were a scam, someone had thought of the perfect crime.

Trying to figure out all the possibilities in the twists and turns of logic was tiring. Hem decided just to play it cool and stay out of harm's way. What the hell.

In a few days, he called Pastor Lemming without checking out anything. "As far as I can find out, this project seems worthy," he told the priest. "You should probably set up a meeting with I.I.I. Depending on what you find out, you can either decline or go ahead. But I must remain anonymous, not directly involved, you understand. If your investment pays off, other clients of mine would feel that I had left them out of the opportunity, which would not be good for my business."

Pastor Lemming thanked him profusely. He had heard what he wanted to hear, that is, Hem's approval. Or thought he had heard it anyway. After the phone call he went over to the church, knelt in the dark sanctuary and prayed for guidance. He had in the meantime received another letter from I.I.I. requesting a meeting at the earliest possible date. Several other churches and charitable organizations were requesting meetings, the letter said, and it appeared that there was not going to be a problem raising the money to build the plant. The letter hoped however that Pastor Lemming would respond soon, because I.I.I. was aware of the "special needs" of the Catholic Church in these trying times, and so wanted Pastor Lemming to have first chance to profit from the venture.

"Oh God," he prayed in an audible whisper. "Guide me in these times of adversity and opportunity. It appears that You have answered my prayers and found a way to help the diocese. But, please God, I will need Your help ever more critically in the days ahead. As you know, I dare not go to the bishop about this investment offer. His Excellency might turn it down summarily, not having the faith in You that I do." ("More likely," he said to himself, hopefully beyond God's hearing, "the bishop would take over the proceedings, and leave me out of the loop.") "You and I know, Lord, that Hem Judin is one smart accountant, not to mention a faithful member of the Church,—well more faithful than those heretics out at St. Philo's anyway—and if he says I should take advantage of this opportunity I am sure that it is You, oh Lord, speaking through him."

Pastor Lemming waited, like the shadowy figure in St. Philo's cemetery had waited, for some sign of acknowledgment. None came, but perhaps the patient expression on the face of Christ in the painting above the altar was actually more of a smile than Pastor Lemming had noticed before. A smile of approval no doubt.

Chapter 16

Mary Barnette tried to pretend that she was being drawn into the St. Philo Festival and Farmer's Market at the end of August more or less against her will. The truth was that it gave her an excuse to see Jack Bump again. He was not easy to get to know, as retiring by nature as she was bold. Also, the idea of selling freshly-ground corn meal from the Bump open-pollinated corn and wheat flour from her own crop was beginning to look promising. In the booth she had put up with Jack's help on the grassy grounds next to the church, she was experimenting with an electric grain mill she had purchased.

"It doesn't seem possible that just by running wheat through a grinder, I can get sixty dollars a bushel for it instead of four," she said to Jack, who was putting up a booth next to hers to exhibit and sell his family's sheep cheeses and Leatherstocking woolen fabrics.

"How do you figure?"

"Do the math. Health food stores are selling packages of whole wheat flour at a dollar a pound. There's nearly sixty pounds of flour in a bushel of wheat."

"Not all profit. Those cute little cloth bags you're selling the flour in aren't cheap, you know. And if you are going to do this on a commercial scale you will have to automate the process."

"If I can sell a bushel of wheat for sixty bucks, I'll fill those bags by hand till my fingers drop off."

"You sound like Grandpa."

"Maybe you should sell the flour cheaper than health food stores do," said Fr. Ray who had heard their remarks as he approached. He was scurrying from one booth to another with words of encouragement for all. "I don't think people in Balem Township will buy corn meal at a dollar a pound. They'll grind their own before they'll to that."

"Well, Lone Ranger, that's what you want, isn't it?" Mary replied. "That's the idea isn't it? To use religion to raise the consciousness of good food." Then she paused and tried to look quizzical rather than sarcastic. "Or should I say use good food to raise the consciousness of religion?"

"I don't care which it is," Jack said, "so long as it sells my cheese. And I'll tell you something, Ray"—he had learned that the priest did not really like to be addressed as "Fr. Ray" but Jack was not quite bold enough yet to call him The Lone Ranger either— "you'd be surprised at how people will spend their money these days. If they know what peas fresh from the garden taste like, they will pay almost anything to get some so long as someone else picks and shells them out. There will always be farmers fool enough to do that work."

"And there may well be a lot more such farmers," the priest added, "if the economy keeps going south."

For Fr. Ray, the Philo Phestival, as he liked to call it in print, was a dream coming true. Some twenty exhibitors had signed on and were putting up tents to sell local food and wares. The countryside was buzzing with anticipation. The Duholland sisters were marketing their fabled Brandywine tomatoes, big as softballs. Dow Kapier was offering his "Ton" watermelons, as he called them, so big "three will not float in a bathtub at the same time." But the Duholland sisters would have to sell them at their booth. Dow could not bring himself to do anything so public. The neighborhood grapevine said that he nurtured his melons on a special liquid fertilizer mixed in milk, feeding the solution by way of a wick into the plant stem. Whether that was true or not, Dow wasn't talking, as usual. When he did talk lately, he exhibited an informed cleverness that surprised his neighbors. Though he was a fixture in the community, no one knew much about him other than his uncommon talent with wood. He had been in the army, in Army Intelligence when he was young. It was said that he knew about all kinds of spy tactics and decoding messages—stuff like that—and now spent a whole lot of time on the Internet. That in itself caused some consternation among his neighbors most of whom were suspicious of the electronic age. One story making the rounds on that subject was about Dobb Henry. His children had given him a computer for Christmas. He did not want to hurt their feelings so he kept it on a table in the living room until it made him feel so uncomfortable that, having sold his hens, he put it in the chicken coop where he didn't have to look at it every day.

Even Hem Judin had a booth. He was pretending to be advertising his accounting business. "Good food requires good accounting," the hand-printed sign said on the counter in front of his booth. No one understood why he was making his presence felt at the festival since he had never before shown much interest in it and had, since the break-in, kept a cautious distance from the more rebellious element at St. Philo's. But Hem knew. He had to keep on the lookout for any rumor, however tenuous, about ethanol plants. If there were an investment firm involved, especially one that apparently wanted the windfall profits to go to worthy religious causes, Hem could leave no church unwatched, especially a closed one.

The news that was bringing the most publicity to the event came from Fr. Ray himself although it was not his idea. Dan Bandy had done a story about the priest's little farm and how the "Lone Ranger" as he was sometimes called, Bandy pointed out in the story, had been in the habit of riding from one of his rural churches to the other on horseback on Sunday to save money in the face of rising gas prices. Bandy also mentioned the Lone Ranger's horse-breaking business after persuading the priest to put on a demonstration at the festival. "How to break a horse without breaking anything," Bandy advertised it. The Toledo Blade picked up the story and now inquiries were pouring in from all over northwest Ohio asking just where this "Philo Phestival" was going to take place. Fr. Ray regretted that he had allowed Bandy to interview him. How would the bishop react?

Fr. Ray's fear was well-founded. Pastor Lemming at the Church of the Resurrection in Bredsocken, had been following the publicity about the festival with mounting alarm and considerable envy. St. Philo's festival had always outdrawn Resurrection's and now it was going to do so even though closed. Pastor Lemming worried that all the favorable publicity for the festival and its weirdo horse-whispering priest just might put pressure on the bishop to open the church again. It was not in Pastor Lemming's interest to let that happen since his parish, Resurrection, was supposed to be benefiting with an increase in parishioners coming from the closed church. It could also jeopardize his ethanol investment opportunity. That might slow down his climb to a bishopric. Something had to be done.

As it turned out, the bishop had been keeping a worried eye on developments at St. Philo's too. He did not at all like the idea of one of his priests being referred to as the Lone Ranger or a horse-whisperer. All the bishop needed was a little push, and Pastor Lemming gave it. This festival and farm market was setting a bad precedent, he told the bishop. "I think you should cancel it or at least combine it with Resurrection's festival. We're only 8 miles apart." The bishop agreed.

With hardly more than a week left before the festival, he called Fr. Ray and lowered the boom. Fr. Ray was standing in front of Pope Mary's booth (everyone was calling her that now, her friends in jest, her critics in sarcasm) when he took the call on his cell phone. Several of the festival exhibitors were enjoying pancakes that Mary was frying in an electric skillet, using batter prepared with her freshly ground wheat flour. Her plans had enlarged from just selling freshly ground flour and cornmeal to include various prepared foods made from the grains. As the priest took the call, the others around him stopped their merry conversation and watched as his face turned pale and agitated.

"Yes. I understand. Yes, I suppose we can do that, although, well, give me some time here. I'll call you back." He flipped the phone closed and stared at Mary. His face looked the color of her wheat flour.

"Are you okay?" she asked.

"He canceled the festival." Fr. Ray's voice sounded as if coming from someone none of them knew. "The bishop canceled the festival."

Mary snorted. "No way."

"You don't understand. He is my bishop. I must obey him."

"And I am your pope," she answered primly, "and I just uncanceled the festival."

Fr. Ray looked at her, marveling at her free spirit. Her dauntlessness flowed out from her and swept over him. He had a powerful desire to embrace her. But then an even more compelling emotion gripped him. He jerked out his cell phone again and with trembling fingers, dialed the bishop's private number. As he waited for the bishop to answer, his eyes never left Mary.

"Ahhh, yes, this is Fr. Ray again, Your Excellency," he intoned. "Ahhh, I don't know quite how to say this, but as an auxiliary bishop, I have made the decision to go forward with the festival."

He could hear Bishop Feering gasp. Then stutter. Then clear his throat. Finally: "Confound it, have you lost your mind? You have not yet received notification to that effect, not that it would make any difference. By whose authority do you make such an outrageous decision."

"The pope's authority," Fr. Ray was still staring at Mary, his eyes widening as he realized that he really must have been appointed an auxiliary. He had meant his remark only as irony.

"The pope?" Bishop Feering's voice cracked.

"Yeah. *My* pope." And Fr. Ray clicked the phone shut. Pope Mary hugged him. The cluster of people around them cheered. The priest shuddered. He had a terrible premonition that the beginning of the schism between the Vatican and American Catholicism had officially begun.

The wrath of the bishop nearly shook the timbers of his country mansion outside Bowling Green. Within a couple of hours of Fr. Ray's manifesto, the driveway was full of cars, each bearing a Monsignor or a lawyer, one bearing Madeleine McMurry, the Bishop's trusted secretary, and one bearing Pastor Lemming and his confidantes on the church counsel, Plover Vitale and Alice Dribble, George Dribble's wife. By the time they had assembled in the expansive drawing room, Bishop Feering was in such a state of agitation that he could barely describe clearly what had happened. He kept interrupting himself.

"I'll have to excommunicate him, confound it," he raged between attempts to spell out Fr. Ray's rejection of his order. "And he knew. Somebody leaked the news. He *knew*."

"Calm down, now, your Excellency," Madeleine said soothingly. "Just sit down and get hold of yourself. What do you mean, someone leaked the news. What news?"

"Why, the notification from the Curia."

"What notification?"

He looked at her witheringly. "Why the notification that he has been appointed an auxiliary bishop. Look at it. Right there on my desk. I just got the letter yesterday. How did he know? There's a spy in my midst, I tell you." And he stared from one monsignor to another, his eyes resting finally on Pastor Lemming who was not a monsignor although he dearly wanted to become one. It had to be Lemming. The scheming little rat was always up to something. But how had *he* found out?

Madeleine took charge, as she always did. "Now, Henry," she said, "Calm down. Are we to understand that Fr. Ray refused to cancel the church festival at St. Philodendron's after we, er, you, ordered him to do so?"

"That's what I just said, isn't it," the bishop snapped.

"And perhaps you should point out to the gathered assemblage why you so ordered him to do so." Madeleine always saw the bigger picture.

"It was getting out of hand," the bishop said, addressing the gathered officials. "This Fr. Ray has been gaining sympathy and adulation because of his, well, for one thing he rides a horse to work, I mean to say Mass at his rural churches. And he's started a sort of religiously-inspired farmer's market that is very popular among the people."

A monsignor cleared his throat. "And what possibly does this have to do with someone getting appointed an auxiliary bishop. Did I hear you say that you had this, ah, horse-whisperer appointed an auxiliary bishop?" The voice was full of dismay.

Bishop Feering's face reflected sheer misery. "Well, the process is ongoing. You were all going to be brought into the loop, I assure you. The appointment is not public yet. But, confound it, Rome knows I was very supportive of Fr. Ray. I thought sure he was right for the job. He seemed to be rock solid. Not involved in any sexual crap anyway. One who would be the steadying hand as we close churches. Confound it, how can I now punish someone I just told the pope would make a good auxiliary? What am I to do?"

"What makes you think that Fr. Ray knows about the appointment?" Madeleine asked. She was once again showing why, and how, she had so much influence in running the diocese.

"Why he as much as said so," the bishop answered.

"What actually did he say?" she prompted.

"Well, he said that the pope had appointed him. How could he know that?"

"Who else knew it, ah, besides me of course." Her stern eyes swept the group, challenging anyone to dare suggest that she had been the spy.

"Well, no one. How could anyone?" He paused. "Surely the pope himself would not have told him nor would anyone in the Vatican. Would they?" His face quavered.

"What exactly did Fr. Ray say," Madeleine continued, used to dealing with a man who often panicked under fire.

"He said the pope had appointed him. *My* pope, he said. "

"*My* pope?"

"Yes." The bishop paused. "Yeah, come to think of it that is sort of strange. The pope belongs to all of us. Why would he say *my* pope?"

"Probably just emotional ardor of the moment," one the monsignors suggested, stroking his chin. "A sort of term of ecclesiastical endearment."

In the silence that followed that remark, which no one quite knew how to assimilate, one of the diocesan lawyers stood up, looked at his partner ruefully, and addressed the assemblage. "You asked earlier for advice, Your Excellency, and we have come to an opinion, although you may not like it at first. We think we should eat a little crow for awhile." He waited then for the shock of that remark to vibrate through the room. Knowing he now had everyone's attention, the lawyer continued. "We have been in serious and protracted litigation with the lawyers representing the opposition, the People For A Democratic Church, as you all well know. We have also been in close contact with lawyers from other dioceses and the problems they are running into defending the closing of churches. What we are finding is that we can't always depend on judges to agree with us that this is a matter of Canon Law, not civil law. And they are not always agreeing, in civil law, that the diocese is the legal owner of a church property. Some of these churches you have closed,"—and here the lawyer felt it necessary to clear his throat— "were built and paid for before the diocese was formed. Already judges have ruled in two separate instances against our position. We think we will eventually win but there is possibility that we won't." He paused again. "The question is, should we run the risk? If a case is ever settled in favor of the people who claim that the church members own the church property, then, well, pardon my language, the shit will hit the fan. That precedent could be used to sue the diocese right and left over closed churches. Do you want to risk that possibility?"

Silence. Pastor Lemming worried that others could hear the thumping of his heart.

The lawyer, waiting for a suitable length of time, then went on. "We are still hammering out the details, but we think it would be wise at some point in the near future, to let those people at St. Philo's get the keys back to the church. I think we can work it so their ownership is only a pyrrhic victory in that the church would no longer be a church in the Catholic sense. Just a building. But whatever decision you make on that score, your Excellency, my colleagues and I advise you strongly to rescind your order about stopping the festival at St. Philo's. Otherwise you will start incurring the anger not just of the parishioners who want title to that property, but the public in general which seems quite in sympathy with these people."

"But won't giving them back the key be an admission that we were wrong?" Pastor Lemming suggested.

"We are going to insist that they sign a document stating that the diocese still owns the property but is willing to give the people possession as a gesture of good will. We think that they will be only too glad to accept that agreement rather than run the risk of losing everything in court."

"But this makes me look very bad, doesn't it?" the bishop said. "Won't this embolden that renegade to challenge me even further?"

"Tell him that he misunderstood your message, that you were talking about his horse breaking demonstration, not the whole festival," Madeleine said. The bishop looked at her in astonishment. For a minute or so he was silent. That might just work. She was the one he should be making an auxiliary bishop.

"But he will surely know that's not true," the bishop replied, half-heartedly.

"He will accept that rather than get into something ugly," Madeleine answered. "He's smarter than most people think."

Plover Vitale was staring at Alice Dribble, something else entirely on her mind. She had come to her own translation of the Bishop's words when he said that Fr. Ray had referred to "my" pope. "My" pope might just also mean that heathen bitch, Mary Barnette. Term of endearment indeed. Plover could hardly contain herself. She had to get back home and check that theory out. Maybe the heathen bitch and the heretic priest were lovers.

Chapter 17

Fr. Ray's hands were trembling so much when he realized that it was the bishop who was calling him again that he could hardly keep the cell phone to his ear. But it was Madeleine McMurry who was actually on the phone. Her tone was jovial. What she said almost dumbfounded him.

"Fr. Ray," she gushed, "the bishop and I were just talking and it occurred to him that you could have misinterpreted his words. You know Henry. Sometimes he gets overly anxious and does not communicate his exact wishes the way he intends to do."

Fr. Ray was having difficulty keeping his cell phone, which he despised anyway, in the right position against his ear to hear plainly what Madeleine was saying. "What do you mean?"

"Well, the way he told *me* what he told *you* made it sound like he wanted you to cancel the festival."

Silence.

"Uh *huh*," she continued, interpreting, or pretending to interpret, his lack of response as an indication that she was right. "I was afraid of that. I just knew it. All this over a misunderstanding. His Excellency only wants you to cancel your horse-breaking demonstration."

A very long silence.

"Surely you will be willing to do that," Madeleine finally continued. "Surely you understand why the Bishop is so distraught these days that he might find public horse-breaking a bit improper for one of his priests. You know. With all the adverse publicity against the Church." She could not keep the pleading out of her voice.

Fr. Ray's thoughts were racing round and round in his head, a supercollider in miniature. Whatever was really going on here, evidently the bishop had changed his mind and if all Fr. Ray had to do was quit the horse thing to get the bishop's blessing to proceed with the festival, well, he had never really wanted to do the horse thing anyway. But the evident fact that the bishop was backing down had several interesting cases of collateral damage for his brain to consider. Had the courts decided in favor of the renegade parishioners? Had he actually been approved as an auxiliary bishop? Could the bishop have been advised to come to his senses and let the festival continue just because not doing so would do nothing except create more ill will? Since that latter idea was the most intelligent of all three possibilities, Fr. Ray doubted it could be the correct deduction. But maybe. Just maybe. Or maybe all three deductions were correct.

"Well yes, I was a bit confused," he finally spoke. Might as well go along with the ruse. "I guess I did misinterpret the bishop. As for that horse breaking demonstration, I had not really wanted to do that anyway. I'd been asked to. I'll be only too glad to call that off." He paused, then laid it on too thickly. "There will be disappointed people but of course my first duty is to my bishop." He almost gagged at his hypocrisy.

Long pause—on the other end of the line this time. Madeleine knew he was playing her game back at her, but that last suggestion of humble prostration was a bit much. He was a renegade priest—officially a renegade in the Canon Law sense. She knew it and he knew it. Now she knew he could also be a very devious renegade priest.

"His Excellency will be very pleased, I'm sure," she finally said. To herself she made a mental note: this man is even more dangerous than I had previously suspected.

Off the phone, Fr. Ray walked over to his DVD player, switched on his favorite piece of music at the moment, AC/DC's "Thunderstruck," leaned back in his office chair, put his hands behind his head, and after a bit, howled along with the music. The last shackles of blind obedience to blind authority shook loose from his soul and he soared into the rarefied atmosphere of true religious freedom. It was not so much knowing that the various gods of institutional religions had no hold on him anymore but also the realization that maybe he, Fr. Ray, was some kind of god himself. Maybe all 6.5 billion inhabitants of the earth were gods. He had to call Mary Barnette.

"Hello, pope," he said. "Guess what?"

His voice was so buoyant she barely recognized it, especially since she could hear Thunderstruck thundering away in the background. Not the Fr. Ray she thought she knew. "What?"

"The bishop has reconsidered. We can have the festival after all." And he howled again, this time imitating how he thought a wolf might sound if overtaken with happiness.

"He DID?" She was not sure that news was nearly as momentous as the crazy way the priest was carrying on. But leave that for another time. Recovering, she responded: "Well, I'm glad to know we can do what we were going to do anyway." There was a hint of disappointment in her voice. It would have been much more fun to put on the festival against the bishop's wishes.

Pastor Lemming had returned from the meeting with the bishop in a purple pique. His carefully plotted path to a bishopric was running amok because of that damned sheep-loving Ray Tulley. He kept running mentally through a list of his worries, trying to figure out how to list them according to their danger to his purposes.

The bishop thought that he, the loyal Pastor Lemming, had tipped off the sheep lover about being chosen to become an auxiliary bishop. Well, he could surely prove that he was innocent on that account because he could prove no one in authority had contacted him about it or anything else.

The bishop was allowing the festival to go on against Pastor Lemming's expressed advice. Well, he could bow humbly and get out of that one without losing too much face.

The bishop was going to open St. Philo's again. Oh my, he did not dare to believe that one might be true.

Plover Vitale pointed out the obvious: if St. Philo's was opened again, it would surely mean that its $200,000 would go back to its account. He shuddered at that possibility. That was the money he needed to save the diocese by investing it in the ethanol plant. Then Alice Dribble, trying as usual to one-up Plover in gaining the priest's attention, pointed out something even more fearsome.

"It might mean that Church of the Resurrection would be closed to make up the difference," she said. Pastor Lemming sucked in his breath and turned even paler. Alice beamed. Mark up that inning: Alice 1, Plover 0.

The priest knew what the two council members were doing, and in fact constantly encouraged them to do so. He loathed both of them for it, but did like the feeling of having two women fighting for his attention. And since they were two of the more accomplished gossips of the parish, having them in his confidence was most convenient. He could use them, use their rivalry, to get all that news that was not fit for a priest to know about. But at the moment he had no use for competitive sniveling. He had somehow to turn the situation to his advantage. Let the sheep priest have his festival. In fact he, Pastor Lemming, would go out of his way to show support. Then he would strike. He would use trash gossip to discredit Ray Tulley, the way the politicians did to each other. He would slyly insert a whispering campaign into the local gossip mill, whispers about why the horse whisperer kept those sheep. If Fr. Ray protested, it would only increase the suspicion.

Such desperateness drove Pastor Lemming to rush into the ethanol investment scheme too. Normally, he would have waited longer but now it was imperative to act before circumstances prevented him from doing so. It might be embarrassing if St. Philo's were opened again and the people found their money had been invested in the ethanol plant, but shortly, when the investment proved so profitable, he would be the hero, right there to take over after the sheep lover was thoroughly discredited. Hem Judin, who knew everything about money, was still positive about the investment. Well, sort of, anyway. Accountants were never positive about anything. So now, pressed by the possible loss of a possible bishopric in the possible future, not to mention the possible loss of a possible parish, he dismissed his last remaining hesitancy. After all, capitalism was a history of the kind of entrepreneurial courage that brought big success. One must have the guts to take big risks. That's why he still had a parish and poor Fr. Ray did not.

He called the number for Intimate Insider Investments. He arranged a meeting. Hem Judin had said he would not go along, nor did he think it was his place to co-sign the cashier's check for $200,000 as protocol called for. No problem. Pastor Lemming called Plover Vitale. As president of the church council she could, literally, fill the bill. Would she come to the rectory, please, for a meeting of great urgency? But of course.

Plover was surprised to find that she was the only council member present. That surely meant that she had finally become Numero Uno in the priest's eyes, not that lapdog Alice Dribble. Her ample breasts heaved an inch or so closer to heavenly realms.

"Plover, I've got to move that St. Philo money to one of the diocese's private accounts," he told her, using his tenderest and most modulated tone of voice which he usually reserved for instruction in the confessional. Plover nodded, eyes wide.

"I have to have a co-signer to withdraw the money and send it on. Could you accompany me to the bank tomorrow?"

Plover's eyes seemed now the size of the moon rising on the horizon. She was nodding in assent even before he reached the end of his sentence. When it became known that Plover was the chosen one, Alice Dribble would surely have a seizure. At the bank, she co-signed the note without even wondering why the bishop's private account was identified as Intimate Inside Investors.

Chapter 18

To Pastor Lemming's surprise, the regional office of Intimate Insider Investments was a rather nondescript house very much like the others around it on a residential side street in Burning Cross, a bedroom community of Toledo. The attractive lettering on the picture window announced the office: "Intimate Insider Investments, Ltd. Funding the Green Revolution and Other Worthy Charities." Since the regional office's mailing address was a box in the Toledo post office, the priest had assumed that the investment company's office would be in the big city's downtown commercial area, but never mind. Burning Cross was a whole lot easier to get to even though he wasn't particularly comfortable about being anywhere near Burning Cross. Its church was being closed too, meaning another raging battle between parishioners and the bishop. He hoped he would not encounter anyone who knew him.

Even before he could press the door bell, the door swung open to a rather frail man, leaning on a cane, wearing dark glasses and a smile, welcoming him inside. There was no one else in the office. The man graciously offered Pastor Lemming a seat in front of his desk and then seated himself. "I am Lester Longin," he announced. "You must be Pastor Louis Lemming from the Church of the Resurrection in Bredsocken. It is such a pleasure to do business with you."

"And I with you," Pastor Lemming beamed. There was a crucifix on the wall behind Mr. Longin and on his desk a snow globe in which a tiny statue of St. Francis of Assisi was encased.

"It's a clever paperweight," Mr. Longin said, noticing the priest was staring at the snow globe. "You know how if you shake one of those things, swirls of snow whirl around. Well, this one"—which he proceeded to shake—"stirs up a flock of birds instead of snow. Very clever. See." He paused. "Francis is my favorite saint. He really wanted to help out the poor."

"Mine too, Lester," Pastor Lemming said, beaming. Good feelings about Intimate Insider Investments coursed through him. No one who loved St. Francis could be up to anything but good.

"I do have some additional information since I last corresponded with you, Pastor Lemming," Lester said. "In case you have any lingering doubts, you might want to read this over." He handed the priest a sheaf of papers. "Apparently the ethanol plant will be built near Bredsocken, and I would surmise that will mean an influx of money into your pastorate, in addition to profits from your investment. The ethanol company isn't saying yet exactly where the plant will go. Announcing that ahead of time might very well run up the purchase price of the land, I imagine. No doubt they are talking to several landowners. The plant is modeled on one in operation in Minnesota, a layout of which is there in those papers. You can find out about that one on the Internet too."

Pastor Lemming leafed through the papers absentmindedly. He had already made up his mind. Mr. Longin was in no way trying to push the issue, was in fact giving him every chance to turn down the offer. Surely an honest man.

"If you have any doubts about the potential profitability of your investment, take a look at these statistics about peak oil," Longin continued. He swiveled his laptop around so the priest could see rows of figures on the screen. "We are at the point where many experts believe we have hit peak oil production. From now on the world will use more oil than we can replace with new discoveries. The market for bio-fuels like ethanol will surely skyrocket." He paused for dramatic effect. Pastor Lemming remained silent. Peak oil was a new phrase to him. The rows of figures might as well have been hieroglyphics. Didn't matter anyway. He knew a good deal when he saw it.

"We do like to point out," Longin went on, "how, after we assure ourselves that an investment really is an opportunity, how we use a percentage of our fee to promote religious causes. Right now that is mainly Catholic churches. The founder of Intimate Insider Investments is a very concerned Catholic and focuses the philanthropic side of his business on rescuing churches in the desperate financial problems that now envelope the Catholic Church. He has a kind of fetish about his charitable donations, however. He goes to great extremes to remain anonymous. He often refers to biblical passages where Christ condemned the hypocrisy of the Scribes and Pharisees, how they performed good works just to gain public favor."

"Yes, and to be honored in the marketplace and given the first place at assemblies," Pasture Lemming added enthusiastically, eager to show his mastery of the Bible. "They wanted to broaden their phylacteries and enlarge their tassels, as Mathew's gospel puts it."

Longin looked suddenly startled but then gathered himself and nodded as if knowingly. "That's why, if you notice, the names of the officials of I.I.I. do not appear on our letterhead or any other public place and our donations to needy causes never reach the newspapers."

"It is in that same spirit that I invest this money for my church," Pastor Lemming said, assuming an air of abject humility. "I too must demand secrecy, at least for now. I don't dare tell the bishop just yet. He is a good man, but overly cautious and I doubt he would go along with the investment at this stage." The priest winked. "We'll surprise him."

Longin seemed to be holding his breath, as if he were afraid of exploding into laughter, which indeed he was. "Oh yes," he finally said. "No doubt about *that*."

Pastor Lemming pulled the envelope containing the two hundred thousand dollar check from his inside coat pocket and slid it across the desk. Longin made no move to pick it up, further convincing the priest of the man's good will. Lots of mutual trust here. He instead placed a folder containing the priest's stock certificates in front of him. Even Longin marveled at them. The wonders one could work with an Office Shop program and a computer.

"We will keep you informed by newsletter as to the progress on the ethanol plant," Longin said. "You have done a very noble and admirable thing here, I want you to know. The people of your parish, all the people under your care, especially out in Balem Township, will remember you forever."

Pastor Lemming tried to look renowned. "My whole purpose in life is to help my Church." Why Mr. Longin mentioned Balem Township in particular he did not know. Probably the man was not aware that it was only the smaller part of his parish.

Investment planner Longin was staring at his computer screen, appearing to study the statistics on peak oil. It was taking every molecule of his will power to remain solemn and subdued. Yes indeed. The money truly would go to help the church. He had just not mentioned the particular church that it was going to help.

Pastor Lemming arrived back home just in time to attend the closing events at St. Philo's festival. It had obviously gone over in a very big way. A crowd still filled the grassy grounds around the church and the people, boisterous with beer and good will, were eagerly buying up the last of the farm produce offered for sale. If he had not been so uplifted in spirit by having closed the ethanol deal, he might have felt a little more envious of the sheep lover who was obviously enjoying the popularity of the crowd. In an enclosure next to the festival grounds, Fr. Ray was ending up a demonstration showing how deftly his border collie could respond to his commands and herd several of his sheep into a parked trailer. Wasn't quite the same as a horse-breaking demonstration, he thought, but in a way more appealing to the people. They clapped and cheered.

But what galled Pastor Lemming even more than Fr. Ray's obvious favor with the crowd, was the way the heathen bitch, Mary Barnette, was carrying on. She was standing up on the table where she had been selling freshly baked bread and pancakes, putting on quite a show. "Step right up here, folks, and help yourselves to the last of Pope Mary's almighty good bread," she clowned. "Goes good with beer." That reminded her of an old folkloric ditty she remembered from childhood, and promptly belted it out: "Oh dear, bread and beer, if I were dead, I wouldn't be here." The crowd roared. Even many DOD's joined in the laughter. Pastor Lemming looked around with alarm. This sort of thing could get out of hand. It could easily become a source of scandal. The non-Catholics would accuse the Catholic church festivals of becoming drunken orgies as they had done in days gone by. But then again, so be it. He would even encourage it. He smiled faintly at one and all. Beer drinking at the festival would make more ammunition to discredit the sheep lover.

Jack Bump, the shy one, tried to join in the fun but Mary's unrestrained ways embarrassed him a little. He wished he had the kind of nerve it would take to jump up on the counter beside her and dance too. He would wave one of the woolen scarves made from his fleeces as he danced, flamenco style, around her. But although he was jubilant too, having sold more cheese and woolen goods than he had ever before done at one night's event, he could not quite make that kind of spectacle of himself.

Nevertheless he watched her in awe. He had never before been so enchanted, so intoxicated. He threw a scarf at her. She caught it, wrapped it around her body, then pulled it away seductively and held it out at arm's length. It was as if she were reading his mind. She became the flamenco dancer, stomping her foot, arching her neck, her hand flung out, holding a loaf of bread as if it were a pair of castanets. The crowd was delighted. If only there had been a band to play some appropriate music, Mary was thinking. But her eyes were only on Jack. Working with him the last few days, she had found herself becoming more and more fascinated by him. Now she swirled round and round precariously on the table top, laughing, almost falling off. Fr. Ray, watching from a distance, felt a twinge of regret. Or maybe it was longing. For a second or two, he wished he were Jack Bump. But enough. It was better this way.

For the first time since she had left Chicago in pain and despair, Mary was laughing with unreserved joy. Jack Bump rules, she was saying to herself. She went into a jerking rock dance. The crowd rocked too. Something a little wild was being let loose on the summer night air and Mary felt it. For one shimmery moment, she was reminded of Fr. Ray's words about the mystical body of Christ, that ancient phrase out of theology books which all Catholics grew up hearing but rarely understanding. Jack Bump was a mystical body, sure enough. And all these frolicking people were a mystical body too, united in spirit. And then Mary, full of reckless happiness, took the metaphor one step too far. She suddenly stopped short in her whirling dervish act, flourished a loaf of her bread in one hand and grabbed up the can of beer she had been sipping earlier in the other. "Welcome to the new age," she shouted, looking up into the night sky. "Welcome to the new Holy Communion." In the hush that followed, she smiled ever so coyly and pronounced in measured syllables: "This is my body,"—she held the bread on high in one hand, then lifted the beer in the other, "And this is my blood."

The Catholics in the crowd went stone cold, stunned to silence. It was perhaps fortunate for Mary that most of them did not, at least immediately, grasp the symbolism she was reaching for. Most of them were merely puzzled. But Fr. Ray understood. He walked swiftly up through the crowd, knowing that he must defuse a possibly explosive situation. Making fun of the Transubstantiation—of the changing of bread and wine into the body and blood of Christ—was worse than the Street Preachers in Marystone shouting that the Mother of Jesus was a whore. Ridiculing the Eucharist was ridiculing the very epicenter of Catholic dogma. It however did occur to him, even in that distraught moment, that the Lutherans and Methodists in the crowd might not be offended, might even see some reverence and propriety in Mary's words since in their Communion services, the bread and wine were viewed as something a bit more symbolic of the body and blood of Christ, rather than the real thing. Maybe there would not be an outburst, in fact. But watching Alvin Farkow, he knew he had to act. The deacon would find it necessary to uphold his office and defend his religion. He was already advancing menacingly toward the table. And Alice Dribble out on the edge of the crowd, hissed loud enough for everyone close by to hear: "heathen bitch."

Farkow jostled his way to the table where Mary stood, she a bit surprised herself that she had said what she said. But when the deacon repeated Alice Dribble's words and made an attempt to climb onto the table, Jack Bump's arm barred the way and there was something so steely tense in his demeanor that Farkow backed away.

Fr. Ray had worked his way to the center of the hostility and now he leaped up on the table and held up his hands.

"Hold on! Hold on!" he shouted. "Let us not ruin this happy day because of a few thoughtless but well-meant words." He could not have imagined himself doing what he was doing even a month ago. Gaining a free spirit had its drawbacks. He glanced at Mary with what could only be described as half stern scowl and half mischievous smile. He was actually quite impressed with what she had said. Or would have been, had she spoken in a less public way. It had taken him all of his 42 years to realize the real significance of the Eucharistic service and had never, until this moment, heard it articulated so well even if, in this environment, it was like pouring gasoline on fire.

"I have some news of great moment." He paused, waiting hopefully for curiosity to subdue anger and confrontation. "The final agreement has not quite been ironed out yet, but I think I can assure you that the bishop is going to unlock the church for community activities and even perhaps weddings and funerals." He of course did not at all know whether he spoke the truth, but if not, the people could have at him later. Right now, he needed to stop a possible fight and figured such a startling revelation might do it. There was a tense silence. People were staring at each other. Finally, here and there in the crowd, hands clapped. Then a few hesitant cheers. Then a full chorus. Even some DODs were clapping.

Across the road, in the shadows of the cemetery stones, a lone figure stood, unseen by the festival goers. There was a look of peace on his face that he had not felt for over a year now. He bowed before the grave of Benedict Berogston and muttered over and over: "Thy will has been done, oh Lord, and my eternal gratitude to you, old Benedict. You just heard Fr. Ray's words. You have answered my prayers. The church is going to be opened again." The dark figure chuckled and melted away into the darkness beyond the tombs.

Chapter 19

Pope Mary was riding high, literally and figuratively. Perched in the cab of her grain harvester as it lumbered across the fields, feeling a little like a pilot of a 747 soaring through space, she once more reviewed her victories. She had helped make the Philo festival a success, which pleased her mostly because she knew that she had not only irritated the Defenders of the Door but more so because it had brought Jack Bump into her life. After her experience in Chicago, she had sworn that she would never fall in love again. But being impetuous by nature, she could not help herself. Jack was the one for her.

But then she had second thoughts. How sure can anyone be about love? She had thought she was in love before. A thoughtful person who has believed in something with absolute certainty and then learned how wrong it could be, was not likely to fall for fervent belief again. But Jack was deliberate and cautious in taking action, the perfect foil for her habit of headlong rushing into things. If he found their relationship sound, and he evidently did, why shouldn't she? When she had told him that what she really wanted out of life was just to have a family and live hidden from the grim reality of the world, an admittance which would have surprised even her mother, he had smiled in agreement. So did he. Also, she was fascinated with new and sometimes strange farming ideas that Jack was constantly bringing up. She knew that delighted him. And they never lacked for conversation or excuses to get together. Most of all, however, he displayed an old-fashioned gentlemanliness toward her that she found utterly charming. He actually would open doors for her. In her previous experiences, men treated women more like business competitors than lovers. And who could blame them. These days they often really were business competitors or were at least competing for jobs. When she had said something to that affect to her mother, Martha only shook her head in puzzlement. She could not fathom being in competition with her husband. He had the barns and fields; she had the house and garden. Never the twain shall meet.

But for Mary, life was good, for the moment at least. In celebration, she sang at the top of her voice inside the grain harvester as it rumbled methodically over acre after acre of soybeans. The beans were another reason for her exultation. She had planted the whole farm to them— bullheadedly defying her family, tradition, and all the other farmers of the county by not planting any corn. The market situation had done about as she had predicted. With so much attention on the possibilities for a good corn market because of rumored demand from ethanol and from third world countries, farmers planted corn on every acre they could drive a tractor on without turning over, as her father liked to say. More corn meant less beans, and so more demand for beans. More corn kept a lid on corn prices at least for the moment; less beans pushed the bean price up. Moreover 2007 had been dry in Vinal County. Beans stood the dry weather better than corn. And since beans cost less than corn to grow, chalk up another gain for beans as input prices soared. At the elevator, around other farmers, Mary gloated without apology.

"Beginner's luck," her uncle growled.

"Just contrariness," Lloyd McTicken added, but not without a hint of admiration.

"Chip off the old block," her father said, although he had opposed her vigorously.

"Wouldn't crow too soon," George Dribble observed. "Some say corn is going up to six dollars by summer."

"And then beans'll be fifteen, " Mary retorted. Knowing it would infuriate the likes of Alvin Farkow, weigh master at the elevator, she assumed a pious voice and added: "God's been good to me."

Alvin, who had kept a discreet distance, mumbled too low for anyone to hear: "God'll send her to hell one of these days too."

As long as the harvest was in progress, the farmers of Balem Township did not have time to pay much attention to the turmoil and conflict that continued to swirl around the church of St. Philodendra. It had not yet been opened again, contrary to what Fr. Ray had predicted. The main topic of conversation still lingered on theories about who had broken down the door. Now that Fr. Ray had openly faced down the Bishop, matters were worsening for him. He was surely going to be excommunicated. Whenever his name was mentioned, sly whispers about the private lives of sheep lovers circulated just beneath the cloud of controversy. The result, however, was not disdain specifically for Fr. Ray, as Pastor Lemming had hoped, but more general disgust with the clergy as a whole. Sheepherder jokes only heightened the rising tide of anger brought on by the pedophilia crisis. Fr. Ray tried to avoid the gossip and controversy by hiding out on his farm as much as he could. He was making a last bit of hay. He had decided to stack it out in the field and was enjoying himself immensely, trying to make his haystack look better than the ones Monet painted. He took his time because as long as he stayed in the field, the less he had to deal with the public. None of the people critical of him for his defiance of the bishop, certainly not Pastor Lemming, or any monsignor, or diocesan lawyer, was going to venture out into the foreign land of a hay field on a blistering hot day, he figured. So until evening, he could enjoy a little peace.

After dinner, or supper as Fr. Ray, like old farmers, stubbornly persisted in calling the evening meal, the farmhouse rectory became a hubbub of religious concern. He forced himself to sit dutifully in his office and face the music. To fortify himself, he kept Thunderstruck playing in the background. Then he would nod thoughtfully at whatever opinion was being voiced but would say little. With his newly-found freedom of knowing that all that church dogma really didn't matter to him anymore, he could endure all statements of religious righteousness with equanimity and after awhile even with supercilious humor. That had always been his strength and weakness, he thought ruefully—making smartass remarks.

One visitor was Dr. Jake, his friend. "You are in deep shit," the doctor said with no apology for his language. "We just about had the re-opening of the church sewed up. Now the bishop's lawyers are stalling. They had pinned their hopes on getting us to sign an agreement saying that they would let us use the church property if we agreed that the diocese was the legal owner. We had no intention of ever signing such crap but were waiting until the very last moment to turn them down. They would have capitulated altogether then rather than go through another bout of stalling around. But now that you have embarrassed them, they want spite. They want the altar removed before they will agree to anything. Timing is everything and you threw it off."

"True of making hay also," Fr. Ray replied. "I got some beautiful stuff in that stack and tonight it is going to rain. If I'd waited one more day, it might have been ruined."

Dr. Jake stormed out, disgusted.

Pastor Lemming was another visitor, not exactly a surprise even though it was the first time he had ventured into the countryside rectory. "I just want you to know," he scolded, "that as a fellow priest, I think you are a disgrace to our ranks. You openly defied the bishop."

"Did not. I didn't do the horse show when he asked me not to."

Pastor Lemming almost made the mistake of admitting that he knew what had really happened.

"Were you about to say something?" Fr. Ray teased.

"I was about to say that you were premature in announcing the agreement to open the church."

"You mean it really is going to be opened?"

Damn, he got me again, Pastor Lemming thought. Then out loud. "Well, not as a church. Just a place for social events."

"Isn't saying Mass a social event?"

Pastor Lemming stood up, irritated beyond disguise. "Just who do you think you are, anyway?"

"I'm the Lone Ranger."

Pastor Lemming stomped out too.

The bishop himself was close to coming down with something that resembled an epileptic fit. "Confound it all!" he stormed at poor Madeleine. "Why does all this have to happen to me." He kept trying to call Fr. Ray, that is, he kept ordering her to call him. Since Fr. Ray was most of the time out in the field with his cell phone deliberately left behind, he could not oblige. In the rectory, however, he felt compelled to answer. He could tell by her tone that Madeleine's message was supposed to flatten him with humiliation and disappointment.

"His Excellency with great regret must withdraw his offer to make you an auxiliary bishop," she said triumphantly.

Fr. Ray chuckled much to her surprise. He couldn't help it. Did they really think he cared? "I understand completely," he answered after he had composed himself. "His Excellency could hardly turn the Lone Ranger into a bishop. Not even with Tonto waiting on the trail ahead."

She hung up.

Dan Bandy visited more than once, always seeking information. But Fr. Ray didn't mind. For one thing Bandy liked Thunderstruck too. And the newspaper reporter always knew things that no one else would tell him.

"The real reason Pastor Lemming is upset is because he wanted to make a big deal out of opening the church up for community activities and handing over the keys. That was supposed to be how he won back the support of all the people. That would persuade them to come to church in Resurrection like they are supposed to do instead of going over to Marystone."

"You mean its official? They are really going to open the church up?"

"Seems likely. But they are going to make the People For A Democratic Church suffer for it." He loved to roll that off his tongue—People-For-A-Democratic-Church. "You are out of the picture completely, for one thing. And they are demanding the removal of the altar as part of the agreement to open the place up for community gatherings. Say it would be sacrilegious for the altar to be exposed to worldly affairs."

"Really? How are they going to get it out the door."

"Guess they'd have to take it apart."

Again the priest laughed. Every new episode in the drama seemed more wildly insane to him than the last one. " I don't believe it and you can quote me."

Dan smiled sweetly. "I've got so much material for columns I'll never run out."

Dow Kapier stormed into the office the next evening. Fr. Ray had not seen him so agitated since the church had been closed.

"They say they are going to take the altar out," he almost shouted. "*Take the altar out!*" His chest was heaving. "That altar is decorated with hand-carvings by immigrant artisans. My great-grandfather was one of them. First they try to steal the windows and now the altar. By God, it'll be over my dead body."

"Now calm down, Dow. I don't think they will do that. Calmer heads will prevail."

"It's a done deal. The only way we were going to get the church opened again was for our lawyers to agree to let them confiscate the altar."

"I wonder if there has ever been another case in history when an altar got confiscated?" Fr. Ray could not keep from laughing again.

"What's so funny?"

"Sometimes laughing is the only sane response to insanity."

"They are going to store it in the basement at Church of the Resurrection for the time being." The anger in Dow's voice made his lips tremble. "In the basement for God's sake. And what the hell does 'for the time being' mean?"

Fr. Ray was studying Dow closely. The man was obviously not as shy as he had previously let on. There was a different Dow coming to the fore these days. "They will probably just take the altar stone out. That is the real sacred part of an altar. Without the stone, the altar is just another fancy table." Fr. Ray shook his head, just thinking about it. Every time he had to explain a doctrinal matter now, it seemed so eerily medieval.

Dow did not immediately answer. Fr. Ray's remark had evidently struck some kind of responsive chord in his mind.

"By God, that's it. That's what I'll do," he finally exclaimed.

"Please?"

Dow smiled triumphantly. "They by God don't know they can't beat old Dow Kapier. That is *just* what I'll do."

"Just what is that?"

"Just never you mind, Lone Ranger." Dow was smiling wickedly. He had never called the priest by that name. Whatever had come to his head had lifted his mood considerably. And again the priest thought that there was something about his manner he had not noticed before. Dow Kapier was more than just the quiet and deprecating janitor of the church and caretaker of the cemetery.

The opening of St. Philo's as a community center was not an occasion of much celebration for the PFDC. The altar was indeed dismantled and removed to the basement at Resurrection. Pastor Lemming had made sure the sheriff was on hand during the removal just in case anyone was tempted to cause problems. No parishioners, not even DOD members, would help. A crowd stood by sullenly watching the entire process. Dow Kapier only showed up as the last segment of the altar was loaded on a truck. He stared stonily at Pastor Lemming and remarked in an acid tone of voice: "What is it costing you to do this?"

Pastor Lemming looked at him sharply but did not answer.

"I suppose you used some of the money you stole from us."

All the people who were close enough to hear, some of them praying the rosary out loud in protest, hushed and stared at Kapier now. Most of them had never heard him say that many words all at once before, let alone such dangerous words. But Kapier's eyes were riveted on Pastor Lemming, boring into him, full of more meaning and intent than the priest could possibly know or understand. Pastor Lemming looked around for a sympathetic eye. None. What prompted Kapier to bring up that money just now? Did he know something? The priest hurried away to his car but heard behind him, as everyone else did, Kapier's dry, bitter, but somehow victorious laugh.

The bishop, helped along by the considerable persuasive power of Pastor Lemming, dropped yet another shoe. He closed St. Clare's as a parish church and demoted it to a mere chapel under the direct charge of Pastor Lemming. Fr. Ray was now without a pastorate and without another appointment forthcoming as far as he knew. Members of PFDC, having spent so much wrath on the closing of St. Philo's and then on the removal of its altar, accepted the change in the status of St. Clare's stoically. Or seemed to. But when Fr. Ray kept on conducting services on a picnic table in the cemetery across from the closed St. Philo's, riding there on his horse just to irritate church authorities, or so Pastor Lemming believed, the former parishioners divided into three groups. Those most obedient to the dictates of Rome bowed to authority and started attending Resurrection in Bredsocken, which is what they had been told to do. The mildly belligerent went to church at Our Lady of Good Patience in Marystone, just to be contrary. The most belligerent contingent either quit going to church at all or transferred their allegiance to one or another of the new Christian Evangelical churches in the area. A few attended Fr. Ray's intermittent lawn services which looked quite like the traditional Catholic Mass. This prompted a telephone call from Pastor Lemming to Fr. Ray.

"If you keep making a public spectacle of the Mass, the bishop has directed me to inform you that you will be stripped of your authority to administer the Sacraments and say Mass at all," he said with a coldness that could not conceal his glee. "You will be excommunicated."

"How do I know you speak for the bishop. He hasn't said a word to me."

"He has now."

"Maybe you're just bluffing." Fr. Ray had never dreamed that, rid of the fear of church authority, he could speak with such careless boldness.

"Satan has possessed you for sure."

"No, just the Lone Ranger."

"I can tell you for sure, Ray, you are out of a job. We've got a place for you, janitorial work in the diocesan headquarters."

"Don't you see what is happening, Louis? Every day you are losing church membership. I know three families that are now attending First Christian Evangelical, and four more that just quit church altogether. Don't you see that you and your poor bishop are committing institutional suicide?"

Pastor Lemming drew himself up in righteous anger. "People who drop out of the church aren't really Catholics and never were. We don't need them."

Fr. Ray had never wanted trouble, but now, filled with a new courage over his conclusion that bread and wine really did become everyone's body and blood and everyone was a god, he lost all patience.

"You are as blind as a fence post." He slammed down the phone. He would continue to conduct his lawn services as long as it pleased him to do it, and there was nothing Rome could really do about it because he didn't care whether he was excommunicated or not. Might be interesting to be excommunicated. He would, by holy bread and wine, start his own church.

At the other end of the line, Pastor Lemming put down the phone and stared at the wall grimly. It was time for the "ultimate action" as he had, in the privacy of his own mind, gotten into the habit of calling his plot to take down Fr. Ray. If excommunication didn't faze him, the "ultimate action" surely would.

Something else was gnawing at the back of his mind ever since that weird janitor had mentioned St. Philo's money which was supposed to be in the bank. He had been trying to ignore the fact that he had not heard a word from Intimate Insider Investments since he had purchased stock in the ethanol plant. But he would deal first with Fr. Ray.

The next meeting of the parish council at Church of the Resurrection was highly charged with suppressed outrage and Pastor Lemming made no effort to relieve the tension. The lockout at St. Clare's had seemed to be accepted by one and all because the church had not been completely closed. But Deacon Farkow who had brought along his lieutenants Dribble and McTicken for backup, was trembling angrily over the news that former parishioners there were attending Fr. Ray's services in the cemetery across from the former St. Philo's.

"What has come over that man," Pastor Lemming said. "He is forcing the bishop's hand. What other course do we have?"

"You mean excommunication?" George Dribble asked, eyes widening. In his mind, excommunication was annihilation. He had grown to sort of like Fr. Ray. The man did not deserve annihilation.

"He is acting almost as if he were possessed by the devil," Pastor Lemming remarked, watching the council members closely.

Plover Venale covered her suddenly gaping mouth with her hands. Alice Dribble gasped in alarm. Could such evil come to Vinal County?

"It does happen, sadly, even in modern times," Pastor Lemming continued softly, almost as if he were afraid of being overheard by evil spirits. "That's why the clergy has been given special powers to drive out devils." He paused, then nodded gravely in the general direction of Farkow. "Even deacons have the power."

Farkow pretended that he had been thinking about that very thing himself and nodded, at the same time drawing himself up with appropriate hauteur. "It does make one wonder," he said. "Especially with what they say might be going on in that poor lost soul's barn."

Everyone knew what he meant, but no one put words to it. Pastor Lemming went into one of his acts, shook his head, as if such a situation were unthinkable, but then nodded and shrugged and wobbled his head around, as if to infer that even though unthinkable, it might be true, which of course it could not be, and yet of course—his head and shoulders kept nodding and shaking every which way, as if to convey that one never knew what to believe in these evil days.

"Just what does that mean anyway, being possessed of devils." As usual, George Dribble was having trouble with strange concepts.

"If you read your Bible once and awhile, you'd know," his wife, Alice, scolded.

Pastor Lemming pretended as if he were going to say something but then pretended to change his mind. He was closely watching Farkow who was staring down at the table top, very intent on whatever was seeping into his mind. Pastor Lemming kept from smiling only with some effort. He had planted the seed just right in the deacon's mind and it did not need any more help. It would sprout and grow all by itself.

"We must proceed with the business at hand," the priest said. "I believe Alice has some new figures on church attendance showing a slight upswing. I would like to discuss some new ideas I have about keeping that trend going."

Chapter 20

"I tell you she is the most contrary thing I ever met," Jack Bump was saying. "I just never know what she is going to do or say next." He was talking to his grandfather Ben, as he so liked to do, and Ben was nodding, knowing he was talking again about Mary Barnette.

"She sounds like your Great Aunt Nan to me, a bit fiery on the surface, but a heart of gold deep down. You should bring her over some time so's I can have another look at her."

"She is just amazing, that's all I can say." What Jack didn't say out loud was that he could see already that being with Mary was never going to make for a quiet, subdued life like she said she preferred and which he preferred, too. But he still wanted to live with her.

"Well, my dear Mary and I weren't always at peace, God rest her soul," Ben said, smiling, reading Jack's mind. "There were moments. Did I ever tell you the time we started a real knock-down fight at the school meeting?"

Jack had heard the story more than once, but he pretended otherwise, humoring his grandfather's love for the old days.

"Course your grandmother was not really in the thick of it like I was, but I have a hunch if I'd started getting the worst of it from that cuss of a Henry Remp, she'd have waded right in too, just like your Great Aunt Nan did." He shook his head, visibly enjoying the memory, and then launched into the story once again, while Jack with an amused look on his face, pretended he had never heard it before.

"I never knew I had it in me, to go up on the stage like that and stare those school boys down, and then throw that Remp clean off the stage whilst your Great Uncle Emmet was settling the Chafer boys' hash. Oh, it was a sight. Sheriff almost arrested us."

"And they say Uncle Emmet really got the better of the school officials by offering free land for a new school if they put it in Gowler rather than Upper Surrey, right?" Jack said, hoping to head off the longer version of the story.

"That's right. Course, it did no good. The state always wins in the end. We got another ten years or so for Gowler school, but the city folk outnumbered us after that, and we lost out. Urban people don't like schools out in cornfields, and they don't like churches out there either. That's the real reason those churches in Vinal County are being closed. The authorities, school and church, want to cram lots of people into one building to make it more profitable. Same as with hogs in barns."

"Mary and I are thinking about starting a new business. Get serious about cornmeal and wheat flour." Jack was changing the subject, not of a mind to discuss education. He figured schooling could all be done over the Internet and would be some day. That was another of his predictions that shocked everyone he told it to except Mary. "What do you think about going into flour milling on a small scale?"

"Well, I think it is just fine and dandy," Ben said with spirit. "That's the way it used to be, you know. We had three, four flour mills in this county when I was a kid and more before that. It's high time we quit sending our grain to Columbus and then buying it back in bread for ten times what we can sell it for grain."

"It's happening everywhere," Jack nodded. "Internet's full of examples."

"Better than trying to make beer and bourbon, I think," Ben added with a wry smile.

"Maybe we'll do that too someday," Jack replied, matching Ben's smile.

"Where you think you'll locate your gristmill?"

Jack shrugged. "Just don't know yet." He paused and then, suddenly, his face brightened. "Oh my, I just had an idea. Oh my, why didn't I think of that sooner." Whatever was working on his mind, his face seemed to reflect a vision of great promise. "Oh yes, this is the best idea yet." He got up and headed for the door, stopped, realizing he was being rude and turned back to Ben. "I gotta talk to Mary right now."

"Well hold on, young feller," Ben said. "What hit you so."

"It's really what you said. About churches having to think like the hog business. Well, not exactly that, but that's what my mind turned on. That church over there, that St. Philo's as they call it, well, the bishop closed it. Not a church anymore. Those folks want to keep using the building for something. They've got that farmer's market going there already. A good place to try out a gristmill. The Evangelicals are using basketball to lure people into their churches. Maybe we can do the same with good food."

Mary hugged Jack when he told her his idea. The hug turned into a kiss. Then a more passionate embrace. Then she pushed away. Time for business, not pleasure. "We were thinking in this direction all along but not seeing where the road led, plain as day," she said.

"We've got to talk to Ray," Jack said.

"Lots of people will balk at the idea of using the church for something other than churchy stuff." Mary replied.

"Well, that's the beauty of it all," Jack said, unencumbered by the traditions of Catholicism. "We'll still call it a church. A church of good food."

Mary beamed, relishing the thought. They had joked about just such a notion before. Maybe it was not a joke. "You are a genius, Mr. Jack Bump."

They found Fr. Ray at his usual Saturday morning chores in the barn. He was, however, not choring but pacing distractedly up and down the aisle in front of the hay mangers.

"You are just the ones I needed to talk to," he said, motioning them on into the barn. "Strange things are happening. Again."

Mary put aside her eagerness to talk about Jack's idea to listen.

"Look at this. Just look." He handed over to Mary a big, brown envelope that he was carrying. She opened it to a billowing flutter of hundred dollar bills. She looked from the envelope to the priest and back again.

"Read the note." Then he repeated himself frantically. "Read the note." She fished it out from among the bills, read it, then looked at Jack and read it out loud.

"As the last pastor of St. Philodendra church, please accept the money herewith offered as a donation to maintain the church building. This money is given to you and no one else but you can use it at your discretion only for the church building. There is more where this comes from, enough to keep the church in good repair and vitality until sanity again returns to the Catholic Church. Ask and you shall receive."

"How much is there?" Mary asked.

"There's five thousand dollars there. Can you believe that?"

Mary sat down on a hay bale, Jack beside her. He read the note again.

"What'll I do now," Fr. Ray sighed. "How can I accept this money?"

"I wonder if it's from the person who broke down the door," Mary said, savoring the mystery. "Maybe this is his way to pay for the damage."

"What am I to do?" Fr. Ray asked again. "Maybe it is stolen money. Maybe someone who thinks he's Robin Hood. Maybe it can be traced. Maybe I'll be accused of robbing a bank or something." His distress was obvious. "And all I ever really wanted was to be a farmer."

"Oh but you must keep this money," Mary said, focusing now, considering alternatives. "It would be wrong not to. Whoever gave this must really care. The church does need the money, especially since the bishop and his pirates took the parish funds. I wouldn't worry too much about it. Whoever gave the money is surely smart enough not to use cash that can be traced so don't worry."

"But if we start repairing the church, everyone will want to know where the money is coming from."

"Well, just tell them the truth. It is coming from an anonymous donor."

"How did the money get here. By mail?" Jack asked.

"No. It was right here in the barn when I came in this morning. Hung right up there on a nail. Someone brought it in here last night."

"Weird."

"We need a plan of action," Mary said, more to herself than the other two. "First of all, we will tell no one the circumstances. Okay? Just say it comes from a secret donor, which is the truth. If the money was here in the barn that means it was someone local and that would raise all kinds of wild speculation."

"Maybe it's some kind of trap," Fr. Ray said. "I wouldn't put anything past that Lemming."

"Well, that's why we have to be right up front about it. People give money this way all the time."

"Hang it on a nail in a barn? I don't think so. But who should be in charge of the money. I don't want to touch the stuff."

"It was given to you so you'll just have to be in charge whether you like it or not. You are part of the community here, whether you like it or not." Mary was almost scolding him. Then she brightened. "When we get organized with the new church, we can have a committee to oversee the money but it will still have to be your decision or whoever is giving it might object. Or quit giving more."

"What do you mean, new church?" Fr. Ray sounded suspicious.

"Oh, yes. That's why we came over here. We've got this idea. We've been wondering where we could put a gristmill, as you know. It occurred to us that the church, now just a community center, would be the perfect place especially since we already sort of introduced cornmeal and wheat flour there at the festival. And now we even have the money to do the necessary alterations, we can think about it as a center for all kinds of food projects. Good heavens, maybe God does exist after all."

"Do not be so sacrilegious," the priest admonished. Then his eyes narrowed. "Pope Mary, are you the donor?" His voice was suddenly full of suspicion.

Mary snorted. "Oh yeah. And I knocked the door down too. If I had that kind of money I'd start my own community center." But then she stopped short, her eyes narrowing, teasing him. "Well, what if I am. How would you know? Or anyone else? Hey, maybe I am."

Now Fr. Ray laughed. "No, you're not. I know you well enough to know when you're bluffing."

"Well, anyway, what do you think of using the church, now community center, for a headquarters for what we're thinking of calling The Church of Almighty Good Food?" She countered. "Jack's idea actually."

Fr. Ray stared at her. Then at Jack. Shook his head in amazement. He never should have stepped out of line with the church. Never should have bucked the bishop. And yet this really was a great idea. He smiled. "On second thought, maybe both of you scoundrels are responsible for that money."

"Well, we aren't but it surely is convenient turning up now," Jack replied. "And really, the food church idea actually came from you in the first place, you know. You are the one always talking about all that weird stuff about bread and wine being body and blood. And the Bible talks about turning water into wine. Hey, maybe you donated that money yourself and are just pretending you found it in the barn."

All three looked at each other and laughed in unison.

"We gotta have a meeting," Mary said. "I'll tell the Duholland sisters to rally the troops. "People are going to be so excited about the money that they might go along with anything."

The church, now St. Philo's Community Center, was jammed for the meeting. The only local leading light not there was Pastor Lemming. But Deacon Farkow was there and his lieutenants, Dribble and McTicken, not to mention Dribble's wife, Alice and Plover Venale, Pastor Lemming's lieutenants. Most of the others were either PFDCs or people not affiliated with either side, but curious about what was going on. Fr. Ray, looking out over the crowd, muttered to Jack Bump, standing next to him in front of the pews: "Never had a crowd this big when this was a real church. There are people here I don't even know."

"That shows we're on to something," Jack replied. "People evidently like the idea of a church dedicated to good food. That group over there along the wall are friends of mine. They could care less about institutional religion. But good food, now, that's right down their alley."

Fr. Ray faced his audience, cleared his throat and fired away. "We are gathered here tonight to discuss a proposal many of you will no doubt find a bit strange," he intoned. He intended to focus on the gristmill idea and play down the money matter. "You are used to thinking of St. Philo's as a church in the customary sense and so you will probably be full of issues and questions as we consider using it in different ways." He paused, realizing that most of the people were barely paying attention. Their glances continually shifted toward Mary Barnette who was sitting with her parents and other members of the Barnette family next to the Bumps across the side aisle. Remembering previous meetings after the church had been broken into, the congregation no doubt figured the most interesting action would come from her. There was even a theory running the gossip vines that she had broken the door down herself and now Barnette money had been advanced to pay for her heathenish ways.

"Okay, we all know why we're here," Fr. Ray said, shifting gears. It was plain that no one wanted to hear his preambles. "Any questions?"

"Do you know the anonymous donor of the money everyone is talking about?" Dan Bandy offered the first question, one of his duties as the journalist in the community being, he always maintained, to act as a spokesperson. The priest glared at him. Bandy, the writer, always knew what mattered most with the readers. The priest would not have been surprised if the reporter knew the identity of the donor himself.

"It's a mystery to me," the priest said, making sure everyone heard him. "I was kind of hoping you'd have an idea about that yourself, Dan."

"What are the details of how you came by the money?" Bandy was not to be sidetracked.

Fr. Ray glanced at Mary, remembering their plan to keep the details secret. He realized now, in the line of fire, that if he told one lie he would have to tell more. Mary seemed to understand his glance and nodded ever so slightly.

"It was in a brown manila envelope hanging from a nail in the barn."

Buzzes rose and fell over the congregation.

"People say you might have donated the money yourself," a voice on the right spoke up.

"I would like to donate money to maintain the church building, but as you know, I don't even have a job anymore. That old saying about being poor as a church mouse applies literally to me."

Some hesitant laughing followed. Fr. Ray's humorous directness, as usual, was the secret of his popularity.

"Folks think the money came from whoever knocked the door down." Another voice from the pews.

"That is a distinct possibility," the priest replied.

Then: "Where's the money now?" This from Hem Judin, the accountant. You might know, Fr. Ray thought.

"The sheriff has it. There's been talk of trying to trace the bills."

"What for?" Don Barnette spoke up. "Why look a gift horse in the mouth." Then he realized that such a statement might indicate to some of those present that the money came from the Barnettes for sure. His brother was glaring at him for that reason, he was sure.

"We hear tell that the note said there was more money available as needed," George Dribble said. "That so?"

"Yes."

"How much more?"

"Didn't say. Just said 'more.'"

"Since this is no longer a church, can we accept money legitimately? Maybe it should go to the diocese." Dr. Jake was talking now, not because he believed what he was suggesting, but to head off opinions of that nature that would surely come from the DODs or Pastor Lemming or diocesan authorities.

"The money was not given to the church as such," Fr. Ray said. "It was given to me for the express purpose of maintaining the church at my discretion. I don't mind saying I am unnerved by that, and one reason for this meeting is to talk about something like a parish council to advise me."

"But the note did say you were to be the final judge in the matter, did it not?" Mary spoke for the first time.

"Yes," Fr. Ray nodded. That woman should be in politics, he thought. He wondered again if maybe she had donated the money, or her family.

"Where in the church are you going to locate the mill?" This from Dow Kapier, always looking at the practical side of things and seemingly wanting to get off the money issue.

"I too have wondered about that," the priest replied.

"I suppose we could just install the mill in the sanctuary where the altar used to be," Ding Duholland piped up.

There was silence. The gathered congregation could hardly be aware of the historic moment in which it was participating. Gatherings throughout history to debate and decide changes in religious belief, or in dogma and doctrine, or in a whole new church organization, had always been conducted by potentates, ministers, theologians garbed in the richly brocaded uniforms of office, amice and chasuble, holding scepters, swinging golden censors of smoking incense, solemn chants rising into the air along with the pungent odor of burning candles. Sometimes the results of these lofty debates were nailed dramatically to church doors as in Martin Luther's case, or shouted out from lofty balconies of cathedrals to the silent masses on streets below. But the scene here in a simple country church surrounded by cornfields was something else altogether. A body of mostly uneducated and certainly non-ecclesiastical people were about to decide on issues that required not only changes in the meaning of church-ordained vocabularies, but changes in the traditional design of houses of worship themselves.

Since the main altar was gone, it was easier to accept new ideas about what should replace it. Although smaller than the average Catholic church, St. Philo's followed the traditional characteristics of the larger ones. All those years the altar with its precious altar stone, its carved cherry reredos looming up over and behind it, had been the material expression of their religious belief. If they had not seen it, every Sunday from childhood on up, they would have realized how quaintly but extraordinarily beautiful the church really was. Niches in the wooden superstructure, the reredos that loomed above the altar table, were intricately carved. They held nearly life-sized statues of St. Francis of Assisi and St. Philodendra, right and left side, with niches above them holding statues of the Archangel Gabriel and Archangel Raphael. The niches themselves dripped with handcarved spools of cherry wood, like wooden icicles. In the center of the reredos, dominating the structure, was a statue of Christ on the cross, and above that in the dome over the whole sanctuary, a congregation of saints and angels painted on the ceiling. The altar itself, now gone, would have been covered with white linen, the tabernacle in the center holding a ciborium of consecrated hosts within its gilded golden brass doors. Candelabra still stairstepped up behind and above where the tabernacle had been. Down three steps in front of the altar, the floor spread out to the communion railing that separated the pews and people from the sanctuary.

On either side of the main altar, along the two outside walls, were two more smaller "side" altars. Over the one on the left in its niche, was a statue of St. Joseph and over the one on the right in its niche, a statue of Mary holding the dead body of Jesus. The fronts of these altars, like the front of the removed main altar, were garnished with finely carved medallions of crosses and sunbursts and *fleurs-de-lis* designs, all in the same jewel-like cherry wood. Even the communion rail was of carved cherry.

No one wanted to be the first to suggest changes to what had been the focal point of their worship for as long as they could remember, a beacon of hope and light. They looked at the bible passage carved into the wall behind the St. Joseph side altar with great affection because it was more meaningful and comforting than most of the ecclesiastical exhortation they listened to Sunday after Sunday. "Come to me, all ye who are burdened, and I will give you rest. Take my yoke upon you, and learn from me, for I am meek and humble of heart; and you will find rest for your souls. For my yoke is sweet and my burden is light."

As they pondered what to do with the sanctuary now, many of the people present realized for the first time that they had never been in the sanctuary of the church except maybe on their wedding day. Though they endured great sacrifice sometimes to get to church, they would then try mightily to linger towards the rear, leaving the front pews for those few who felt duty-bound to stand at the head of the table, so to speak. The sanctuary was for the priests. That's why they endured priests—someone to fill the front lines between God and His more sinful followers. They grew up believing it was a mortal sin not to attend church on Sunday, but once in church, they were more comfortable staying as far away from the action as possible.

Some of them remembered ascending the steps of the altar to light candles when they were altar boys or altar girls, but as adults, the altar had been off limits. Even as children lighting candles, they had felt constrained from so much as peering into the tabernacle even when the opportunity to do so presented itself. This was God's sacred territory into which only an ordained minister was allowed access, and that was fine with the rear pew population. Awed and mystified by the whole doctrinal conduct of godly affairs, they did not want to come near the altar. All they sought was the comfort of sitting in a quiet place on a Sunday morning and letting someone else do the work for a change.

"Wouldn't a flour mill up there be a sort of desecration?" A voice spoke from the crowd. Long pause.

"Well, we do have the blessing of farm crops in the sanctuary, so I guess we can grind grain there too."

A few uneasy titters and grins. Public gatherings always drew out the humor of rural people, a way, no doubt, to cover uneasiness for having to be there.

"I think we should do the milling in the back of church, in the vestibule back there. We can close off the vestibule during grinding. Otherwise, it will get awfully dusty all over the church."

"Well, look how dusty that stable in Bethlehem must have been."

It was clear that no one had thought much about the details of the church interior before, beyond noting the lettering below each stained glass window that denoted who had donated the money for it. For those who knew the genealogies of the community, and most of the older church members did, those names gave a fairly good notion of who still ran the church: Barnette, Dribble, Farkow, Kapier, Duholland.

"A grain grinder is kind of loud for a church."

"Would hardly drown out Rita playing Adeste Fidelis on the organ."

Rita Traxe's eighty-year-old face reddened but the smiles flashed her way were all of good will so she felt mollified. As she always said whenever a new pastor had come along and hinted ever so gently that she was hitting the crescendoes a little bit on the heavy side: "These folks are used to tractors and such. Some of them are half deaf. They like their music loud."

"What kind of mill are you thinking of getting?"

"Well, that's something we need to rethink, actually," Fr. Ray said. "Now that we have the money, we probably ought to think of a bigger and better one, even a stone mill. Could be expensive."

"Well, like you say, there's more money where the five thousand came from," Dow Kapier said. For him that was almost a speech and, in case anyone doubted, showed where his sentiments lay.

"We will have to have enough room not just for the mill but for packaging or sacking the flour," Jack Bump offered. He was hesitant to speak for fear he might be resented. People might say that he was "not from here." But nothing ventured ... "Should we be thinking of maybe removing some of the pews?" he asked.

"Maybe we should be thinking of using part of the space for making fruit juices, even wine," Pope Mary said, as if that had just now occurred to her. "You know, bread and wine, body and blood." When others, particularly from the DODs, stared at her skeptically, she quickly changed her direction, having made her point. "What we really need room for is banquet tables. This new church is about food, remember." She wanted to say something about food churches not requiring any kneeling before invisible gods, but decided, for once, to curb her tongue.

"Well, we just can't get rid of these pews. They are priceless."

"Not get rid of them," Jack said quickly. "Just rearrange them around tables. Maybe just turn around every other row of seats to face each other and put long tables between them. Maybe use the kneelers in making the tables."

Much to Fr. Ray's surprise, most of the people nodded after giving that a thought or two. A novel idea but practical.

"My old prayer bones are tired of kneeling anyway," someone mumbled. Those who could hear that remark laughed. Fr. Ray was heartened. The meeting was going much better than he had expected.

Ding Duholland stood up, sat back down, stood up again, raising her hand. She had something she deemed important to say but wondered if the time was appropriate.

"Yes, Miss Duholland," the priest acknowledged her.

"Mabel and I have an announcement apropos to this subject." Mabel looked up at her sister sharply. She did not think Ding knew that word, apropos. "We are making available acreage from our farm next to the church on the east side of the road, for anyone and everyone who wants a garden plot. A free garden plot. What is a church of almighty good food without gardens around it?"

The murmur of voices that followed sounded positive and approving. Even Deacon Farkow, who had come to the meeting prepared to object to anything proposed, realized the appropriateness of the idea and smiled almost graciously.

Fr. Ray beamed. "Well, Ding, that is certainly a wonderful offer. Just exactly what we need in this endeavor."

Pope Mary was beside herself for not thinking of garden plots. But she would not be outdone. "And Barnette Farms, which owns the land south of the church, will donate five acres for a community orchard. More if needed." She glanced at her uncle, Tom, who actually owned the land, and dared him with her eyes to disagree with her. He just looked at her, mildly vexed. She got the better of him every time.

There was now a subdued hubbub throughout the community center as the mostly rural people seized upon the possibilities that gardens and orchards suggested.

"And we can use part of the church, er, community center, for a canning area, like the Frelins are doing at their market garden over by Marystone," another voice spoke up. "People who want to can their garden stuff can come here to do it or get instruction in how to do it."

"Yes, yes," Pope Mary said, jumping up excitedly. "Do the old can can!" And she kicked up a leg suggestively. Even Venale Plover laughed now.

Deacon Farkow was about to stand up to make some kind of formal objection but by now he had forgotten what it was. He could not deny his rural culture. This all made sense. Fr. Ray, catching the spirit, allowed as how people might keep chickens at his farm. They might even develop a steady supply of fresh eggs at the community center.

"How about a cider mill," someone else suggested. "The commercial one over at Bredsocken is about to go out of business, I hear tell."

Again nodding and murmurs of approval.

"We will need to have someone in charge, to coordinate everything," Pope Mary said. "And we know who needs a job." She turned sweetly toward Fr. Ray, who blushed.

"Well, of course," said Dr. Jake before the priest could object, as if he and Mary had planned it all. "How fitting that our former pastor take on this assignment. We can pay him on a percentage of sales."

Fr. Ray looked embarrassed. "Well, I don't mind saying that I would welcome the job seeing that at the moment I am out of work, but perhaps for now we should just kind of settle on some general resolutions. First of all we need to vote on the general idea. If the majority approves, we can get to the details by and by."

Dan Bandy, who had not come to the meeting overly in favor of anything, had caught the vision of a church dedicated to feeding people materially as well as spiritually. "Looks to me like we can do it with a show of hands," he said. And before anyone could object, he asked. "All those in favor of the Church of Almighty Good Food, raise your right hand."

A few hands went up. Then a few more. Seeing that those in favor were obviously in the majority, even most of the DODs finally raised their hands.

"Motion carried," proclaimed Bandy, and headed out the door to file his story. He was thinking now that it was such a good story it might gain national attention. Could anyone ever have imagined a Church of Almighty Good Food? He could win a Pulitzer with this. He drove eighty all the way back to his office.

Chapter 21

Stopping at the Farm Service Administration office to take out insurance on the 2008 crop, as many farmers were doing, Mary happened to notice a new wrinkle in the government program. She read through the new details and then read again. FSA regulations were always confusing, written that way, she believed, to justify the army of FSA personnel needed to translate them into practical English for farmers.

"You mean you are insuring corn at $5.40 a bushel if we have losses?" she asked, not believing her eyes.

"That's the spring price, yes." The woman on the other side of the counter wore an expression of everlasting patience. She had been answering farmers' questions like this for twenty years.

"You mean if I take out this coverage and have a crop loss of say 40 bushels per acre under my farm's crop history, that the government will pay me $5.40 for those bushels lost up to 80% of the whole?"

"Well, yes." The FSA official replied with a certain wary aloofness in her voice. She was used to answering questions from male farmers who despised government subsidies but always took them. Having to talk to a female, especially one with Mary Barnette's reputation, was a bit unnerving. "But we're expecting the corn market to rise dramatically. And it's expensive insurance, you understand." Her tone indicated, at least to Mary, that it was an alternative only for really big farmers, out of Mary's league.

"What will it cost if I cover a thousand acres of corn this way?"

The FSA official started pecking away on her calculator, one eye on the Barnette farm's crop yield history for corn which was 152 bushels per acre and one eye on the details of the insurance program. Long before she came up with an answer, Mary had figured it out in her head but she remained silent.

"Right at $40,000," the translator of government edict finally said. She figured that would be the end of it. "If you have a normal crop, you're out that much money. Even if you have losses, you have to figure that we only cover 80%."

The cogs of Mary's mind were whirling away at high speed. Forty thousand dollars was a lot of money. But if corn prices stayed high and went higher, as obviously the government was anticipating, believing its own propaganda that world demand for grain was going to skyrocket, and then, on top of that, a bad crop year followed, say a 30 bushel per acre loss, that would be five dollars plus times thirty bushels or something more than $150 an acre of insurance payment. On a thousand acres, that was something more than $150,000. In case that ever happened, the $40,000 premium seemed well worth it. If the crop were normal she would gross over five dollars a bushel on 152,000 bushels, or $760,000. So what if the insurance cost $40,000. Chicken feed. To Mary, it seemed like neither the government nor the farmers really grasped just how much money was involved in five dollar corn. And what if it went higher? There was no way she could lose. And then she thought of something else even more sensational. She stared at the government translator.

"I'll take that coverage," she said.

The translator's eyes opened wide. So far no other farmer in Vinal County had opted for this expensive insurance. Mary Barnette thought she was so smart but this was one time she was going in over her head. "OK, Mary. Sure hope you know what you are doing."

"I am the pope of Balem Township," Mary said, trying to keep a straight face. "Popes don't make mistakes in matters of faith, and corn is a matter of faith in Balem Township." Then she smiled as if she knew something that the FSA hadn't figured out yet. Which was true. But she would not dare tell anyone. Well, maybe Jack.

Pastor Lemming choked on his pizza when he heard what had happened at the meeting at St. Philo's. "The place is going to turn into an evangelical Whole Foods store," he pouted. "What has gotten into those people anyway. Don't they know they are desecrating a holy place."

"But it's not a holy place any more. You said so yourself," Alice Dribble pointed out, a little surprised at herself for challenging her pastor.

"Well it's just not right. A church of almighty good food. God Almighty, that's desecration."

"But, you know, in a sort of strange way, there's something to be said of the idea," George Dribble spoke, his faith in the faith of his forefathers wavering a bit of late.

"What do you mean?" Deacon Farkow barked at him. "This has got to be nipped in the bud."

"Yes, indeed," Pastor Lemming said. "Fr. Ray, if I can still call him Father, is obviously a dangerous man. He not only disobeys his bishop. He is now making fun of the holies of holies, the Eucharist. I do believe the man is possessed."

Deacon Farkow's eyes narrowed. A plan had been brewing in his mind ever since Pastor Lemming had first brought up the matter of possession by the devil and that one of the powers of ordained deacons was that they could conduct exorcisms. He had been studying up on the subject. Google was full of references. And he and his lieutenants had been doing some planning and organizing. By God, when it came to dealing with devils, he was the right deacon for the job. Maybe he'd drive a devil or two out of Pope Mary while he was at it.

"I do believe he is possessed too," he finally said. "Maybe I can do something about that."

"We must at least make everyone aware of the danger and pray fervently for deliverance," Pastor Lemming responded piously. He did not want to get too involved on the subject. The official Church took a dim view of devils these days, another sign to him of the deterioration of Catholicism. But he meant to keep the sprout of suspicion in Deacon Farkow well-watered.

Even as he drove home from the meeting, the deacon was on his cell phone, calling together what he referred to as his "posse" in the sense of the old western movies. If Fr. Ray thought he was being funny by calling himself the Lone Ranger and by riding horses to church, maybe he wouldn't feel so cute when a posse showed up to relieve him of a devil or two. Farkow could not call a meeting at his house because Dora, his wife, would not brook any such talk. She thought he was crazy anyway and had already told him that if he didn't quit talking about this devil nonsense she would join the Church of Almighty Good Food just to embarrass him. He wouldn't be surprised if she had a devil in her, too.

"Lloyd, the time has come," he muttered into the phone.

"You mean to do it?"

"Yes. Get the posse together. We meet tomorrow night on the old covered bridge as planned. Soon as it's dark."

The old covered bridge over the Tymock River, hardly a mile from St. Philo's, had always been a favorite meeting place for young people operating on the ramparts of polite society. Now that the road had been redirected over the new, modern bridge beside it—farm equipment had grown too big to fit through the old bridge—the latter suited the purpose even better. The county commissioners had not yet had the heart, or the money, to tear the old bridge down, so without traffic, it was an even more private-public place on the lonely country road for such questionable practices as underage drinking, pot smoking, and sexual encounters. Even in past times the bridge had been a gathering place. Local folklore was full of stories of night riders and Klu Klux Klanners meeting there to hatch out plans to burn down a Catholic barn or lynch an unfortunate black man who thought he had escaped to freedom in the North. So it was a logical place for Deacon Farkow's posse to gather and work up the courage it would take to face down the devil.

They came armed with crosses and holy water, as Deacon Farkow had directed. Lloyd McTicken even brought along a strand of blessed palm leaf left over from last Palm Sunday. What exactly a devil might do or not do they weren't sure, but if crosses and crucifixes would stop vampires and witches, as they had learned from movies, maybe Deacon Farkow knew what he was talking about. Vampires, witches, and devils were all about the same anyway, weren't they? But in case these defenses proved inadequate, the posse had brought along several six packs of beer to bolster their fortitude. They were understandably uneasy, especially George Dribble who was not too sure he believed what he said he believed, anyway. They were the kind of men who worked hard for a living far from the protective assurance of higher education and even farther from the kind of knowledge that reading books might have brought them. What they knew about the spiritual world was what they heard in church, teachings which they accepted unquestioningly because Momma wouldn't lie even if a priest might. Devils roamed the land for sure, and the Catholic Church was the one safe refuge from them. That's what their elders had told them, and the elders before that had told their elders, and so on and so forth as far back in time as they could imagine. They listened now, arms folded defensively over their chests, to what Deacon Farkow was saying.

"As we have discussed earlier, we are faced here with an unfortunate situation. A priest of God who has gone haywire," Farkow said in a low voice, although there was not anyone within a mile of the place. "Father Raymond Tulley has disobeyed his bishop, will soon be excommunicated, doesn't seem to care, demeans our religious beliefs, and worst of all, appears to be carrying on with sheep." Deacon Farkow stopped and blessed himself at such a disgusting thought. Other members of the posse mimicked him. What could possibly be more evil than carrying on with sheep. "But we must think only kindly of Fr. Ray because, you understand, he is not in charge of himself. When he speaks, it is the devil speaking. When he acts, it is the devil acting."

He waited for reactions. None came so he resumed. "The church has prescribed ancient rituals to drive devils out of people and has given this power even to deacons. I am about to undertake one such effort. According to the instructions, I will don this stole, a symbol of my office as deacon, and attempt to drape it from my neck to the unfortunate soul's shoulder." He opened the little suitcase and pulled from it a purple, scarf-like length of cloth, one of the vestments that priests and deacons wear at various churchly celebrations. In the bag there was also an alb, another of the churchly vestments, a crucifix, candles, a shaker of salt, a bottle of wine and a holy water sprinkler. The posse gaped.

"I will sprinkle this salt on the poor victim when we confront him. Salt is symbolic of purity," the deacon explained. "The wine represents the blood of Jesus and I will splash a little on him if I can. You will hold your crosses in front of you and keep repeating the name of Jesus, which is very frightening to devils."

The posse members stared silently, eyes as round and bulging as cue balls. George Dribble drew back farther into the darkness. "Gotta take a leak," he said. The others stared at him. Most of them would have just unzipped and let fly, not even necessarily turning their backs. This is the way real men lived when women weren't around. Maybe George was having the piss scared out of him.

But George disappeared into the darkness for other than bodily urges. He wanted to call Pastor Lemming on his cell phone and didn't want the others to know. It seemed to him things had gone too far.

"Pastor Lemming, this is George Dribble." He barely whispered, still walking away from the others.

"George?"

"Just thought you ought to know. Deacon Farkow is going ahead with the exorcism thing."

A pause. "You mean actually doing it?" The priest sounded incredulous.

"Yes. He's assembled a group, and they are as of now headed for Fr. Ray's place."

"Actually going ahead with a real exorcism?" The priest asked again. He had not thought that idiot Farkow had the guts to actually do it. "How does he know what to do?"

"He found it on Google."

"Google? What's that?" It sounded like one of those satanic names in the bible to Pastor Lemming.

"You know. The Internet."

"You mean there's things like that on the Internet?" Pastor Lemming replied, outright amazement in his voice.

"Everything is on the Internet, Father."

Pastor Lemming laughed drily. Things were not going his way these days. He had only wanted to instill distrust and ridicule. But if he tried to call off the exorcism, it would mean involving himself openly. That would not go over well with the bishop.

"Serves Fr. Raymond right. He asked for it," he finally said and then hung up. But just to be safe he decided he had better drive out to Fr. Ray's rectory and at least cruise by slowly.

George stared at his phone. Now he had more misgivings. Perhaps someone else needed to be tipped off. But who? The last of his courage slipped away. What the hell. The die was cast.

McTicken grinned when George returned to the group. "Beer must really work fast on you. Doesn't even have to change color going through, right?" Everyone laughed at the old joke, except Farkow. This was no time for old jokes.

"The main thing is that we must all be free of secret sins," Farkow continued his lecture. "What the devil likes to do during exorcism is to shout out the sins of the exorcist and his assistants to confound us. So if you haven't been to confession lately you might want to drop out now." He stared from one to another of his posse. They were expecting Louie Latt to excuse himself because it was rumored that he was paying inordinate attention to Dora, Farkow's wife, when the latter was off doing his deacon things. But Louie Latt did not budge. So much for that rumor. Dribble was tempted to use secret sin as an excuse to get shut of the whole weird night, but then everyone might think he was the one spending time with Dora.

"Mount up," Farkow said dramatically as he headed for his car. "Fr. Ray should be finishing up chores about now."

That was indeed the case. The priest who wanted only to be a farmer had just emerged from the barn and was standing in the soft glow from the light inside as cars pulled into his driveway. He was expecting Jack Bump, Pope Mary, and Dr. Jake, but there were more cars than that. Puzzled, he forgot to close the gate that held in the sheep.

The occupants of the car, seeing him in the light, gathered in a group and advanced toward him, some lighting candles, others lighting cigarettes, one or two coughing nervously, a few muttering what sounded like prayers. Fr. Ray was mystified. What in the world …

When they got within the light, he saw with astonishment that in the lead was Alvin Farkow and he was wearing—yes—he was wearing liturgical vestments, a lacy, white, full-length alb and a purple stole. He was also holding up a crucifix. Totally mortified, Fr. Ray could only stare in silence. The world of humans was surely insane.

"Do not be alarmed, Fr. Ray," Farkow intoned. "We are here on a mission of mercy. We are here to save your soul." Fr. Ray gazed around wildly. The others were silently standing by with their candles and cigarettes, and did not approach close enough for him to recognize them. He edged away from the barn, toward the house.

"What is going on?" He asked in a very bewildered voice.

"Remember now," Farkow said, turning to his posse. "What you hear coming from this poor wretch may not be his words, but Satan's. Do not be deterred. Begin praying, as I have instructed you."

They immediately began a muttered monotone chant: "Jesus, save him. Jesus, save him. Jesus, save him."

Deacon Farkow removed the salt shaker from his black bag and shook it in the general direction of the priest, who had taken a few more steps toward the house, wishing, for the first time ever, that he had a cell phone on him. Then the deacon moved closer, brandished the holy water sprinkler and liberally irrigated the barnyard around them all. Farkow half-expected the evil spirit to shriek in pain when the holy water splashed on Fr. Ray, as the experts on Google said frequently happens during exorcisms. Instead, Fr. Ray took a few more steps toward the house. When members of the posse moved to block his way, he shrugged, turned up the five gallon bucket he was carrying, sat down on it, and laughed helplessly. It had dawned on him what Farkow must be doing.

"That is the devil laughing," Farkow remonstrated his men. "Keep praying." He then approached Fr. Ray and held out the crucifix. "Will you please take this crucifix, Father Raymond Tulley, in the name of the Lord Jesus crucified, and pray with us."

"You are really pathetic," the priest finally found his tongue. But he was growing alarmed. He recognized most of the men after getting a closer view, and though they were the kind not to cause trouble ordinarily, this was not an ordinary time. He could smell beer. This could be mob time. Hopefully Doc and Pope Mary would soon arrive. If nothing else, they would surely find this scene uproariously funny.

"That is the devil talking," Deacon Farkow again warned his posse. "Hold fast to your crosses and rosaries. Keep praying."

Fr. Ray noticed, as he studied the men closely, something even more startling than their actions. None of them, not even Farkow, were displaying the least bit of malice toward him. Quite the opposite. There was only sympathy and concern in their faces and in their body language. They really thought that they were doing God's work, the priest could see. The full force of that realization overwhelmed him. He was witnessing the ultimate irony and sadness of religion. Pitiful superstition could hold in thrall a human nature that really did want to do something good. He knew, clearer than ever, why he had lately abandoned the embrace of organized religion. Wrapped in doctrinal belief, ignorance could perpetuate itself, a parasite inside the human inclination toward virtue. The priest felt an immense pity for all human beings including himself. He had been a fervent believer too. He could understand. Helplessly, hopelessly, he held out his hand and took the crucifix from Farkow and bowed his head. Might as well humor the idiot.

"I know you mean well, Alvin," he said. "Let's go to the house and talk this over for awhile."

Farkow's eyes bugged. He had expected devilish obscenities to foam out of the poor priest's mouth, not such kindly words. Must be a really clever devil. But with the crucifix now in Fr. Ray's hand and his head bent in what looked like abject humility, it was time to go on the offense. He bent over and draped one end of the stole that he wore around his neck over the shoulder of the seated priest, raised his eyes toward the dark skies and cried out in a loud voice:

"By the power of the Universal Church invested in me, I command you, Satan, in the name of Almighty God and Jesus his son, whom you must obey, depart from this poor man!" The members of the posse now raised their calloused hands holding their crosses and brought their chant to one word, repeated dully over and over: "JesUS, JesUS, JesUS." So intent were all parties on the proceedings that no one noticed the sheep. With the gate still open, some of them, including Sam the Ram, had emerged from the barn to see what was going on. Deacon Farkow and most of the posse now stood between the priest and the barn, their backs to the sheep, the better to see the tormented priest in the barn light. Fr. Ray sitting on the bucket with his head bowed, did not see the sheep either or he might have warned one and all that it was not a good idea to turn one's back on Sam. At the same time, adding more confusion to the scene, another car pulled into the driveway and its occupants, no doubt seeing the shadowy figures by the barn, pulled across the barnyard, the car lights flooding the scene.

Deacon Farkow, having not elicited any reply or reaction from the devil or devils in possession of Fr. Ray's soul, decided to give it another try. This time, still bent over, he read from a prayer book of Holy

Scripture, using the light of a candle that Lloyd McTicken extended to see the printed words. "Matthew, Chapter 9," he intoned. "Now as they were going out, behold, they brought to him a dumb man possessed by a devil. And when the devil had been cast out, the dumb man spoke; and the crowds marveled." The deacon paused, flipped a page and read again. "But if I cast out devils by the Spirit of God, then the kingdom of God has come upon you." He paused. Still no reaction except Fr. Ray staring at the ground, shaking his head in mournful embarrassment. Deacon Farkow flipped to another page: "Luke, Chapter 7: For He was charging the unclean spirit to go forth from the man... And Jesus asked him, saying, 'What is thy name?' And he said, 'Legion' because many devils had entered into him. And the devils entreated Him not to command them to depart into hell. Now a herd of many swine was there, feeding on the mountainside. And the devils kept entreating Him to give them leave to enter into them. And He gave them leave. And the devils came out from the man and entered into the swine; and the herd rushed down the cliff into the lake and were drowned." Deacon Farkow's face was wreathed in a satisfied smile. That passage would surely be enough to scare any devil back to hell.

But there was only silence coming from poor Fr. Ray.

"All right then, I have no choice but to use the last resort," the deacon exorcist said. He flipped the pages again, took a deep breath, read wrathfully: "Leviticus, chapter 20: He that will copulate with any beast or cattle, dying let him die! The beast also ye shall kill."

Fr. Ray was by now nearly out of his mind in desperation over what to do. He raised his head, unable to think of any response. At that moment, however, utter pandemonium descended upon them all, causing the priest to cry out, too late, a warning. Bearing down on the still bent figure of Deacon Farkow was Sam, head down, going like a ram out of hell and aimed directly at the deacon's rather voluminous rear end. Ram head met man butt and the deacon was bowled over into McTicken, both going down to the ground while the candle and prayer book sailed into the night.

There was at that very moment an almost unearthly shriek piercing the darkness. The posse scattered. Sam's attack was reason enough, but some of them, like McTicken, were absolutely sure that the cackles and screams were emanating from the devil leaving Fr. Ray. Deacon Farkow also thought that was the case but he had little time to enjoy the moment as he tried desperately to scramble on hands and knees away from the ram who continued to belabor him with head butts. Another banshee wail split the night air, and the deacon in spite of his harrowing circumstances, smiled, thinking for sure that he had indeed rid Fr. Ray of the devils and they had gone into the sheep, as they had gone into the swine in the bible.

Sam finally tired of his frolic and raced with the rest of the flock around the barnyard, as if indeed possessed, before tumbling back into the barn. Deacon Farkow, realizing that he was not seriously hurt, wobbled to his feet and ran toward his car. Things had not gone quite the way he had intended. And now his way was blocked by a trio of human figures and another eruption of shrieking laughter. He stopped, speechless and stunned. Standing in front of him was Mary Barnette. It was she who had been rending the darkness with spasms of uncontrolled laughter. The devil had gone into her.

"If only I had caught that on video," she was saying, directly in his face. "I could sell it to television and retire. No one would believe it." And, in her usual free-spirited way, she whooped again, pounding on Jack Bump's shoulder beside her.

"Out of my way," Farkow muttered.

"I don't think so," said a crisp voice, full of authority, behind Mary. It was Dr. Jake. "You are not going to leave just yet. I have something to say after you round up your gang of idiots." Something in his tone of voice brooked no disobedience. Dr. Jake waited as members of the posse limped out of the darkness. Fr. Ray had secured the sheep in the barn by then and returned to the group, still not believing what had happened right in front of his eyes. Unnoticed by anyone, a solitary figure had parked a car out along the road and approached to within hearing distance. Dr. Jake, who did not seem to think the affair nearly as funny as Mary did, was in fact, quite as angry as he had ever remembered being. His anger, however, was more with himself than over what had just transpired.

"Nobody leaves here tonight until I have my say," the doctor began. "I should have spoken out sooner but had hoped common sense would prevail. It has not." He clipped out the last three words as if he were lopping slices of cucumber with a corn knife. "And I am not talking about your stupid little devil act." He paused. The posse all stood there, heads down, numbed with beer and fright.

"I have Fr. Ray's permission to tell you this, although I thought all along that it would not be necessary, since it is of a very personal nature." He paused, obviously distraught, and let his eyes linger for a moment on each of his listeners. "You have all been guilty of passing around the neighborhood a vicious, stupid lie. I don't know who started it, but I do know who has encouraged it." The figure out on the edge of the light quavered and looked back at his car.

"For your information, Fr. Ray sustained an injury as a young man which has left him with erectile dysfunction. In your language, that means his joy stick don't work very well; his gun won't fire." Again he glared at the men, each in turn. "He couldn't screw a beautiful young woman if he wanted to, much less a sheep."

Out on the edge of the light, the shadowy figure slunk into the night. He made it to his car unnoticed, eased away as quietly as he could, did not turn the car lights on until he was well down the road. The only thing that would save him now, he was thinking, was how his investment in the new ethanol plant would be so profitable that the bishop would forget all else.

But the person even more shaken by Dr. Jake's revelation was still in the barnyard, even after the posse had gone home and the others gone into the rectory. Mary Barnette stood there all alone, stunned by the information she had just heard. Now Fr. Ray's way of treating her finally made sense. He really wasn't interested in her sexually. She knew she should feel relieved by that as she edged closer and closer to a permanent attachment to Jack. But to her consternation, she did not.

Chapter 22

The news raced through Balem Township faster than rumors of unintended pregnancies. Fr. Ray could not screw a beauty queen even if he wanted to. Quote and unquote, Dr. Jake, more or less. All that talk about carrying on with sheep had been nothing but tongue trash, about what you'd expect from the likes of Alvin Farkow. And what's this? You say Pastor Lemming was party to that trash too? That milksoppy, lily-livered excuse for a priest ought to be excommunicated, not Fr. Ray.

As is almost always the case, bad things rarely happen singly. Human turmoils run like raindrops gathering into rivulets and trickling down a gentle slope. The water oozes along until it hits a bit of blockage and only when enough raindrops in aggregate build up and deepen do they spill over, all at once. Then the trickle moves onward again to the next point of blockage, builds, and spills over again. So do the strivings of mankind trickle and spill, rolling on not steadily but by fits and starts, each little act of virtue or vice needing the help of other little acts to build up force enough to move on. So in the summer of 2008 the various little misadventures of erratic behavior in Balem Township reached another point of maximum density and spilled over again.

The great exorcism adventure had finally been laid to rest, more or less, but what took its place in local gossip was even more shocking. There was not going to be an ethanol plant in Vinal County after all. Dan Bandy broke that story in his newspaper column, gloating that what happened was exactly as he had predicted. Even with the government providing a subsidy of a dollar and a half a bushel for corn, there was just not any profit in trying to run cars on whiskey. The fact that corn prices were inordinately volatile didn't help the situation either. The economy was in upheaval and talk of a second Great Depression was on everyone's lips.

Vinal County was actually lucky. Many ethanol plants were declaring bankruptcy.

The times were, to put it mildly, not good for Pastor Lemming. Not only had the exorcism business discredited him in the eyes of even his most faithful parishioners, but now the very thing that he thought would enhance his position in the eyes of his fickle congregation, not to mention his jittery bishop, was in grave jeopardy. He had to get the $200,000 back from Intimate Insider Investments immediately, before anyone knew what he had done.

He called III's number. The phone had been disconnected. Hmmm. He tried to find Lester Longin in the phone book. No listing. Hmmmm. He called the headquarters of the Minnesota ethanol plant for which III had done consulting work. They said they had no knowledge of anything called Intimate Insider Investments. Hmmmmm. He called the bank where his cashier's check had been deposited. Yes, there was a record of that transaction. Yes there was a Social Security number to validate the account. But the account was closed out. Hmmmmmm. The money had been withdrawn intermittently in amounts of about $7000. Nothing unusual about that. Business as usual. As a matter of fact, quite a few people were withdrawing money because of fear of a bank collapse. "Of course we're not publicizing that fear. Don't want to start a panic," the bank representative said, panic clearly in his voice.

With growing alarm, Pastor Lemming jumped in his car and sped off to Burning Cross to find Mr. Longin and straighten the matter out. But when he arrived at the house he thought was the right one, there was nothing to indicate that it had been anyone's office. The attractive sign in the window was gone. There was a For Sale sign in the yard.

He decided he was on the wrong street. Or maybe just the wrong house on the street. He hadn't been too observant of the surroundings on his first visit. All the houses looked about the same anyway—all built on the same nineteen-fiftyish model—modest houses for returning veterans of World War II. He drove systematically from one street to another in the vicinity, all much the same, and finally came back to the house he had been sure was the right one, the one that now had the For Sale sign on it. He knocked on the door. Peered in the windows. The room he had surely entered previously was bare to the walls. He called the realtor's phone number on the For Sale sign. The woman who answered wanted to tell him all about the house and what a great buy it was in these hard financial times. No, the house had not been rented to anything called Intimate Insider Investments as far as she knew. But the realty company had clear title to the property and it was a terrific bargain. Make us an offer.

Pastor Lemming put the phone down slowly. The dream he had been having lately ran before his mind's eye. In the dream he was caught under a huge rock on an ocean beach and the tide was creeping in. He could not budge. And over the roll of the incoming waves, he could hear a voice saying: "Upon this rock I will build my church and the gates of hell will not prevail against it."

He began to sweat. His breathing came in short spurts. Could the whole thing have been a scam, after all? He sped back to Vinal County. His destination: Hem Judin's office. Hem had said the deal looked good. Hem was a smart man. He would know what to do now. Or how to bring in the law and investigate. After all, it was really Hem's advice that he had taken, or so he now wanted most earnestly to believe. He realized that he was already drawing up the defense he feared he would have to make before a diocesan tribunal. He was in deep trouble, But Hem would know what to do.

Hem Judin sat in his office, his elbows on his desk with his hands clasped under his chin, and listened with rapt attention. The sad tale that Pastor Lemming was telling him was music to his bored mind. All his life he had secretly disdained clients who acted so righteously in public, hanging out flags to show their patriotism, then using ever conceit and deceit they could think of to cheat the government out of paying their taxes. Making sure he was always free of blame while he helped them, he loved to see them get caught.

"I cannot get in touch with Intimate Insider Investments," Pastor Lemming was saying for the third time. "It is as if it never existed. And that fellow who said he was Lester Longin seems to have totally disappeared along with his office."

"Disappeared?" Hem said, trying very hard to look shocked and concerned. "What do you mean?"

"*The office isn't there, that's what I mean.* I went round and round the block and the streets all around and it's not there."

"You mean you can't find the house? Come on, Father."

"Oh, you know how it is. I was all excited that day. I didn't look around. The houses on that street all look about the same anyway."

"Well, you had the address, for heaven's sake."

"Yes, but the house is empty. And the window doesn't have that nice sign in it. It is all bare inside. It's for sale. The realtor says she had no record of an investment company renting it."

Hem did not say anything.

"And the company phone number has been disconnected. And the post office box has been closed. And the people at the ethanol plant in Minnesota never heard of III, so they say. And the account at the bank has been closed out."

"Well, there's gotta be a record of who had that bank account."

"Well yes, there's a legitimate social security number involved but the transaction was so much business as usual that nobody seems to have checked it out."

Hem scratched his cheek. "It's real easy to make fake I.D.s on Photoshop."

"What's Photo Shop?"

Hem stared at him in amazement, then looked out the window while he shook his head. How was it possible that so many people, even people in responsible positions, were Internet illiterate. "Never mind. Something on computers."

"Shouldn't we call the police?"

Hem was slow to answer while he let his mind turn over all of what he had heard. Finally he replied. "I don't think you want to bring the law in just yet. What did this Lester Longin look like?"

"Lots of hair. And beard."

"Maybe it was fake hair?"

"How in the world would I know?"

"Just thinking." Hem's mind was racing. "Isn't going to matter anyway, I fear. You will want to talk to the bishop first, I think. Before you call in the law."

"But I can't tell him what has happened. I'll be ruined."

"It will be the end of you for sure if you don't. Calm down now and think with me. If it turns out the money has been stolen there is no way you can keep this secret, even if the law is able to get it back. Especially if it gets the money back. I have a strong hunch that when the bishop thinks it over, he may not want to pursue it. That $200,000 is just peanuts compared to the ramifications if this story gets out. You invested church money in what appears to be a notorious scam. Can you imagine what the press would do with that? On top of all the other church scandals? The bishop may want to keep the whole thing a secret. You might just get out of it that way."

"I am still ruined."

"It could be worse if the news gets out."

Not even Madeleine McMurry could calm the bishop this time. He stomped back and forth in front of the hapless Pastor Lemming. He sat down at his desk and beat his head with his fists. He roared and snorted. He got up again and paced. He threw his cell phone on the floor when it buzzed. He left the room but shortly stalked back in. The monsignors bowed their heads. The lawyers bowed their heads. Pastor Lemming trembled and mopped his brow with a wet handkerchief. Madeleine followed the bishop around in his tirades, trying to mumble reassurance. Once she even patted him on the shoulder. Snarling, he jerked away from her.

"Confound it. You were one of my most trusted priests," he raged at Pastor Lemming. "How in the name of God could you do anything so stupid." Pastor Lemming's eyes darted swiftly from one Chancery member to another, from one lawyer to another, looking vainly for some sympathy.

"I only had the good of the diocese at heart," Pastor Lemming whimpered.

"Oh sure you did, you imbecile."

"Our accountant thought it was a good move."

"Confound it. Your accountant does not run your church affairs. You do," the bishop roared.

"Well the man from the investment company had a statue of St. Francis on his desk."

That gem of a detail sent Bishop Feering into a near foaming rage. He stormed out of the room, repeating over and over under his breath words that sounded like "a statue, for God's sake, a confounded statue," and only Madeleine knew for sure that he was not going to attack the hapless Pastor Lemming physically. Why was all this happening to him. He had always been a model prelate. What had happened to the church? Pedophilia, bestiality, scam investments, the whole economic world tumbling down around society. "I just wanted to be a good bishop," he said to Madeleine, begging now for sympathy. "Where have all the good people gone, confound it anyway? Where have all the good priests gone?" He looked up at the ceiling, as if talking to God. "Oh give me back my yesteryears before the world filled with evil."

Back in the Chancery office in front of poor Pastor Lemming, he seemed to have regained his composure. "What are we to do now?" he asked, eyeing Lawyer No. 1. Lawyer No. 1 stood up, cleared his throat, knowing that what he was about to say would either lose him his job or secure it forever. It depended on how smart the old fox really was underneath all that episcopal funk.

"Your Excellency," he began. "In view of what has happened, and after discussion with my partners here, we have a suggestion which we ask you and members of the Chancery to give some serious thought to, as unpopular as it might sound. We have here a grave breech of authority which is going to come back to haunt you forever, whatever you do. The buck stops here, as they say. To be sure, we must consider the possible loss of a considerable amount of money. But, your Excellency, have you considered the consequences of trying to retrieve that money? There is a good chance that we won't be able to get it back, first of all. But let us say you do. Does $200,000 make up for the scandal that will become common knowledge, once this gets out in the media? It just might be the better part of valor to pretend it didn't happen. To cover it up."

Pastor Lemming could scarcely believe what he was hearing. That sneaky little creep of a Hem Judin was smarter than he had given him credit for. Bishop Feering was silent for a long time. By God, the sniveling lawyer standing in front of him was making a good point. His glance went from one Chancery member to another, one monsignor to another. They were all nodding assent, although only very slightly so that later if necessary, they could say they were not nodding. Then he looked at Madeleine, the only one he trusted. She nodded too.

"So be it," the bishop finally said. He waited dramatically for objections. None came. "And it goes without saying. If this gets out of this room I'll have your hides. Every last one of you." He paused. "As for you, Father Louis Lemming, you are relieved of your pastoral duties as of right now. We have made a position for you here at diocesan archives where we can keep an eye on you. You're more dangerous than those damnable pedophiles."

At that moment, Pastor Lemming showed why he had risen from the ranks and why he just might make bishop someday after all. A sudden realization gripped his ever-conniving mind. Although still trembling, and although his voice still shook with fear, he replied.

"I don't think so."

The bishop, who was gathering up papers and preparing to leave the room, stopped short. His voice was so cold one might fancy his face had been chipped from ice.

"You don't think *what?*"

"I don't think you are going to want to remove me from Resurrection." Pastor Lemming's teeth were actually chattering, but his whole liturgical life was over if he backed off. All the people in the room were staring at him.

"If you try to remove me from office, I will spill the beans. I'll tell everyone what I did." Pastor Lemming thought he might faint as he squeezed out of his throat the last words. If secrecy would protect the bishop, it would protect the priest too.

"And I will excommunicate your little ass right out of the church, confound it anyway."

"You do and I will call in the media."

The bishop slumped back in his chair, turned to a ghostly white, than slowly to crimson. "Are you all right, your Excellency?" Madeleine rushed to him.

"Get that man out of my presence," the bishop said malevolently. "*Get him out of here before I throttle him.*"

Pastor Lemming almost smiled. He knew that at least for now, he was safe.

Chapter 23

Mary Barnette, alias Pope Mary, was in a dither. As is true of many people who outwardly bubble over with seeming self-confidence and show a flagrant disdain for the world in general, she often felt, inwardly, turmoil and unrest. For reasons not entirely clear even to herself, the revelation that her Lone Ranger could not screw a beauty queen even if he wanted to was not as much a relief as she thought it ought to be. She had always felt comfortable around him precisely because he had not shown any real or even furtive sexual interest in her. Or so she had told herself. Now she realized that she was not so happy with that situation after all. She had believed, without ever saying it even to herself, that no man could resist her when she really turned on the charm, even if they suffered from erectile dysfunction. Finding out that she might be wrong about her assessment of herself did nothing for her ego. Something in her had desired, unconsciously perhaps, more from the priest than friendship. Or something less than friendship, she corrected herself, since she had decided, after she had been dumped by that rathead in Chicago, that friendship was more valuable and meaningful than sex.

But where did one end and the other begin? Could two people, especially male and female, really, *really*, be close friends and not think about culminating the relationship with sex? What if sex were really not much different than having breakfast with someone. Breakfast was a pleasurable act whether you really liked the person you were dining with or not.

As usual, this kind of thinking tied her mind into frustrating knots. Did one enjoy having breakfast more with one's sexual lover than with, say, one's mother? Depends on how tasty the food, her inner voice replied sarcastically. Moms generally cook better than lovers. But the complexity only began there. She had read in the news that behavioral scientists were predicting marriage between humans and robots some day. So much for meaningful sex. Could one enjoy breakfast with a robot? She laughed out loud and tried to dismiss the whole dismal problem. But the contradictory voices inside her went on arguing.

No, I didn't ever really think of him as a potential lover.

Yes, you did. Don't try to kid me.

You thought that he thought that you were hot. Now you're upset because he doesn't care whether you're hot or not.

I like Jack Bump better.

So now you can have them both. One for sex and one for breakfast.

But Jack makes good breakfast too.

Well, count your blessings.

Humans are such pitiful creatures. She remembered that the news had recently reported that someone was even having sex with corpses.

For Jack Bump, the revelation of Fr. Ray's "condition" as everyone was now referring to it, was also not as much of a relief as he would have liked it to be. He could not deny that he had felt from the beginning a kind of sexual tension between Mary and the priest, which had translated into tension between himself and both of them. He had tried to tell himself that he was just being jealous for no good reason. Now apparently that was the case so he should be feeling fine about it all. So why wasn't he? The truth was that he had always noticed when all three of them were together, that Mary paid more attention to the priest than to him. Only when he and Mary were alone did she seem to address herself without reservation to him. What was he supposed to make of that? And why would it be any different now with Ray's "condition" common knowledge? What if Ray and Mary really were in love and now they could play the big martyrs. That would be even harder for him to handle than if they were having a real affair. Why did everything have to be so complicated?

Fr. Ray, who seemed to have benefited from the revelation of his condition, was also troubled by it all. He too had told himself, over and over, that he had no intimate sexual feelings for Pope Mary, but now, with the whole business out in the open, he did not feel as self-contained and satisfied as he thought he should feel. He really did like that woman, and just maybe he liked her sexually more than his mind or even his body wanted to admit. He also now realized, much to his chagrin, that he had rather enjoyed being Jack Bump's seemingly innocent rival for her attention. He knew how, with his skill for clever wittiness, he could keep her attention more on himself than on the shy Jack. He had actually enjoyed doing that. And thinking of himself as a rival to a younger and more attractive man. So he was evidently just as much a peacock as any man. Good grief.

But the whole affair, if he dared use that word, was all vanity of vanities. First of all, he knew what the others didn't know and probably wouldn't believe. Erectile dysfunction was but a part of his presumed problem. Even as an adolescent, before his injury, he had not felt all that interested in sexual relationships as other boys seemed to be. And he had learned since then that there were other people like himself, whether society wanted to believe it or not. For them privacy was everything and sexual consort was about as un-private as one could get. His mother had been fond of saying that when she contemplated the behavior of human society, she found herself preferring the company of cows. So did he. Maybe in some weird way, he was guilty of the pernicious lie about him. Sheep were so compliant, accepting, and predictable. Maybe he had a platonic bestial relationship with them. He grinned devilishly at the thought.

After years in the confessional and learning how terribly afflicted and conflicted the human race was about sex, he had become convinced that it was more burden than benefit. There were moments, yes, but in the long run, he was glad to be shut of the whole sweaty process.

But at least with Fr. Ray's secret no longer secret, the uninformed would not think him abnormal, just unfortunate. That made him chuckle. His "condition" took all the grandeur out of celibacy. If a priest remained celibate voluntarily, he gained respect because he was thought to be suffering pangs of unrequited desire. But if he weren't suffering, what's so great about not screwing beauty queens? The thought so amused him that he had to call Dr. Jake and tell him.

With all their internal agonizing over the situation, Fr. Ray, Mary and Jack found themselves uncomfortable enough that they found reasons, however slight, to avoid each other in the days following the Great Exorcism Attempt. Each waited for one of the other two to initiate the conversation that would resolve the issue. It was easy to find excuses not to do so. There was plenty to keep them occupied. Although there was every sign on the financial horizon that the country was falling into a deep recession, farming seemed immune to the situation. To continue her reputation of contrariness, Mary planned to plant all corn come spring, just as she had planted all soybeans the year before. But fertilizer prices continued to skyrocket, making profits from a highly fertilized crop like corn look iffy.

"We should just not use fertilizer at all," Mary said. "Then the crop would be short, prices would go up, and we'd make the same amount of money while the fertilizer boys went broke."

Her father shrugged. "Not use any fertilizer? You just don't think like a farmer."

"The way farmers think these days is what's killing them. Do you realize it wouldn't matter anyway. I've got insurance coverage of $5.40 a bushel. If we didn't make our usual yield, we could collect some insurance. We could just say it was bad weather caused the loss not lack of fertilizer. Who could prove otherwise? I would just say I put on most of my fertilizer for this year last year. Lots of farmers double up that way. And anyway, not a word was said when I took out that insurance about fertilizer."

Her father stared at her. "You aren't as smart as you think you are. More bushels is always better than more insurance. And lowering your yield will bring your crop history yield down the next year, don't forget." But he couldn't keep the admiration out of his voice.

The summer of '08 was one to try a farmer's soul in Balem Township. In April and May, rain seemed to fall every day or nearly so, holding back planting. The situation was particularly grim for corn which needed to be in the ground in May, so Mary's decision to plant all corn was not looking so brilliant. Then in June, the rains stopped. What corn had gotten planted had rooted only shallowly in the early wet weather, and now with what turned out to be nearly three months with hardly a shower, the roots couldn't get to moisture deeper in the soil. Stalks quit growing and leaves curled. At first no one minded much, because corn prices were rising, which could make up for a short crop. That was why many farmers did not buy crop insurance. If the crop were bad, prices would go up, a sort of built in insurance coverage.

"Let the drouth come," Mary told her father gaily as he stewed over the condition of the corn. "We've got insurance." But she still didn't tell him the details. If he had known that she had spent $40,000 on insurance, he just might have a heart attack. In all his farming life, he had never bought one cent of crop insurance.

"You know something, Dad?"

He looked at her, wondering what was coming now.

"Do you realize that you could be the best farmer in the country and if you didn't play the market and the government right, you could end up a failure."

Jack Bump had reached for the phone to call Mary so often that he had lost count, but had not quite worked up the courage to do it. But he could not keep his mind on business, on the planning that desperately needed doing as his corn leaves curled from dry weather. His kind of farming was blessedly free of the angst and anxiety of trying to beat the government like Mary was doing. He sold most of his corn and wool directly to his own customers and so did not depend on the whims of government so much. He had also lucked out with a nice rain shower that missed most of the rest of the local area so his corn was growing a little better than the average in other parts of the county. But that did not mean he was free from worry. Would enough small farmers still want to buy his open-pollinated corn for seed when it was a known fact that it did not weather drought as well as hybrid corn? Would the high food prices continue and turn consumer attention toward growing their own in which case he could sell more seed to them. Or if they merely wanted cornmeal, would he be able to grind enough to keep up with demand? He needed to be working also on preparations for the big food fiesta at the Church of Almighty Good Food that was only a couple of months away. Last year's success was encouraging a much bigger affair this year.

He had come up with an idea more bizarre than starting a distillery, a perfect excuse to call Mary because it was loony enough to override any need to discuss the personal issues they had to deal with. His open-pollinated corn often sported exceedingly fat cobs and it occurred to him that they could be hollowed out quite nicely into corncob pipes. If they could make corncob pipes in Missouri, he surely could make them in Ohio. The idea had occurred to him when he happened to notice that a carton of cigarettes was selling for upwards of $40.00 A man smoking a cheap pipe and cheaper pipe tobacco rather than cigarettes could save a heap of money and pipe smoking wasn't as apt to cause lung cancer, so the statistics said. With the recession going into high gear, saving money might suddenly get popular again. He finally made the call.

"Mary!" he almost shouted when she answered the phone.

"Well, where have you been?" she replied, trying to sound as if matters were the same as they had always been. " I've missed you." The relief in her voice was almost palpable.

"I've missed you too, hon. Listen, I've got this perfectly absurd idea I just had to share with you."

Before she could say anything, he launched into his corncob fantasy. That allowed Mary to giggle and not have to pretend that things weren't any different than before the exorcism fiasco. He concluded his rather long-winded defense of corncob pipes by pointing out that all the info was on the Internet because, of course,—and they both said it in unison—"everything is on the Internet." Then they laughed in unison too, and both knew, just that fast, that they were back together solider than ever, despite, or perhaps because of, Fr. Ray's "condition."

"I am surprised that you aren't thinking about growing some tobacco too, to go along with the pipes," Mary said.

"Hey, maybe that would be a good idea. Grandpaw Ben says the old timers used to grow tobacco around here, just for personal use. Kept a leaf or two in their hip pockets for an occasional chew. Hey, maybe we should look into that."

"You are crazy," Mary said, still chuckling.

"Afraid so."

"And that's why I love you."

Getting back together with Fr. Ray also turned out to be easier than any of the three had expected because of what happened next. Fr. Ray went out to his barn one morning in July and found another manila envelope stuffed with hundred dollar bills. Five thousand dollars more. The note was brief: "Get the rest of the roof fixed."

"It happened again," he said to Jack on the phone. "Five thousand more dollars. What on earth am I supposed to do?"

"Get the rest of the roof fixed."

Pause. "Wait a minute. How do you know that's what the note said? Jack Bump, are you behind this?"

Jack laughed. "No way. Everybody knows the north side of the roof needs repairs too. If I were forking over money, it would be to get the church interior ready for the food fiesta."

"Well, anyway, whoever is giving the money knows the situation close at hand."

A week later, the priest called Jack again. "All right, Mister Jack Bump, now I know it's you."

"Please?"

"I got more money. This time the note says for remodeling the interior of the church. Ten thousand this time. I've never seen so many hundred dollar bills at one time."

"If I had that kind of money, I'd be asking Mary to marry me." The statement just slipped out before he could haul it back in. To Jack's great relief, Fr. Ray was so totally unsurprised that he didn't even comment.

"Well then who the heck is it?"

"Was the money in the barn?"

"No, this time it came in the mail. Postmarked Toledo but that doesn't mean anything. Whoever is doing this could mail it from any post office. It's somebody right around here, I tell you."

"Well, whoever. Don't look a gift horse in the mouth, Ray. Get busy. Move those pews around. Get some tables. Get hold of Mary. We should meet with Dow Kapier. He'll know about remodeling."

"Will do." Fr. Ray was relieved that Jack told him to call Mary rather than say he would do it himself. That surely meant Jack did not consider him a rival anymore.

When he talked to Mary, Fr. Ray tried nobly to keep the conversation on the mystery money. But every time he hesitated, there was awkward silence. Mary wasn't cooperating. She was not cooperating because her mind was focused on how to bring up the unmentionable topic. Finally she did it in her usual head-on, embarrassing way.

"You mean you could actually go to bed with me and just go to sleep?"

The priest smiled. Pope Mary really was a real case. But no one was going to beat him in the wisecrack game. That was his department. He replied almost immediately.

"Depends on how loud you snored."

She laughed. How could she not love him? She wrapped her arms around him and hugged tightly. Then in his ear, she whispered: "There are times when the impossibility of sex is a great blessing."

He laughed too and gently withdrew from the embrace.

"Actually, Mary, my inability in that area is not the whole story or the most important part of it. If you remember your church history, and I know you don't, Tertullian, an early father of the church, overcome with sexual desire, had himself castrated following the biblical injunction that if a part of one's body scandalizes thee, cast it out. To his chagrin, he learned that he was still sorely tempted."

"So much for a literal interpretation of the bible," Mary said sarcastically.

"Point is, while I do have a physical problem, it doesn't mean necessarily that I am devoid of sexual feeling."

"So I wouldn't have to snore to keep you awake."

He laughed. "Hey, I can't really explain it. I was not much interested in sex even before my injury. Doesn't mean I don't like people. Doesn't mean I don't like pretty girls. I just feel, like, well, I am just more comfortable in an asexual world if there is such a thing. If I have a problem it is too much shyness, too much love of privacy. I am quite happy with a lot of solitude in my life."

"Maybe you're the sanest one of us all."

"Or the most selfish. But that's my best way to deal with life. I suppose that's the reason I became a priest in the first place." He paused to stare at her closely. "I have a feeling that for all your seeming self-confidence you wonder if you really are in love with me like you are with Jack."

She drew back, taken off guard. She could think of nothing to say.

"I thought so," the priest said. "But I can tell you something for sure. If you were in love with me like you are with Jack, you would be bawling your eyes out over my listless attitude toward sex."

She just kept staring at him in wonder. There really was such a thing as love between the sexes that had nothing to do with sex. She hugged him again, impulsively, then hurried to her car and drove away.

As it turned out, Dow Kapier already had drawn up a blueprint of the changes to be made in the church and was particularly pleased to announce that he had come by some very nice cherry wood to make the tables to match the pew seats. He also had contacted local roofers to get busy again on the roof. No one thought it odd that he showed no surprise when new contributions appeared, because Dow never expressed surprise about anything. That would require more talking and Dow was rarely given to more talk.

From last year's experience, Jack suggested that the food fiesta be structured around a corn roast. There was now corn enough growing in the garden plots around the Church of Almighty Good Food to feed half an army. And this year the beer garden would sell only local home brews along with local wines. There was some discussion of whether to have people buy directly out of the garden plots or to have booths set up around the church. Finally they agreed that both ways of selling would be appropriate.

The congregation did not argue as much with the changes to the church interior as Fr. Ray had feared. Many of them were newcomers, some who had not previously gone to any church and some from the several newer evangelical churches in the area. They had no sense at all of the traditional sanctimony that attached to Catholic or High Protestant churches. For example, the main space in the newest evangelical church north of Bredsocken, from which new members of the Church of Almighty Good Food came, was designed to be used as a basketball court first and church services as almost an afterthought. The pastor there had his own sense of theology. He said basketball was a more effective way to keep young people "scoring points for Jesus" than any church service.

Other parishioners, former members of St. Philo's and St. Clare's, were so curious about where the money was coming from, that they gave little thought to how grinding grain and canning vegetables "right there in church for God's sake" as Ding Duholland liked to say, might violate orthodoxy. In a way, the diocese's spiteful removal of the altar made the transition easier. Without the altar present, desecration seemed less imminent. And after all what was more sacred than an ear of boiled sweet corn seeping butter? Go ahead and turn the church into a food pantry, the general opinion seemed to be. They all pitched in to help prepare for the food fiesta, sharing rumors about where the money might be coming from. There were plenty of rumors.

"It's the Duholland sisters, I tell you. They have every cent they ever made and every cent their father made too. They're loaded."

"Nope. Those gals have squeezed their money so long there's no way they can let go of it."

"Well I can't imagine Tom Barnette doing it although he could afford to, the old tightwad. Now he's saying we're in for a second Great Depression and it's going to be hell to pay."

"He's been saying that for twenty years."

"I don't think it's anybody around here giving that money. Has to be somebody rich who was born here but lives far away. You know how they do. They get to feeling guilty about going away and always talk about coming back. Finally they come home in coffins."

This last theory enchanted George Dribble and Lloyd McTicken. Here was work for the Private Eyes of God to sniff out. Something to bring them a little respect after becoming the laughing stock of the Great Exorcism Attempt. But they could not interest their leader, Alvin Farkow. He was a changed man. Rumor had it that he had resigned his deaconship and was spending all his free time at home in spite of his wife's rantings. Occasionally he was seen in the Yellow Room Saloon but he refused to talk to anyone.

"Guess we'll just have to go it alone," George said.

"I think we should make a list of people who have gone away from here," Lloyd said. "We could profile them." He looked wisely at George. He had learned that from television. "Have to be Catholic, I think. And making tons of money. And probably feeling homesick for the old ways they wouldn't go back to if you paid them. Probably somebody stuck on the eat-local food craze. Some libral."

There were two people in the community who were almost sure where the money was coming from, but neither was talking. Hem Judin's theory was that whoever pulled the scam on Pastor Lemming was now relaying the money back to the church. Robin Hood had returned from the dead. When Hem was alone in his office, the thought made him often pause, slap his knee and erupt into chuckling as if he had just heard the funniest joke of his lifetime. But he dared not tell a soul or he would surely be implicated. And besides knowing secrets he dared not tell was what made him feel important. That's why he was an accountant. Being an accountant, it was also easy for him to decide that if the Bishop knew that he had been scammed out of $200,000, he would pretend not to be missing anything. That had so far proved to be the case. Whoever had perpetrated the scam had committed the perfect crime, first because returning the money to its rightful owner was not a crime, and even if it were construed as such, it was one that was more or less victim-less. The whole affair was just too, too hilarious. If the donations stopped at $200,000 that would prove Hem right for sure. But then he realized that whoever was doing this would be much too clever to let the two figures match. That would be too obvious a clue. But then he realized that was wrong too. The donor actually would stop at exactly $200,000 just so no one would be in doubt as to where the money was coming from. And again, Hem Judin cackled in a very unaccountant-like way.

The other holder of this theory was Pastor Lemming himself, of course, only he had arrived at that conclusion much more slowly. When it finally dawned on him that there was a good possibility that the thief who had taken the money was giving it back to St. Philo's, his utter inability to do anything about it brought him close to mental if not spiritual breakdown. He had been thoroughly outwitted. And when the bishop had so decreed that the diocese was going to pretend no money had been stolen, he had agreed or lose his position. If he ratted on the bishop, he might even be excommunicated.

If ever the weeping and gnashing of teeth were heard outside of biblical times, it could now be heard in the rectory of the Church of the Resurrection as Pastor Lemming paced back and forth in his study, cursing and swearing in a very un-pastorly way. He even lost his temper occasionally in public, like when he told Plover Venale, who kept bugging him for details of his last meeting with the bishop, to go home and tend to her own business. With the same kind of impatience that he had rarely exhibited before, he scolded Alice Dribble for always trying to win his favor. She and Plover suggested to the Ladies of the Altar and Rosary Society that the poor man seemed to be having some sort of nerve problem. Maybe the whole experience of losing out to Fr. Raymond over the closing of St. Philo's was affecting Pastor Lemming's mental health. They should all keep an eye on him, Alice said, not unkindly. The Ladies all nodded grimly and although he would not realize it right away, the day of Pastor Lemming's dominance was gone whether the bishop removed him from office or not. He had violated the first rule of running a Catholic parish: never, never alienate the Ladies of the Altar and Rosary Society.

He was sleeping hardly two hours a night and as a result fell asleep in the sanctuary during a sermon by a visiting missionary priest—right up there where everyone could see him. When he jolted awake from his noddings, he could see all the children in the front rows trying to suppress their giggling. He glared them into composure only to notice farther out in the congregation, adults were glancing at each other with knowing smiles. He had reached the bottom of the pit for men of his ambition. He had become an anachronism.

He spent his time mostly plotting his revenge. He decided that Fr. Ray himself had run the scam. A joker like Tulley was quite capable of something like that and no one would suspect him. Pastor Lemming would watch closely the amount of money that was coming from the so-called secret donor, which would be easy to do because it was not being kept a secret. If it amounted up to $200,000, his suspicion would be true. And if it only amounted to, say, $180,000, that would mean that Fr. Ray was keeping some of it for himself. He, Pastor Lemming, would use the knowledge to effectively destroy the heretic. But then he realized, again gnashing his teeth, that he would in doing so, reveal that he, Pastor Lemming, was the one who had been scammed.

If Pastor Lemming thought the tide had turned against him, it was nothing compared to the despair that was descending on Balem Township as the shallow-rooted corn shrivelled in the summer drought. Farmers secretly hoped for a devastating hurricane, a repeat of Katrina which had brought misery to Louisiana in an earlier year, but moving on north brought salvation to Ohio agriculture in the form of three inches of rain. To feel relieved even while New Orleans was all but destroyed, made them all realize what hypocrites they were. But they had always known. "Yes, we are a bunch of selfish sonsabitches," Tom Barnette said. "We secretly rejoice if Iowa has a drought and we don't, but don't think Iowa doesn't rejoice when we have a bad crop and they don't. If it weren't for bad weather, none of us would ever make any money."

So once again a hurricane boiled up out of the Atlantic Gulf and slammed into Texas. Once again Ohio farmers went into their little act of bereavement for the people adversely affected while they yearned for the winds to bring them desperately needed rain. Only Pope Mary seemed untroubled.

The righteous would say that what actually happened was God's way of punishing greedy grain farmers. The hurricane roared north all right but for reasons even meteorologists found mysterious, by the time it crossed the Ohio River, it had turned into all wind and no rain. In Vinal County, seventy mile per hour winds raked across the shriveled, shallow rooted corn and laid some of it on the ground as neatly as if a mower had cut through the stalks. Harvested yields in some areas were only a little more than half of normal.

Only Mary Barnette did not go around with dour visage, and her uncle wondered why. "Why do you look so unperturbed?" he finally asked her.

She at first seemed unwilling to answer and then, pride getting the better of her, she told him. "You are not going to believe this, but by not thinking like a farmer I am going to be just fine."

"How so."

"I bought crop insurance this year."

"So? About everybody did."

"I bought a lot of insurance."

"What do you mean, a lot?"

"It cost $40,000, but now it is going to pay me $5.40 a bushel for every bushel we lost up to 80% coverage. I think you can do the arithmetic."

Her uncle could only stare at her.

"That's not the best of it, Unc," she went on, obviously enjoying herself to the fullest. "I didn't use but a little bit of fertilizer. It would have been a waste, the way things have turned out."

Tom's jaw was working but no words came forth.

"You have to understand this modern kind of farming, Unc. You take out plenty of insurance, skip the fertilizer, and hope for a crop disaster."

"Over the long haul that wouldn't work. More bushels is worth more than more insurance."

"That's what Dad says but who knows what the long haul will bring?"

"You are just plain lucky, that's all."

"No, I am the pope of Balem Township and in matters of corn faith, I am infallible." She grinned roguishly and went to find Jack and tell him how, in the mad world they lived in, crop failure can be good news for a farmer.

Chapter 24

A rural church surrounded by working farms owes much of its charm to its bucolic isolation. There is little else around it to arrest the eye, unless one is a farmer interested in the crops growing roundabout. On the other hand, the crush of urban growth around churches in cities almost swallows them up, obscuring their architectural beauty in a landscape of the junkyard society: traffic jams, used car lots, gas stations, fast food restaurants and real estate offices. One of the commonest streetscapes of big cities is the lovely, quaint old church dwarfed by huge, faceless hotels looming over it.

The Church of Almighty Good Food, alias the late Church of St. Philodendra was, in addition to its isolation and the natural beauty of the farm fields around it, eye-catching in its design. New rural churches being built in the area often looked like glorified Morton buildings—one near Upper Surrey was indeed often referred to as St. Morton's in the Fields. But the former St. Philo's was a traditional brick Gothic edifice straight out of late medieval Europe where its design originated, its lean, clean spire shooting far above the corn tassels. Ignoring the wealth of lumber around them, the early farmers cleared the trees off their land and burned the wood to bake the bricks for their churches and very often their houses. Fr. Ray never ceased to wonder how that simple rural economy, closer to barter than to banking, could have afforded such magnificent churches and mansions only the richest could afford today— and so many of them. In western Ohio, he knew of one barnyard at least, where he could stand and by simply turning 360 degrees, see four such churches at various points on the horizon. He was sure that never again in the history of mankind would there be a combination of spiritual fervor and material wealth to make such a feat possible. Of course, he reminded himself with a smile, it could happen again if more churches dedicated to the good life of good food brought a renaissance to both religion and economics.

He could not keep from smiling because the Church of Almighty Good Food was surely a harbinger of such an improbable turnaround in history. What he had always hoped for under the old rules and rites of religion was actually materializing in front of his eyes, spurred on by new rules and rites. His church, if he dared call it his, hummed with activity, a human beehive of communal effort. The pew seats had been rearranged to face each other, two by two, with tables positioned between them, turning the body of the church into a large dining hall. A kitchen replete with all sorts of food processing appliances filled one sacristy off to the side of where the altar had stood. The grain mill went into the left sacristy, that choice being made because the room could be closed off from the rest of the church to keep noise and dust at a low level. The motor powering the mill was placed outside the church.

Dow Kappier had insisted that the main area of the sanctuary, where the altar had been removed, remain empty. He gave no particular reason for his insistence, but everyone agreed that it was the proper thing to do, out of memory for the altar that had once been there. Other than that, Dow kept a low profile and delegated the remodeling work to others. Indeed, he had been living even more like a hermit than usual for the past months, keeping to his workshop, denying entrance to everyone. He would only say he had a surprise for the big food festival in late August.

The garden plots around the church burgeoned with vegetables and fruits and even a few little plots of grain. Tom Barnette declared that if the whole township were cultivated this way, it could supply all the food needed for the whole county and then some. He even went so far as to pull the pencil stub and day book from his bib overalls and start making some calculations as to what might be his profit if he rented out garden plots on his land rather than grew corn and soybeans. More people, some enchanted by the hum and thrum of so many others gardening and visiting side by side, asked for and received garden plots for the next year from the Duholland sisters. Others, worried about a second Great Depression, also reserved plots.

Fr. Ray was in his glory. The new board of directors did indeed offer him the job of manager. Assured that his pay would come from a percentage of the monies generated by the food products sold, and none directly from the mystery money, he accepted the position. He now became what he had once thought impossible: a true shepherd with two pastoral flocks, one human and one animal. He could now literally follow the biblical admonition that had prompted him to become a priest in the first place: "Feed my lambs; feed my sheep." It was some kind of miracle. Even Pope Mary agreed.

And more miracles followed. As he was doing chores one evening, he was aware that someone else was in the barn with him. Finding uninvited guests in the barn had so often happened over the past year that the discovery did not even startle him, although when he recognized who was shuffling hesitantly toward him, he backed warily away.

"Well, well, Mr. Farkow," he said when he had regained his composure. "I daresay you are about the last person I ever thought would come to visit me again." He could not quite keep the sarcasm out of his voice.

"Evenin', Father." Nothing more. Alvin was obviously finding it difficult to speak.

"And what brings you out on this fine evening?"

When Alvin still did not respond, Fr. Ray tried to help.

"Haven't seen you around recently."

Alvin tried to grin. It came across as a painful grimace. Still no words.

"What do you think of all those gardens around the church?" Fr. Ray tried to help some more.

"I want to go to confession," Alvin mumbled. It was the last thing Fr. Ray expected to hear. He looked sharply at the forlorn man in front of him.

"Why would you want to do that, Alvin?"

"I'm sorry for what I did to you," Alvin blurted. "I am sorry for being such an ass."

"Well." At first the priest could think of nothing to say. "Well, that's very decent of you, Alvin. Your apology is accepted."

"I want to go to confession."

"Alvin, you just did. And you just admitted that you made a mistake. It takes character to do that. I forgive you. That's all the confession you need. Anyway I can't even hear confessions officially now. I've been suspended from administering the Sacraments."

"Once a priest, always a priest."

"Let's do it this way," Fr. Ray said. He extended his hand in offer of a handshake. Alvin took it.

"You are forgiven, Alvin. Let's just forget the whole stupid business."

Something very much like a smile came over Alvin's face. He felt an urge to reciprocate in some way.

"I would like to join your church," he said, "but I am already a member at Resurrection."

"Alvin, that's fine. That's okay. We should all be members of all our churches. You are welcome to old St. Philo's anytime. There are no exclusive clubs or membership fees in the Church of Almighty Good Food."

Alvin nodded as if he understood, turned and walked quickly from the barn into the gathering darkness.

As preparations for the food fiesta progressed, Pope Mary found herself, much to her chagrin, more and more the person in charge. At first overall direction came from Dow Kapier since he had long been custodian of the church and caretaker of the cemetery. But since he had all but disappeared into his woodworking shop which stayed locked to all visitors, someone else had to make decisions. Fr. Ray was expected to assume a leadership role since he was now officially the manager of the church, but it was soon evident that he did not relish making the kind of quick, spot decisions that were constantly necessary as the church struggled to transform itself from a place of divine worship to a sort of divine food pantry. He was good at going around from one garden plot to another, or one market booth to another, saying just the right things to encourage people to greater effort, but when it came to making decisions, he was inclined to philosophize rather than solve problems. Jack was the best-informed of them all on growing and marketing food in this manner, but he shied away from public notice in general, and from giving advice or orders to anyone at the church in particular. He understood the politics of rural society—how precarious it was to come from a neighboring county and appear to be putting on airs. Doctor Jake might have assumed some leadership role, but he declined, saying he didn't know enough about farming and marketing to keep a mouse from starving.

So it was Mary making day to day minor decisions, mostly because she could not remain silent when a question needed answering. The words would just pop out of her.

"No, we won't insist on uniform prices. Every marketer will charge what he or she desires. What do you think this is, communism?"

"Well, of course the meal we serve featuring roast corn will have a price—whatever has been charged for the sit-down meal in earlier years. No, a little more. Most of these people don't know how good really fresh sweet corn tastes and when they find out, they'll pay anything."

"No, we aren't going to remove the Stations of the Cross from the walls. They add ambience to the scene. You ashamed of your religious roots or something?"

"Yes, we'll put posters in store windows roundabout. Dan Bandy is in charge of publicity. Talk to him." She had not bothered to consult with Dan about being in charge of publicity but he was doing it regularly in his newspaper column anyway. Besides she knew he would oblige if no one tried to tell him what to put on the posters.

"No, we won't sign people up as members of the church. Looks too calculating. Too hierarchical." Pause. "Wait a minute. Here's what we'll do. Set up a website. Pass out little cards at the food fiesta with the website address and an invitation to get better acquainted with The Church of Almighty Good Food. Dow can do that. He knows everything about the Internet."

"If we need extra parking, we will use the land where the orchard is going in. Won't hurt the trees. No, don't worry about rain. It has been so dry it could rain five inches and no one would get stuck."

After every question, the person doing the asking would nod and scurry off to carry out the orders. Mary turned to Jack after the question about rain and laughed. "Now I understand the psychology of having infallible popes. That's what people crave. They want someone to tell them what to think. It is just so reassuring. The real joke is that there are people around like me dumb enough to assume the mantle of infallibility. Yep. Pope Mary. That's me. But if it rains on festival day, I'm outta here."

Jack laughed. "I love you, you scamp."

"I love you too, and I guarantee you that's an infallible statement."

Representatives of government health bureaucracies made life miserable for all of them. Tipped off by Pastor Lemming, someone from the health department showed up to inspect the gristmill. "You can't sell cornmeal and wheat flour without special permission and it may take awhile," the food policeman said. "But you can sell grain."

Pope Mary whirled on him. "So it's okay to sell the grain and then charge costumers to make meal out of it?"

"Yes. That will work. Just don't tell me the details."

Pope Mary laughed helplessly, but Jack, with more experience along these lines, stepped in. "Well thank you so much, sir, for your help and advice. We are most appreciative."

To Mary, after the inspector had done his duty and left, he said. "Government inspectors are people too and often they are aware of the stupidity of the government position. If you make them think they are being helpful, they will almost always lean your way."

A similar problem came up when a dairy farmer wanted to sell raw milk at the festival. When Pastor Lemming got wind of that, the food police again descended on the church.

"You can't sell raw milk to the public," their leader informed Jack and Pope Mary.

"Isn't it true that I can drink my own raw milk?" Jack said.

"Well, yes."

"It is my understanding that if the people drinking this milk have purchased shares in the cow, they at least technically own the cow, so they can drink their own milk."

"Well, that's how people are getting around the law." The food policeman looked uncomfortable. "The governor has so ruled for the time being. But if you sell milk to the public here, that is pretty transparently not going to be the case."

"Wait a minute. Wait just one very big old minute," Pope Mary said, bulldozing her way into the conversation. "Did I hear that correctly? I can drink my own raw milk and the Health Department doesn't care. But I can't *sell* my raw milk?"

"No, ma'am, you can't, That's the law as of now."

"You don't care if I die from drinking my own raw milk just so long as I don't sell it and compete with the pasteurized milk industry." She rolled her eyes. The world was indeed a strange place.

The big day finally arrived and even before noon it was obviously going to be a very big day indeed. The orchard parking lot was already full, and cars were beginning to line the narrow country roads leading to the church. It looked as if the farm sale of the century was in the offing. Pope Mary made one of her split-second decisions to allow parking along the lanes in the cemetery which soon meant cars just about everywhere that the absence of tombstones allowed.

"I have a question for you, Jack," she said. "If a pope prays for fair weather and it rains, is God telling him he's not infallible after all?"

The festival officially opened at 1:00 PM with Dow Kapier insisting on doing the honors. As he unlocked and pushed open the big front doors of the church, he cried out with more drama than anyone had ever thought he was capable of.

"I promised you a surprise and here it is!"

He walked up to the front of the church, the flow of visitors following. Some object, about the size of a car and draped entirely with a cloth covering, stood in the center of the empty sanctuary. Ceremoniously, Dow flung off the cover to reveal a model of the altar that up until a few months ago, had stood there for a century. Exclamations of awe rose from the crowd. The altar was somewhat smaller than the original but otherwise the carvings on the front were almost exactly like the ones everyone remembered. Not even Pope Mary or Fr. Ray had known this was coming,—Dow had paid several farmers, after swearing them to secrecy, to help move the altar into the church in the middle of the night. All day visitors trooped up into the sanctuary to stand before the altar. They did not speak, but many of them wiped tears from their eyes.

Mary went away to find Jack, and led him by the hand to the little altar. Fr. Ray was still standing there, alone now, full of a kind of joy he could not quite describe. There really had to be some sort of God or mystical body, or *something* to account for this happy outcome to all that had transpired in the last three years. Now he even had his altar back. He realized suddenly that he liked it just as much as he liked his barn. His life was complete. He could still be a priest of sorts without being a hypocrite. He did not even notice, at first, that Jack and Mary had joined him in front of the altar.

Jack, used to Mary's unpredictable impetuous ways, did not know exactly why she was making him stand there, admiring Dow's handiwork. She was obviously expecting him to say something. He stared at her. She stared at him. Finally, impatiently of course, she snapped: "You are supposed to ask me to marry you."

"I am? Right here? Right now?"

"Yes, I want to be married in front of this altar."

"You want to be married in front of an *altar?*" Fr. Ray could not believe his ears.

"I said that if you started a new church I might be your first convert."

By four o'clock, when the volunteer cooks began to serve dinner, the church and churchyard teemed with activity. The heavenly smell of roasting corn drew the people to the tables and the quaint pew chairs. As quickly as one diner left, another sat down. The line stretched all the way out of the church. Jack and Pope Mary were selling corn and wheat as fast as they could grind it into meal and sack it. The cider, home brew beer, and homemade wine were going fast—much too fast, Fr. Ray worried. Shoppers sauntered passed the garden plots and food booths, their pocketbooks in their hands. Tempting them was a bewildering array of onions, lettuce, potatoes, tomatoes, squash, fall raspberries, sweet corn, eggs, cheese, butter, melons, sweet potatoes, cucumbers, garlic bulbs, apples, peaches, pears, dry beans, string beans, lima beans, even a cage of chickens and another of rabbits. Jack Bump, sweating profusely, looked over at Mary once and exclaimed: "This is just like the Amish markets over in Holmes County. I never thought it could happen here."

"The Amish were the real pioneers in building churches of almighty good food," Pope Mary replied. "They just use different words."

By the time the sun went down, there was not a stomach nor a car trunk not loaded down with food and drink. Pastor Lemming had tried to get the Private Eyes of God to take pictures of what he planned to tell the bishop was a "drunken orgy" at the food fiesta. However McTicken and Dribble and now Farkow, newly restored to the trio, declined to get involved, mostly because all three of them were looking forward to spending time around the home brew booth themselves. Abandoning his usual caution, Pastor Lemming decided he would have to do his spying in person. He was dying to attend the food fiesta anyway, but thought he needed an excuse to do so. He would sift through the crowd incognito, he decided. He would wear dark glasses and that silly Hawaiian shirt his sister had given him for Christmas. And he'd wear a ball cap. He never wore a ball cap so that would increase his chances of not being recognized. He had one with fake gull droppings on it, the kind popular along Lake Erie but which Pastor Lemming found corny in the extreme. The bishop had given it to him on a fishing trip in happier days. The bishop thought the bird-dropping hats were funny, you might know.

By the time the incognito priest arrived at the festival, the mood of the people there was so high and riotous that he would hardly have needed a disguise. Even if he had been recognized, who cared? Good will and love, at least for a few brief hours, hovered over the crowd. Good humor was so rampant that Pope Mary found she could even speak kindly to Alvin Farkow. Pastor Lemming, under his gull-decorated ball cap, soon found that he was enjoying himself too and it made him feel guilty. He didn't have to be sneaky about taking pictures. Everyone was taking pictures, including members of the press from around the area, guaranteeing that the Church of Almighty Good Food would be heard about around the state, maybe even around the world. A few drinkers at the home brew booth were even entertaining other customers by striking goofy poses for the cell phone cameras. Pastor Lemming moved in on them. They would provide perfect evidence to the diocesan tribunal that food festivals ala The Church of Almighty Good Food were bad for the general morality. One beer-drinker in particular seemed perfect for Pastor Lemming's purpose, a portly, middle-aged gentleman, also wearing dark glasses and a ball cap with fake gull crap on it. He was ludicrously waving a bottle of home brew in one hand and an ear of corn dripping butter in the other, while an elderly woman beside him watched anxiously. Pastor Lemming moved in, smirking and clicking away. This was perfect. Then, horrified, he recognized the person he was photographing.

"Confound it, Madeleine," the man was saying. "This is the best damn roastin' ear I've ever eaten!"

Out in the dark cemetery, away from the merry crowd, a shadowy figure was talking to tombstones again. Only now, he was not addressing the grave of Benedict Berogston, as he had been wont to do previously, but a very small stone inscribed Lambert Closk. "Once again I want to thank, Mr. Closk, for your wonderful help. God has indeed answered our prayers and brought justice finally to the church of our forefathers. I want you to know that this very night I did deliver to Fr. Ray's barn the last of the $200,000 that the church authorities tried to take from us. Without your help and especially without your Social Security number, this would not have been possible. I am sure you rest in the lap of the Lord." As the shadowy figure turned and walked away, lights from the festival caught his face for a brief second. It was Dow Kapier, his visage wreathed in a cherubic smile. "That old man over in Rome thinks he runs things," he said, out loud, to no one in particular. "He has no clue."

Chapter 25

And so it came to pass in the Year of Our Lord 2009, or Year 1 of the Church of Almighty Good Food, that out in the cornfields of Vinal County, Ohio, a new kind of religion, or lack thereof, did sprout and begin to grow. No one at the time actually realized that this unheralded upstart approach to universal sanctity would go on to attract followers from around the world but then neither did the early Christians or Muslims or Buddhists know what lay in store for them.

The first indication of what was going to transpire happened almost immediately. The thousands of pilgrims who annually came to the shrine at Our Lady of Good Patience a few miles away, also took time to stop by The Church of Almighty Good Food, just out of curiosity. Tasting for the first time what truly fresh sweet corn is supposed to taste like, they spread the good news by word of mouth back to the inner and outer cities of Detroit, Cleveland, Toledo, Pittsburgh and elsewhere. *Yes, there is salvation and it is near at hand.* Glad tidings also spread by newspaper, television, and the Internet where of course all things real and imagined can be found. The board of directors at the Church of Almighty Good Food had no choice but to begin enlarging their facilities to accommodate the increasing number of visitors. Local folklore claims that Tom Barnette actually made his farm fortune from renting out garden plots, not from corn, soybeans and the stock market, although that is hotly disputed in the everlasting water holes of the Yellow Room Saloon in Bredsocken, and Sheepshit Golf Course in Gowler.

Subsequently, at first sporadically but soon regularly, whenever a traditional church was abandoned or closed, Good Food Apostles, as they called themselves, showed up and laid claim to it, beginning the slow process of changing the edifice into a glorified food pantry. Sometimes they took over abandoned schools too, and finally, in the most profound symbol of the new era, even abandoned farmsteads. Officialdom did not seem to object very much, especially bishops and prelates of various persuasions. Being very practical leaders or they would hardly have become bishops and prelates in the first place, they soon realized that this development was good for business. It did not conflict financially with institutional religion—seemed in fact to enhance it. As far as thorny issues of theology, allowing churches to be turned into gatherings for the glorification of good food did not violate any institutional religion's dogma and could actually render knotty matters of faith and doctrine more palatable to the increasingly skeptical members of all sorts of Mystical Bodies of Christ. As crafty old Bishop Feering often pointed out, it was a way to get rid of church buildings without losing either money or favor with the people. Who was going to object, really, to a Church of Almighty Good Food in the neighborhood? In fact, in the way that history often turns on absolutely irrational contradictions, Bishop Feering was eventually appointed an archbishop largely in recognition of his contribution to the movement. Well, it did start in his diocese under his jurisdiction, did it not?

Pope Mary and her prince Jack Bump did indeed eventually get married—and in front of Dow Kapier's altar, and with Fr. Ray officiating. God did not send a bolt of lightning down to interrupt the ceremony as Pastor Lemming had grimly predicted.

Pope Mary remained notorious locally not for her questionable contributions to religious progress or religious decline, depending upon one's view, but for her farm accomplishments which were at least as controversial as her work in the realm of theology. She first of all proved to all the men in Vinal County that she could survive in farming as well as any of them. But more amazing, she could survive while being just as contrary in her tractor cab as she was in church. She would go down in history as the first farmer ever in the county to plant, in 2007, all soybeans and no corn. Even more unbelievable, she survived the next year too, when she became the only farmer since 1942 to plant corn without hardly any fertilizer of any kind at all. Not only survived, but collected over $162,000 in crop insurance and still made money on the corn and beans that the weather did not destroy.

"You can't grow corn without fertilizer," the FSA official told her.

"Well, I did."

"Then we can say your yield loss came from that, not from bad weather."

"Prove it."

The officials of course had no way of proving their contention because other farms in the vicinity, using fertilizer, had suffered losses like hers too.

"And furthermore," Mary went right on, "show me where in your insurance program it says anything about insurance payments being dependent on what fertilizer I used. Maybe I fertilized with Holy Water like the Catholics used to do on Rogation Days."

Mary had grinned as evilly as she could. "The government expects farmers will always do what it wants if it bribes us enough. You outfoxed yourself this time."

It was hard to argue with her. Her 2008 corn crop averaged 120 bushels per acre, 30 bushels less than her crop history. Insurance paid her $5.40 a bushel for 80% of those bushels or $129 an acre or $129,000 on 1000 acres without her so much as having to lift a finger. She also saved in fertilizer about $150 an acre by 2008 prices, or $150,000 altogether. The crop she did harvest she eventually sold for enough to add $40 per acre more to her overall profit or, $40,000. So the take for the year, because of the abnormally high market prices and her abnormally low costs was roughly $319,000.

She and Jack purchased her father's farm, using that money as a down payment. Her parents moved to town in time-honored fashion, and Mary was quite happy to turn over the day to day farming activities to Jack. They raised three children while living a rather traditional farm family life, except that their main crops were cornmeal, wheat flour, and increasing oat products from their own hull-less oat varieties, another of Jack's ideas that turned out to be a little more practical than making smoking pipes from corncobs. Also, unknown to almost everyone, he kept experimenting with a small, farm size ethanol generator. Only he was actually learning how to make bourbon.

"I'm just continuing the legacy of my great-grandfather who paid for his farm with moonshine," he loved to say to Mary when no one else was around. She in reply would add, mimicking her uncle Tom: "A farmer has to be ready to jump in several directions at once just to survive."

Fr. Ray became a well-regarded breeder of fine-wooled sheep, and he was very fond of describing himself in just those words, always with a bit of a smile. For reasons not ever officially stated, his much-rumored excommunication never quite came through. Because of the strange doctrinal logic that the Catholic Church must use when faced with the need to save face, a ruling came out of diocesan headquarters that while no priest was allowed to say Mass or administer the Sacraments in the Church of Almighty Good Food, a deacon could conduct weddings and funerals there. Alvin Farkow was only too glad to take over that assignment and Fr. Ray only too glad to be rid of it, so the sheep-whisperer passed out of official church attention without further fanfare. After that, what happened at the former St. Philodendra's seemed to be ignored by the official Catholic Church. But privately, not a few of its local dignitaries, not to mention a few imams from the Toledo area, were among those who kept standing orders for fresh vegetables and fruits with the Church of Almighty Good Food.

Neither the Private Eyes of God, nor the sheriff, nor Hem Judin nor Pastor Lemming, nor even Dan Bandy ever did find out for sure who broke down the church door, or who engineered the $200,000 scam that saved the Church of Almighty Good Food at its conception. Pastor Lemming remained for the rest of his active life, trapped by his own connivance as pastor of the Church of the Resurrection, where he was only a figurehead under the stern eye of the Altar and Rosary Society. He went to his grave convinced that the sheep whisperer had scammed him out of $200,000, although of course no evidence of that ever revealed itself. Only one person ever knew for sure who worked the scam, and he was, as usual, not talking much. He was too busy taking care of the cemetery and making fine furniture in his woodworking shop.